THE CAVERNS OF

MARS

D. B. DREW

Published by Martian

An imprint of HLA Publishing LLC

To my wife, Wendy: You are an inspiration,
without which I could never have written this.

Acknowledgements

Very special thanks to Heather Z, Shelly W, Shelly B, and Dawn D for early read-throughs.

Cover design and layout provided by Mischievous Designs.

Contents

Chapter One

New York 2082

Marty walked out of the cantina and into the elegant lobby of the swanky Manhattan hotel. The furnishings blurred as her mind spun with the day's revelations. The echo of her boots hitting the floor faded until she could hear little else but her own thoughts.

She ran a hand through her short, black hair, all the new information fighting for attention, her mind a chaotic mess. She needed to organize her thoughts and figure out what all she had to do to prepare for leaving the planet—but that conversation with Larry. When her friend, Larry, better known at the United Earth Space Research University as Professor Lawrence Wellington, had requested her presence on a long-term research trip to the International Mars Base, she knew he'd been holding something back. However, she hadn't been prepared for a secret of this magnitude.

An alien ship found in a cave on Mars—what the fuck? It's been there for a billion years. A billion years. It's an easy enough number to understand, but hard to wrap your head around.

Reverse engineering the advanced technology had unlimited possibilities. The alien craft might only be a small automated one, but the implications and technology could change virtually anything—maybe even everything.

It was already going to be awesome getting to see Mars and hanging out with Larry. Fuck, She'd missed Larry lately. Between preparing for the trip and his wedding before they leave, she didn't get to see him much. He and Smita probably won't leave their quarters the entire time they're on the ship.

The only thing that could make this better is if she met a little cutie to spend time with. That's going to be a tall order though. A lesbian who—no actually any orientation where she is attracted to women would work—but also around her age, attractive, gets along with her, isn't an ex and happens to be going to Mars soon—well, she might as well be hoping to find a pink unicorn.

Marty doubted there would be much for her to do there professionally. Securing the network, server maintenance and all that stuff the university neglects won't take that much time. Marty figured she would probably have to hack the corporations there to find out what they know. But mostly having some fun—trying out her mixed martials arts moves in Martian gravity—and what about that pink unicorn?

Marty couldn't help but worry, since at least one of the three corporations on Mars at least knew something about the alien ship. No telling what they would do—or be willing to do, for that matter.

They would love to get their hands on it. Once patented, the monopoly on the resulting technologies would bring about a record amount of inequality. It would have to be done by the university, so all of it would remain in the public sphere.

It had been weird putting all her stuff into long-term storage. It was even weirder telling clients she wasn't going to be able to handle any consulting jobs for a while.

The Mars trip was exciting and the result of her technical skill. She excelled at her consulting business and one of her clients was the United Earth Space Research University, specifically Professor Lawrence Wellington, who later became her best friend.

Nearly five months had passed since Larry first mentioned the Mars trip. It was the same day she won a regional powerlifting competition. She only placed third at the New Jersey state women's championship. They were all within a few pounds of each other though. Marty vowed to take first in 2083.

Fuck, my mind keeps wandering. I have too much to think about.

Marty imagined it must be worse for Larry, as he was leading the mission and getting married shortly before they were due to leave.

Marty came to the end of the hall, where it joined up with the lobby. There was a guest lounge, with table space, refreshments, a partial kitchen and other amenities.

It was getting late so only one person remained inside. The woman looked young, early twenties and her big, green eyes, sparkled like fine cut emeralds, adorning her round face. She ran a hand through her silky, medium blond hair. Most of it just a little longer than Marty's, but much longer at the top, combed over one side of her face, covering her left ear, extending to her jawline. She sat at a table shutting down a small mobile device. A very compact physical keyboard lay in front of her, an empty cup off to the side.

She is absolutely gorgeous! Her face was so beautiful with wide eyes and full lips. Her large bust was alluring as well, as it pressed against the table. Marty especially liked the way her hips looked seated on the chair. The woman glanced up and had this subtle expression as if she liked what she saw, but Marty perceived some shyness there as well.

"Hi," said Marty. "I hope I'm not disturbing you. I just checked in earlier today, so I was having a look around."

"That's all right, I was just finishing up in here anyway," said the woman. "I have this Mars trip I'm preparing for."

"What a coincidence, so do I. I'm Marty, by the way. I guess you must be Dr. Bierbrauer," she said, nodding toward the nametag adhered to her top.

The woman looked puzzled for a brief moment then looked down and giggled a little as she removed the label. "Oh, I left my nametag on! I had a seminar earlier this evening. Officially, I'm Dr. Bierbrauer, but you can call me Mia." She held out her hand and they shook. "Nice to meet you."

Marty couldn't help noticing how smooth and soft Mia's hand was as it clasped hers. She let it go, albeit with some reluctance. Mia continued in a somewhat nervous voice with the cadence a bit too fast. "Marty is an unusual name for a girl. Is that short for something or were you named after your father?"

"Yeah, it's short for Martina. It's nice to meet you as well, Mia." Marty leaned in and smiled, her interest showing through her lack of subtlety. "So, are you going to Mars with anyone special, or just on your own?"

Mia looked a bit overwhelmed for a brief moment, then smiled broadly and got this wide-eyed, mischievous look on her face. "Oh, I know who you are," she said laughing. She relaxed and leaned back in her chair. "I know exactly what sort of information you're fishing for with that question," she said pausing, her smile wide, filled with apparent glee.

Marty was confused. She didn't appreciate being at such a disadvantage, but she liked Mia's smile, her dainty voice and her cute little laugh.

"You're Professor Wellington's friend. I should have made the connection as soon as I heard your name. I have a lot on my mind and I'm a little absent-minded to begin with," she gathered up her belongings as she continued.

"Well, you'll be pleased to know I am indeed single and I'm also gay." Mia, with her hands full of everyday tech, stood and looked directly into Marty's eyes. "Does that mean you're thinking of asking me out, Miss Barbotti?" Mia asked in a teasing tone.

"Well, I didn't want to be so obvious," said Marty sheepishly.

"It's actually better this way," said Mia. "I am usually rather shy, but I've heard a little about you from Professor Wellington and this situation kind of breaks the ice a bit too."

Marty smiled. "In that case I think I will ask you. How about tomorrow around seven? We can maybe have drinks in the cantina and get to know each other."

"That works for me," said Mia. "Let's exchange contacts before we head up to our rooms."

They pointed their mobile devices at each other. Both devices beeped indicating success as they headed toward the lobby. All the rooms for everyone involved in the University's Mars trip were at least somewhat close together. It turned out Marty and Mia were just down the hall from each other. They chatted a little on the way up. Marty couldn't help but check out Mia as she walked. She thought she saw Mia glancing at her too. They said goodnight at Mia's door and Marty walked down the hall to her room.

A trip to Mars, billion-year-old alien tech to reverse engineer and now a new woman to explore—the future was definitely looking up.

✳ ✳ ✳ ✳ ✳ ✳ ✳

As soon as Mia closed the door she began to take off her clothes. After a long day, she couldn't wait to get her bra off. "Time to free the girls," she said quietly to herself as she unhooked it. It was quite a relief after having to wear it all day. In the time it took to walk from the door to the bed, she went from fully dressed to wearing only panties. She dropped her clothes in a pile by the bed and picked up a big, comfortable, over-sized nightshirt to put on.

She enjoyed meeting Marty and was looking forward to their date already. *She is absolutely gorgeous.* She could have gotten lost staring into Marty's dark brown eyes—so dark they looked black. They were rather large but her eyelids hung down slightly—bedroom eyes they were sometimes called.

She looked so strong and athletic too. Mia could just imagine being held in Marty's strong arms, kissing her full red lips. She couldn't help but look at Marty while they were walking. She didn't generally stare at other people's bottoms, but Marty's was too tempting to ignore.

Mia was feeling a little turned-on and she hoped Marty felt the same. She thought she had noticed Marty checking her out. The thought of being desired turned her on even more. She was only slightly overweight, but she had always been somewhat self-conscious about it. It was a consolation knowing she was quite curvy, but she still wasn't entirely comfortable with her body. She climbed into bed thinking pleasant thoughts about her chance meeting with Marty and what the future might bring.

* * * * * * *

Marty had slept in late and then spent much of the day taking care of personal business online to prepare for her upcoming trip to Mars. It was getting to be late afternoon and she was attending to the last thing she needed to do.

She had to sign some paperwork and have it notarized at her now former landlord's corporate office. It was in downtown Newark, so she had taken the subway over.

While it was still called "the subway" like the mass transit of a century ago, it was a magnetic levitation train, just like the maglev, but adapted for short distances with more frequent stops. It travels underground and then through underwater tubes when it crosses bodies of water.

After signing the paperwork, she started walking back toward the subway station. On her way, she saw four men in suits get out of the rear of a fancy car with tinted windows. One man was about 50, thin and a little short. He walked in front of the others, carrying a briefcase. Marty had a bad feeling about this, as the other three men moving in her direction looked like hired muscle.

"Hi, Martina," said the older man as he approached. "I'm Charles Mantis with Amalgam Global and these are my associates, Gus, Herb and Francis. We have a business proposition for you."

Gus and Herb were large, bulky guys who stood side by side behind Charles. Francis stopped a little short, staying in the back watching. He wasn't quite as big as the other two henchmen were, but he seemed like the particularly dangerous one. Marty put on a poker face and played dumb.

"I'm going to be tied up for quite a long time. Depending on your needs though, I could certainly recommend another consultant for you. Also, this is not a method of contact I appreciate. You'll have better luck acquiring technical services by going through the proper channels."

"Actually, Martina, you already happen to be going exactly where you will be needed. We are just going to need you to gather information and do some minor tasks. It will be very easy and we're willing to pay you quite a bit," said Charles opening his briefcase to reveal a holo-display showing a large three-dimensional payment form.

"That's an incredible amount of money, but I still must decline," said Marty, trying to maintain her business-like demeanor.

"I'm prepared to give you this now and as much again when we're done and we're not going to take 'no' for an answer," said Charles, his voice becoming stern and forceful, with a hint of anger.

"That's a whole shitload of money," said Marty, dropping the business-like demeanor for her 'Jersey girl' attitude and vernacular. "But it isn't fucking happening, so you might as well piss off now."

Charles snapped the briefcase closed stepping to within a couple feet of Marty, pulling a small pistol from inside his jacket.

"Like I said, we're not taking 'no' for an answer," said Charles coldly, as he pointed the gun at Marty.

Marty immediately smacked the gun with the back of her hand, sending it flying across the road into traffic, landing between lanes. Before anyone had time to react, she jammed the heel of her other hand into Charles' nose. There was a snap and a crunch as blood erupted. Charles fell flat on his back, catching Gus and Herb off guard. They quickly came around him, reaching for Marty from either side, trying to grab hold of her. If they got their hands on her, she would not be able to overcome their strength. She would have to be fast.

Gus got to Marty first. She dodged to his side, got her hands behind him and pushed him hard into Herb. He fell forward bumping into Herb who stumbled back, almost falling. With Gus on the ground, Marty jumped and dropkicked him right in the back of the head. His face slammed against the pavement. With Herb off balance, Marty was able to punch him in the gut as she bounced off Gus's head. A kick to the side of Herb's knee landed with a loud crack. The lower leg swiveled to the side in an unnatural motion. Marty kicked Herb in the mouth, blood and teeth flying out.

She turned her attention to Francis, but it was too late. There he stood, right in front of her. She tried to dodge, but Francis connected with half of his fist, pounding the side of her face. Her head flew back and to the right. The force of the blow knocking her to the ground.

Francis grinned at her, but that quickly disappeared. Marty did a kip-up and was back on her feet swinging. He dodged to the side and counter-punched. Marty sidestepped then pivoted to avoid the next blow. She tried a left and then a quick right and he blocked them, pushing them away with his arms and then ducking a kick that was coming straight for his face.

He punched out as he ducked, but Marty moved her mid-section back, bending at the hips. The blow didn't connect until his arm fully extended. It produced little force. This move brought Marty's face forward and he tried to connect with his foot, but she was expecting it. She caught his foot for a quick moment, but he was too fast for her to hold on. It was long enough for her to sweep his other leg though, knocking him to the ground. She followed up with a savage kick to the ribs. They crunched as the steel toe connected.

Francis responded by trying to slam his heel into the side of her knee. This forced Marty to jump back, giving Francis time to get up on his feet. Marty lunged at him trying to land a few punches. Francis blocked them and tried to respond with a high kick. Marty caught his foot. As soon as she had a grip on it, she kicked him hard in the crotch and simultaneously bent his foot roughly to the side, snapping his ankle. She pulled on his leg so he came forward and rammed her fist into his gut, right under his ribcage. She pushed his leg upwards with as much force as she could, so he landed hard on his back.

The pain of the crotch kick, plus the blow to the diaphragm and another to the lungs had him stunned and gasping for air. She knew she would have almost a full minute's head start before he could even get up and the ankle would have him limping slowly.

Charles finally got up, blood pouring from his face. Marty kicked him hard in the chest, sending him back to the ground and then took off running for the subway station. Within a few minutes, she was there.

The wait for the train was the longest five minutes of her life. She looked around to see if anyone was following her. When she was seated and the train was headed back to New York, a wave of relief paralleled the draining tension. There was tight security on board, so she should be all right. The hotel wasn't far from the station either.

There was a message from Larry on her mobile device telling her there were major security concerns and everyone going to Mars from there, had been instructed to stay in the hotel. For her own safety she needed to return ASAP. When she activated the phone function and called Larry to inform him of her new "friends", he was concerned, but glad she got away without any serious injuries. She kept the call short, as she wasn't in a talking mood at the moment. She figured she could give him all the details when she got back.

With the immediate danger over, her thoughts turned to her upcoming date. She was looking forward to seeing Mia again. She would have just enough time to have a chat with Larry, grab a bite to eat and get ready for her date. Her thoughts continued to drift, as the train sped back to New York.

Chapter Two

Marty met up with Larry in the lobby of the hotel. He was a well-built, tall man of African ancestry, with a short, full beard, the same length as his hair and a smooth deep voice. He usually spoke with a calm tone, like a cross between Carl Sagan and a Buddhist monk—but not right now. His voice, hinting at agitation, matched the look of worry on his face.

"I'm glad you're okay, Marty. I know you can take care of yourself, but these incidents—it really has me worried."

After giving Larry additional details about what happened to her earlier, she asked, "So, what's the scoop here Larry?"

"We've spotted some suspicious looking people lurking around the hotel. Some of them are snooping around inside, while others seem to be scoping the place out."

"It's probably related to what happened in Newark a while ago," said Marty.

"Yeah, we were starting to get the idea that at least one of the corporations with a Mars base had discovered something. That's been a concern for a while now. Your story confirms that," said Larry.

"I just hope they aren't waiting outside to pick us off, or worse, coming in after us."

"There is a security detail here to take care of that. We just have to stay inside. Otherwise, we can go about our business."

"Hopefully they aren't biding their time, waiting for us to leave either," said Marty.

"They don't know when we are leaving, or where we are going. We'll be fine as long as we can keep that confidential."

✻ ✻ ✻ ✻ ✻ ✻ ✻

Marty walked out of her room a few minutes before seven and was halfway down the hall when she saw Mia emerge from her room. Mia walked toward her, looking sexy and beautiful. Hair fixed and makeup on, she wore an outfit that complimented her curvy figure quite well. They greeted each other as they neared and finally met in a warm embrace.

"I was so relieved to hear you were all right," said Mia. "I was very worried when I heard you were out. Of course I've been at least a little anxious most of the day with the possible danger we face."

"It was a long ride home," said Marty. "I was nervous that I was still being pursued, even in the presence of the transit security. Plus I couldn't wait to meet up with you tonight."

They walked to the lift and Marty couldn't help but sneak a glance at Mia. She was just stunning, every inch of her. Marty couldn't help but notice the prominent posterior, wiggling provocatively as they walked.

When they reached the cantina, about half the tables were full, with people drinking and chatting. They sat down across from each other at a small table toward the back and a young woman took their drink order.

"Well, I guess this is the part where we get to know each other better," said Marty. "One thing I've been curious about is that you lock quite young to be a PHD. Did you go to college early?"

"Yes, I did. I started college at thirteen. That's even a year earlier than Professor Wellington. My parents were obsessed with me being a gifted child. They really pushed me."

The server returned with their drinks, setting them down and excusing herself with a polite nod.

"That sounds difficult."

"Yes, it was," said Mia, sipping her fruity cocktail and pausing a moment before continuing. "I had to take full schedules and even summer semesters the entire time. I got to choose my classes and work toward a degree at my own pace. It was all studies all the time though. I had my first PHD in advanced engineering at twenty. Because of the overlap, it wasn't hard to get a second PHD in mathematics a little over a year later. I left school and started working for the university about a year ago—I'm 22 now."

Impressed, Marty leaned forward. She took a drink and then looked up at Mia.

"I'm amazed by people who can handle so much formal learning. I couldn't stand school and took as little as possible. I dropped out and got a GED at sixteen, took a fast track course at a technical school to get an associate's degree and a couple technical certifications. By eighteen, I was working as a consultant mostly doing system and network security, but also programing and a little systems engineering. I learn fast on my own. I do quite well at my consulting business."

"That is impressive being independent at such a young age." Mia raised a hand, absently pulling her smooth, blond hair behind her ear. Both her fingers and her ears were nearly absent of jewelry, her nails unpolished. A small ring and a pair of tiny studs were the only exceptions. So many of the women Marty dated had a number of tattoos and piercings that Mia's lack of embellishments was quite striking in their simplicity.

"So tell me," Mia continued, "how do you know the professor?"

"Larry was one of my first clients and we ended up becoming close friends later. Other than our high level of intelligence and our penchant for drinking, we couldn't be more different. We just get along so well though."

They chatted for a while, asking and answering questions as they got to know each other. They discussed growing up with difficult parents, their likes and dislikes, their hobbies and everything that came to mind. The subject eventually turned toward relationships and sex.

"I've only had one relationship," said Mia, looking down at the folded napkin in front of her. "There wasn't much time until I got out of school. So I never experienced sex with a partner until just last year."

Mia was obviously uncomfortable. He innocence was both refreshing and endearing at the same time—not to mention a huge turn on.

"I guess you could say I'm fairly experienced. I'll be gentle with you though," Marty said with a wink and a smile.

Mia giggled a little, asking, "So did you always know you were a lesbian, or was it something you struggled with?"

"It was hard initially," said Marty. "I had sex with boys at first. I always found girls attractive though. When I first discovered masturbation, it was while thinking about girls. Despite that, I assumed that dating a boy is just what you end up doing."

"That sounds unpleasant and confusing," said Mia with a look of concern.

"Yeah, I suppose it was. I tried to fantasize about guys, but I couldn't usually get off unless my thoughts returned to girls. Even after a few years of that, I tried to date guys and have sex with them. It didn't quite work out though and when I was seventeen, I started seeing girls."

"So, you were able to accept yourself for who are then?"

"Not quite. Right after I turned 18, I took one last try at being with a man. It didn't last long. At that point, I was finally able to accept that I was a lesbian though."

"That's good. Did you feel a lot better when you came out?"

"Well, sort of. I was in a traditional Italian, Catholic household, so that made it harder. It wasn't as bad as it used to be, but it still wasn't exactly acceptable. I was also dealing with the fact that I found all their religious beliefs to be a load of nonsense. I never was able to fit in and get along there." Marty paused, feeling uncomfortable. "How was it for you?" asked Marty, redirecting the conversation.

"It was pretty easy actually. My parents were easy going other than the education thing. They raised me without religion too, so I never had to deal with that. I sort of always knew I was a lesbian."

"Wow, that sounds easy and awesome."

"Yeah, it was. I didn't fully understand until the sexual feelings of puberty hit me though. But, I never even thought about guys. I kind of thought about girls in a romantic way, which became sexual later and—well you know," said Mia becoming a little self-conscious.

"Yeah, I understand."

"Oh, it's getting really late now," said Mia, noticing the time.

"You're right. We better head up to our rooms."

They left the Cantina and took the lift back up. At Mia's door they hugged and held each other tight as they said goodnight. However, they didn't let go and just stared into each other's eyes. Marty leaned her head forward, as Mia's full red lips parted slightly. Marty pressed her lips against Mia's and they kissed. Their tongues touched, exploring each other's willing mouths. Then it slowly subsided as they eventually leaned back.

"Mia, that was every bit as good as I imagined it would be," said Marty.

"I really enjoyed tonight, and, well, THIS," Mia blushed, waving her hand vaguely between them. She seemed flustered by the intimacy. "It's a little soon to be moving forward right now, but let's get together again tomorrow after orientation."

"Trust me, I won't be able to think of anything else," smiled Marty.

When Mia went into her room, Marty walked toward hers feeling quite aroused and excited by the idea of seeing Mia again the next day.

Chapter Three

Marty and Mia met up on the way to the orientation. They hugged and then walked down to the conference area. They headed over to where the United Earth Space Research University logo was.

The UESR was a global university headquartered in Geneva, Switzerland. Established in 2030, they had campuses in every country. They would pick one city per country and partner with an existing university, in order to share resources. Switzerland was the exception, as they had campuses and a secondary headquarters in Zurich. In the US, they partnered with Columbia University in New York. It had begun as an exchange of campus space in return for access to the specialized science courses, as well as the research they did. It also had the side effect of connecting universities all over the world, pooling resources and sharing research data.

This arrangement had greatly increased the effectiveness and resources for all areas of scientific research. It resulted in a large increase in the rate of technological advancement, especially in areas related to space exploration. The space programs in turn yielded technologies that could be applied in various unrelated ways. Chief among them was the development of fusion reactors and their continued improvements. That, as a follow up to hydrogen, wind and solar, revolutionized the energy industry and solved many of the problems, which had plagued the world in the early part of the century.

Quantum computers were an additional technology they developed and refined and soon became integrated into practically everything. That led to the Quantum Entanglement Communication, or QEC technology. QEC connections were created with entangled particles, much like the quantum computers. An entangled quantum pair would be split and installed in different devices. Each one was a connection. The connections formed networks that allowed instant communication. So, people could make calls between Earth and Mars with no time delay.

When they arrived, they saw Larry and Smita there, along with a few other people.

"Hi, Marty," said Larry waving to her. "I see you've met my colleague, Dr. Bierbrauer. I was planning on introducing you today, but I see you're already becoming friends."

"Yeah, I met Mia the first night I was here actually," said Marty.

"It was while I was in the lounge finishing up some work after the conference I spoke at," said Mia.

"So you must have met after talking to Larry and me in the cantina the other day," said Smita in her posh west London accent.

Dr. Smita Patel, an Indian woman from London, was a medical doctor and Larry's fiancé. She was about thirty, with thick, long black hair and big dark eyes. Marty quite liked Smita. She was the best thing that ever happened to Larry. She made her friend so happy, which in turn made her happy as well.

"That's right," said Marty. "I went looking around the hotel for a while before going up to my room and that's when I met Mia."

"This is Dr. Brian Wong," said Larry, motioning toward one of the men standing there. "He's a fellow physicist and works with me in the lab. This is his husband Evgeny Petrov, who will be taking over as head of security on Mars."

"Nice to meet you, Marty," said Brian in what sounded like a Southern-California accent.

"You can call me Yev," said Evgeny in a heavy Russian accent.

Brian and Yev both looked to be in their early 40's. Brian was average height and thin, starting to get a little gray in his black hair. Yev was enormous, probably just a couple inches shy of seven feet, with veiny, muscular forearms larger than most people's lower legs. His upper arms were much the same, stretching his shirtsleeves.

"These are my two assistants and former students, Jorge Gonzalez and Zahra Khatami," said Larry.

"Hi, Marty," said Zahra.

"Pleased to meet you," said Jorge.

Jorge was slightly chubby and a little short, with longish black hair and a Van Dyke beard.

Marty thought Zahra's Persian features were quite beautiful. She had a unique and very striking face.

"They also act as Dr. Wong's assistants," continued Larry.

Both Jorge and Zahra appeared to be in their early twenties. So, they were likely somewhat recent assistants, graduated within the last year or two.

When the introductions were completed, they joined all the other people in a sort of general orientation about traveling to Mars, scheduled for the first half of the day. There appeared to be about forty people in all. A handful of them were children, going along with their parents.

A gray-haired man with bushy eyebrows of the same color, took the stage. He appeared to be about sixty and walked with the aid of an exoskeleton on his lower body. It was like a flexible metallic belt attached to full length stockings made of a similar flexible metal material. It had sensors that monitored muscle contraction and moved the exoskeleton in the intended direction.

"Good morning, I am Tobias Keller, director of Mars projects at the New York campus. This morning I will be outlining what you can expect on your upcoming trip to the International Mars Base. Those of you who are not attending Professor Wellington's meeting will be free to go after lunch."

Professor Keller told them all about the Mars base. He talked about how it was built in sections over many years, that it was like a small indoor city and even mentioned the three corporations with nearby bases. He then changed gears to a discussion about the trip itself.

"Earth and Mars are very close right now. They reached the closest last month at about thirty-five million miles and it's not much further now. It will only take a week to get there. One day to go down to Miami and take the shuttle up to the ship, about five and a half days on the ship and then a few hours shuttling down to the base. You have a little over two days of constant acceleration, which will give you just a bit more than twenty percent of Earth gravity. Then the ship is allowed to coast for a day, where you will be weightless. Finally, the ship slowly rotates around the other direction, the fusion rockets fire again in the new orientation and the ship decelerates for the same period of time, with the same gravity as the acceleration phase."

Professor Keller spoke for the rest of the morning and then they broke for lunch.

Marty and Mia snuck off together to eat lunch, just the two of them. They both wanted to discuss plans for the trip. They sat at a table off to the side, trays of food sitting between them.

"I'm glad we were able to pick our roommates for the ship. Maybe we should see how we do together. That way we are at least somewhat used to it before we are in the small room on the ship. I think they are only eight feet square," said Marty.

"Oh Marty, I want to so badly, but things are moving awfully fast." She paused for a second. A look of indecision and even a little apprehension was clear on her face. "It really makes sense though, so we know what to expect before getting on the ship," said Mia.

Marty looked into Mia's eyes reassuringly, placing a hand on her upper arm.

"It's all right. Trust me, Mia. I won't do anything you're not comfortable with. I know how it is when you don't have much relationship experience. I think I know exactly what to do to keep you at ease."

Mia relaxed a little and started to smile.

"I trust you, Marty, thank you. That makes me feel a lot better. When the afternoon meeting is done, how about you bring some comfy clothes with you and come over to my room. We can order some room service and maybe watch something on the holo-display."

"That sounds perfect," said Marty smiling.

✳ ✳ ✳ ✳ ✳ ✳ ✳

"Well look at you two," said Larry in a teasing voice.

Smita was standing next to Larry, laughing a little.

"Hey, fuck you, Larry," said Marty teasing him right back.

Mia looked a little embarrassed.

"I'm sorry," said Larry turning to Mia. "I didn't mean to put you on the spot like that. I just had to give this one a hard time," he said, nodding toward Marty.

"Oh, that's all right, Professor," said Mia

"And no more of that," he said. "It's about time you start calling me Larry. You're seeing my best friend now, after all. I'll call you Mia if that's all right with you."

"Of course," said Mia smiling. "Larry."

Larry told them about the alien craft and how Dr. Magnus Petersen, who heads the science team on Mars, has been working on the translation project. Dr. Alistair McDermott, a cryptography expert and Dr. Jean Pierre Dubois, a linguist, assisted him. The team was nearing completion and should have it translated by the time they reached Mars.

He brought them up to date on the reverse engineering project and the attempts to conceal the ship from the corporations. It appeared those attempts had not been entirely successful in light of Marty's attack. This meant they were all at risk.

✳ ✳ ✳ ✳ ✳ ✳ ✳

What a weekend it had been—it seemed like they just got out of the orientation Friday and now suddenly it's Sunday night. Marty felt relaxed and drowsy as she lay there with Mia on the bed they had been sharing.

Marty was ecstatic even though they technically hadn't had sex yet. It had been three fun nights and the anticipation of going even further with Mia was exciting. Mia was very inexperienced and shy though and Marty had promised to take it slow.

The first night had been unbelievably erotic. The two of them lay next to one another, each with their hand down their own pants, their breath ghosting the other's cheek. Marty told Mia exactly how to touch herself, how to explore and massage her body bringing her right to the edge and then back. Seeing the excitement and pleasure take over her body as she followed Marty's orders drove her wild. Watching Mia come, seconds after calling her a naughty girl had sent Marty crashing over the edge as well.

The next night, after Larry and Smita's wedding, they couldn't wait to get back up to their room. Mia had been even more comfortable together, willing to both give and receive touch—at least in the beginning. Still self-conscious about her body, she'd been okay with removing some clothes, but not quite everything.

Instead of frustrating Marty, she'd found it extremely arousing. It'd been intriguing for her, finding Mia's comfort level then helping her relax and become more familiar with both of their bodies.

When they'd gotten off it'd still been by their own hand, but the flash of partially clothed flesh along with Mia's surprised gasps somehow made it more satisfying than some full-on sex she'd had.

As Marty thought about it, it occurred to her that it was just like the start of any relationship. The only difference was that instead of masturbating together through a hologram chat, they were in the room together.

I'll trade nudity for a live make-out session, any day. Besides, we finally got to the naked part tonight.

On the surface, stripping for each other and watching the other achieve orgasm was typical of a hologram session. But live, together, with Mia, it'd been completely different. Touching her smooth skin and feeling her return the touches with soft, hesitant strokes of her own. Strokes that soon became bolder, more aggressive.

It was like a masturbation marathon tonight.

"So you usually sleep naked?" asked Mia.

"Yeah, I always do. This is just the first time because you weren't quite comfortable with full nudity yet."

"I'm comfortable with it now," Mia said, trailing her fingers up and down Marty's arm. It was as if now that she'd given herself permission to touch Marty she couldn't stop. "I still prefer to wear panties and a night shirt though."

"I certainly enjoyed seeing your gorgeous body earlier." Marty leaned in, kissing Mia's now covered shoulder.

"I was nervous about it but you made me feel at ease. You made me feel beautiful and desired."

"I liked what I saw. You got me so excited."

"Yeah, it helps knowing you like a pair of big, floppy boobs and a fat, jiggly ass," she said, with a small laugh.

"Hey, don't make fun. You have amazing boobs," Marty said, cupping Mia's large breast, her thumb brushing over the erect nipple. "And a spectacular ass." She reached around giving it a light, playful smack as Mia giggled.

"I like how we've done this," Mia said. "These last few nights, doing a little at a time. It was sexy. Watching you and being watched--it made me feel both safe," Mia paused. Marty watched her hand as she stroked down Marty's bare breast, "and incredibly aroused." Mia looked up. "It got me ready to be with you, without holding anything back."

"I enjoyed getting to know more of you a little at a time these three nights—four if you count our first kiss. I even got to see your birthmark. I've never seen a birthmark on the inner lips of a vulva before."

Marty stopped. "Hey. Wait. Back up. What was that about not holding anything back?"

"I feel ready. The next time we're together, up on the ship—I want you to take me, hold me in your strong arms. I want to feel your hands and lips all over me. I want to taste you," said Mia, gliding her hand over Marty's back.

"If you're ready, then that's exactly what I'm going to do. I've been longing to massage you, bring you to orgasm, taste you. I want to feel your tongue on me."

"That sounds amazing. I can't wait."

They cuddled under the covers together and soon fell asleep. It would be the last night they slept on Earth for quite a long time.

Chapter Four

Marty and Mia headed down to the lobby where everyone was gathering. Larry waved a quick hello as he went around making sure that he accounted for everyone. When he had done so, he addressed the group.

"Good morning, thank you all for making it down here so early. The bell-bots should be bringing your luggage down to the shuttle now. In just a few minutes, we will be boarding as well. That will take us to the maglev station, where we have an express train booked to Jacksonville Florida. That will take a little over an hour even at the express speed. Then a short wait and an hour flight to Miami. You all should have been off solid food since midnight and you must stop drinking as soon as we leave here. If you would all line up over there, Dr. Patel and our two nurses, Ben and Hilda will give you each a pressure injection with your first dose of the myostatin inhibitor, along with an anti-emetic in case some of you don't tolerate the launch."

"Better than giving us the anti-emetic in case we don't tolerate the lunch," Marty whispered to Mia, as she laughed.

Mia laughed as well. Larry smiled at them, but everyone was lining up for the injection, which went through the skin by the force of high-pressure air.

"Unfortunately I have actually eaten at a place where I could have used an anti-emetic to help me tolerate the lunch," said Larry with a chuckle. Then he added, "Marty, Smita got your records updated in regard to the myostatin inhibitor, as well as any supplemental treatment that may prove necessary to prevent atrophy in the low Martian gravity. So you'll still be able to compete in the natural, tested, power lifting contests when we come back."

"Thanks, Larry," said Marty.

Injections also sent out a broadcast message to the person's nanobots, updating their medical data. Everyone had nanobots injected in them as infants. The nanobots contain a person's medical records, which can be scanned by doctors. They also monitor health and are augmented, reprogrammed and replaced occasionally as needed. In addition to monitoring health they can fight off many common communicable diseases, including all sexually transmitted ones. They can even be programed for male or female contraception.

When everyone had their injections, they headed out to the shuttle, which was really just a full size, automated bus.

$$* * * * * * *$$

When they arrived at the maglev station, everyone waited until all 40 of them were off the shuttle. Marty was at the back of the crowd with

Larry, making sure everyone was accounted for. Mia followed close behind them.

As they ushered everyone into the outer doors of the station and toward the gates, men in suits suddenly ran at the people in the back of the group. Two came from one side lunging at Marty and Larry. Marty was ready, dropping low to dodge her attacker and sweep the legs out from under Larry's assailant.

Turning quickly back to the man in front of her, she punched him right under the breastbone while he was off balance and then jammed a knee into his groin. The other guy started to get up. With a spinning kick, the toe of her boot tore through some teeth, going right into his mouth. She was off balance after that move, but recovered quickly. Not quickly enough though.

Another man was between her and the rest of the group. He pointed a pistol right at her face, his finger on the trigger. She heard a loud bang and for a split second, thought it was her last moment. She felt a shower of blood spraying her face. Her attacker, now missing most of the right side of his forehead, toppled over, hitting the ground face first.

Yev was standing a few feet behind him holding a large handgun. Mia screamed. Marty looked over, seeing that a man had grabbed her. His arm around her neck, holding her in front of him. He had a handgun pointed at her. At first Marty thought it was a plasma gun, which was illegal for civilian use, but it turned out to be the old fashioned, common sort—still deadly though.

Another man drew a weapon, aiming it at Marty. Yev had pushed through some people and shot that guy twice in the chest and third to the head as he fell back. The guy who had taken a boot to the mouth was making a run for it, holding his bleeding mouth. The Man holding Mia was starting to back away, still holding Mia with a gun to her head.

"Mia!" Marty screamed in desperation. "No!"

Mia let her legs go limp, the gun pointed up and away from her, as he struggled to regain his grip on her with his other arm. Marty ran at the man who was almost 10 feet away. At the same time, the attacker she knocked to the ground earlier was up and had surprised Yev, slapping his gun away. Yev rendered him unconscious with one devastating punch to the face.

Marty dove at the man. One hand at his face, the other on his wrist, as she slammed into him. Mia fell backward and to the side, hitting the pavement with a thud.

Marty had the guy by his face, slamming his head into the pavement, as her other hand did the same to his wrist. The gun flew out of his hand and the man appeared a little dazed, but still trying to grab at her with his other hand. She was screaming as she jumped up, her face red, adding to the blood spatter that covered it, tears coming from her eyes. She bared her teeth in a snarl, like a provoked wolf. She savagely stomped his face and started kicking him brutally in the ribs, stomach and groin. Thick treads and steel toes pounding away as hard as her powerful legs could kick.

Two more men had been trying to circle around to separate a couple of them from the rest of the group. They were fairly strong and grabbed onto Marty, pulling her off their comrade. However, Yev pulled one away, allowing Marty to free herself from the other.

Yev punched the guy hard in the gut, then wrapped his thick, beefy hand around the man's throat and lifted him right off the ground. The man struggled and Yev gave him a quick jab to the face. He then allowed the man's feet to rest on the pavement and loosened his grip a little, as the guy had been unable to breathe.

Marty faced off against her attacker who took a couple swings at her, missing as she quickly moved to either side. Marty was still in a rage, countering his next blow with a punch to his throat. As he gasped, she gave him a spinning kick to the ribs, which landed with a crunch. She let out a horrible half scream, half growl, grabbing the man's face with both hands, pulling down hard, slamming his head into the pavement. He was out cold. A small amount of blood trickled from his head.

Marty turned to see Yev holding the last attacker standing, by the throat and Mia starting to pick herself up.

"Mia!" yelled Marty, as she ran for her.

Marty could hear Yev attempting to question the man, "Who do you work for?"

"Charles....Mantis," the man croaked.

Marty scooped Mia up in her arms, tears leaving small lines of skin washed clean, in the running blood spatter of her face. Mia was scared, shaking and starting to tear up a little. She had some abrasions on her left arm.

"Mia, I thought they were going to take you away from me. I thought I might never see you again," said Marty starting to regain her composure.

"Marty, I was so scared," said Mia still shaking. "I was hoping my little stunt would let you get the upper hand."

"I should have stayed with you until we got in—I got you back though," said Marty.

"You can't be ready for everything," said Mia.

"I know," said Marty. "I just....well—I'll never let anything happen to you. I don't care how many I have to fight off—"

"Everyone stop right there," said a commanding voice on a loud speaker. "You are all surrounded and you will submit immediately to transit security personnel."

A man in a uniform, weapon drawn was approaching Yev, saying, "You will unhand our prisoner immediately!"

Yev let go of the man without delay, taking a step back.

"Get on the ground now! Hands behind your back!" barked the security guard.

A man in a slightly wrinkled gray suit walked from the outer doors of the station, holding a cup of coffee, with a guard on either side of him.

"What the fucking hell is going the fuck on here?" yelled the man. Then going from raging to fairly calm between sentences he said, "I'm supposed to be running a maglev station."

The man took a sip of his coffee, continuing, "You know, that's a little hard to do," he said pausing and switching back to full rage mode, "When not one single fucking train, can budge one goddamned, motherfucking inch!" he yelled and then calmed suddenly, but with ever increasing sarcasm. "Because the whole station just went on security lockdown."

One of the guards spoke to him for a minute, too quietly for others to hear.

"Oh, from the university...." the transit administrator said trailing off and sipping his coffee.

The administrator's face got redder, his lips curled into a scowl and he threw his mostly empty cup roughly to the ground.

"Those brazen fucking, slick-dicked, corporate, cocksuckers! What the fuck—ah fuck me running—right outside the station...." he said trailing off.

Larry started to speak, "We're really sorry about all this—"

"No, no, that's all right," sighed the administrator. "I guess I should have posted some guys outside. It's just that I never had to fucking do that before. Look, we got this on holo-vid from multiple angles, so you guys are all free to go—except the big guy there. He's not going anywhere until we verify he's got a license for that thing and he better have been planning on checking it at the gate. We'll have the trains running again soon."

Yev walked over with a mobile device, pointing the display at the administrator.

"Okay, looks legit, now clear out of here," said the administrator.

Upon hearing that, they all started heading for the outer doors of the station.

The administrator pointed to the prisoner, "don't bother with a holding cell. The cops will be here soon."

As Marty turned and walked with everyone, over toward the doors, she heard the administrator continuing to talk. "Just watch that cancerous fucking anal tumor until they get here and keep an eye on Sleeping—fucking—Beauty here and his drowsy fucking dwarfs—oh and don't let anybody walk through here. The last thing I need is something getting disturbed before the cops arrive and having that to deal with on top of explaining all the delays. Oh and call over to Jacksonville, so they can tighten security. Huh? Oh yeah, the Dwarfs were Snow White—his sleepy fucking stepsisters then. Whatever, classic cartoons aren't my fucking strong suit...."

Once they were inside, the administrator's voice was completely inaudible. Everyone was scared and shaken as they walked to the gates, but nobody was seriously hurt. Smita walked Marty and Mia over to the restroom, while everyone else went through weapon detectors at the security gates.

Marty washed her face, as Smita wiped antiseptic on Mia's abrasions. Marty couldn't stop thinking about what had happened earlier—the terror she felt as Mia was dragged away. She had never seen someone killed right in front of her either—well not that close anyway. In her presence— yes, unfortunately—but not right in front of her like that. That guy had it coming though, if Yev wasn't there, she'd be dead and who knows what would have become of Mia. The other guy was further away and she didn't really catch but a brief second of his final moments, with everything that was going on. He was at the very least, planning to take a shot at her though.

"I have a big bruise on my hip. It's a little sore, but I'm all right," said Mia interrupting Marty's thoughts.

It was only then that Marty realized Smita had asked how Mia was doing. Marty put an arm around Mia, as they walked back to join the others.

"Marty, you were so brave and I couldn't believe how fast you were moving—and I knew you were strong, but—once I saw you run toward me, I knew I'd be all right and you would save me," said Mia squeezing Marty tight.

"I'm just glad that's over and you're right here with me," said Marty, kissing Mia on the cheek.

When they were all inside waiting to board the maglev, Marty walked up to Yev, his husband, Brian, standing by his side.

"Thanks, Yev, you really saved my ass back there—twice," said Marty.

"I wouldn't even have been able to pull gun from holster if you hadn't taken out first two. It was amazing how fast you dropped them. You were very fast, like in movie—you are even stronger than you look," replied Yev.

"Talk about like a movie—you lifted that guy off the ground with one arm," said Marty.

"Lots of weight lifting and eating—makes me big and strong. You lift too, don't you? You fight too? A little MMA?"

"Yes, on all accounts," said Marty. "I've been into power lifting for years. I won some local meets and took third in my weight class at state. I'd probably be kind of famous if people paid any attention to women's power lifting," said Marty smiling.

"That's cool," said Yev. "So how did you end up getting into MMA?"

"I did plenty of fighting, lessons at different martial arts from childhood and then got into MMA later. The rough neighborhoods I was in gave me plenty of opportunity to fight as well. I was really good at MMA, but I just did the sparing, where you have thick pads everywhere. I won the few actual matches I was in, but the rate of injury just wasn't worth it. There isn't much money to be won, unless you're a man in the higher weight classes. I wasn't about to suffer all the injuries, all the recovery time, just for a fucking plastic trophy. So, no more real matches, not for a long time."

"That makes sense," said Yev.

Everyone started boarding the train, so Marty went back to where Mia was, so they could stick together. She wasn't going to let Mia out of her sight!

✳ ✳ ✳ ✳ ✳ ✳ ✳

After taking the maglev down to Jacksonville and then a quick flight down to Miami, they were picked up by an automated bus, almost half-full of armed, security personnel from US Mission Control. It dropped them off at a building next to the launch pad.

They all changed into flight suits, while their luggage was loaded onto the space shuttle. Once everyone was in their flight suits and ready to go, they walked out to the launch pad.

The triangular-shaped shuttle sat on the launch pad. The widest part at the bottom contained the fusion engines, which were specially designed for escaping Earth's gravity. The cargo area was on top of that, which is where you board, then stairs and ladders led up to the passenger areas. The seats were back to back, so the row of five on the bottom had ten seats, above that was another row of five. Then the next two were rows of three and the next two were rows of two. A cockpit sat atop the shuttle, with two pilot seats, sitting side by side, with controls in front of them. Once everyone was on board, the pilots verified they were strapped in and then climbed up to the cockpit.

Chapter Five

After waiting for the system checks and the countdown, the engines finally started increasing thrust rapidly and they started lifting off the ground. They accelerated faster and faster, as the g-force pushed down harder on them. Finally, they reached escape velocity and the g-force let up. They maintained speed as they cruised upwards. After a while they started feeling lighter and then weightless as the shuttle left Earth's gravity.

Even though they were going just a bit slower than before, they were still moving very quickly, as the pilots maneuvered into an orbit that continued to move them further from the Earth. It wasn't long before they pulled alongside the ship, in geostationary orbit. They slowly approached and then cables from the ship and the shuttle locked onto each other. The docking anchors extended, connected and then locked in place. Finally, the airtight seal was in place and the ship's crew signaled that the airlock had been pressurized.

One of the pilots climbed down and when he heard the outer hatch of the ship open, he opened the hatch on the shuttle. They sent people over ten at a time, going through the procedure of opening and closing doors, so that the inner and outer doors were never open together.

It was crowded at first, as there were people leaving. The entire group of forty went into the common areas, while those departing pushed their stuff out of their rooms. The crew put it all in the airlock, which closed again. Then when it finally reopened, their stuff was in its place. It all had to be crammed into the common area with them. So they floated up as the crew pushed their stuff in under them. The other passengers went over to the shuttle in three separate groups. There had been maybe twenty-five or thirty of them.

Once the shuttle was undocked, they got their room assignments, while the crew put all their stuff in the rooms.

A tall, thin man in his fifties floated over to them.

"Good evening, Captain Oliver Johnson," the Captain said in an Australian accent. "Welcome aboard. We'll get you all a bite to eat, instruct you on the use of the bathroom facilities and then show you to your rooms shortly."

A short and somewhat stocky Japanese man of about forty floated over by the Captain.

"This is my first mate, Hiroto Matsumoto. I'll leave you in his capable hands," said the Captain, pushing off the wall and floating away.

"Hello, I'm the first mate, Hiroto Matsumoto. I manage the day to day operations on the ship," said Hiroto with only a very slight accent.

Hiroto continued, saying, "You can call me Hiro, which is nice and easy, since it's just like the English word, 'hero'. I'm even fine with 'Matt'," he said chuckling.

Everyone else chuckled a little as well. Hiro gave everyone bags of water they could suck through a straw. He also showed everyone where the bags of food were and how to heat them.

While they ate, he told them they would reach the right orbital position to depart in about three hours. Then instructed them on the bathrooms, how to secure their luggage and finally to secure themselves in their bedding and wait for the gravity that would result from the acceleration.

"You can head to your rooms when you're ready, but be in them in an hour at the latest. You all need to be ready for when we depart. We'll announce it, so you know when to expect the feeling of gravity," Hiro said with a wave, as he floated off.

✱ ✱ ✱ ✱ ✱ ✱ ✱

After about half an hour people were having a look around the ship. It had two decks that were double size, about sixteen feet from top to bottom and a third that was eight feet. The deck of standard height was on the top and they only just got a quick look through the doorway, as it was for the crew. It had crew quarters, a small lounge and the flight deck.

A couple common rooms and a galley comprised half of the bisected middle deck. Since people would be moving around more in those larger areas, they kept the ceilings high to avoid the injuries that might result from people bouncing around in the low gravity during the flight. It wasn't wasted in zero-g either, as people could just float up higher to make use of the space. The other section contained the rooms with stairs leading to walkways, to get up to the rooms on top.

The bottom deck was also in sections, but not bisected like the main deck, with the engines in the middle area and engineering rooms between them. The engines took up the whole height of the deck, while conduits ran over the top of the engineering rooms. On the sides were cargo areas with bare grating separating them into two separate levels. All of the cargo was held down by straps running through the grating, or through hooks in the walls and ceilings.

In a back cargo area by an engine, Marty, Mia, Larry, Smita, Brian and Yev met to discuss the events at the maglev station. Mia and Smita each took a different spot to watch and make sure nobody else was listening in. This allowed the other four to talk undisturbed.

"What do you think, Yev?" asked Marty. "Did someone in our group betray us?"

"I am pretty sure that is so," said Yev. "I think someone at the Mars base is in on it too—probably more than one. Not just the corporate guys trying to poke around where they're not allowed. I mean more trusted people."

The International Mars Base was public, so the people from the corporate bases would come there for various reasons, but at least two thirds of the base required some sort of special access, of varying levels. Some access, any resident could get, as well as other access levels that got more and more restricted.

"I can't think of anyone who would do that among us on this ship, although Mars base is another story," said Larry. "How about you, Brian?"

Brian thought a second and then replied, "Same here. Nobody comes to mind. We will need to find out who it is though, both here and on the Mars base."

"We'll add that to the list of what we need to find out, which includes what the corporations know about the situation there," said Larry.

"We also need to find evidence that will tie attacks to Amalgam Global," said Yev. "The guy I was holding by throat—he confessed he works for Charles Mantis, one of the bosses in charge of dirty side of operations."

"Yev," said Brian in a teasing sort of mock whisper, holding the vowel sound much longer than usual. "Definite article."

"All right, all right, Brian! Geez," said Yev teasing back. "I forget—the—lessons sometimes when I get excited. I'll work on using—the—definite article more often—I'll remember when I need—an—indefinite article too," he said, making a face at Brian where he widened his eyes.

Brian moved his lips in mock speech and then stuck out his tongue at Yev. Larry and Marty were stifling their laughter watching the interaction.

"Well, I guess I got my work cut out for me," said Marty. "That's a whole lot of stuff I have to find out."

"Brian and I will help as much as we can with the internal stuff, since we know pretty much everyone at least a little," said Larry.

"I'll be in charge of....The...." Yev paused briefly and looked at Brian, who rolled his eyes. "Security forces. So I should be able to help with some of that."

"We should probably get back up there now," said Larry.

Yev grabbed Brian by the shoulders pulling him closer in mock aggression. "All right, little man, I think it's bedtime."

"Uh-oh," said Brian in a kidding tone, "Is—The—Big, Russian, Giant going to drag me off and have his way with me?" Brian paused for a second, turned his head and continued in a higher, overly dramatic tone, "Oh, whatever shall I do?"

"That's exactly what's going to happen," said Yev.

"Well you can start with this," said Brian as he grabbed Yev by the ears, planting a kiss on his lips.

They kissed with a little passion, but only for a couple seconds. They looked sheepishly at the others as they floated toward the stairway leading up to the main deck.

"I can't say anything," said Larry. "Smita and I are guilty of a PDA or two....or ten."

"I let it all fucking hang out. You can call me Martina PDA Barbotti," said Marty, laughing. "It causes a scene too. Most folks just have offended old people to deal with, but when attractive girls kiss each other....Fuck! Half the men that see it start losing their fucking minds, whistling and cheering and shit. Well, I guess it's really only a few, but it feels like half while it's happening. It doesn't take much searching to find a short holo-vid of me kissing this hot Mexican chick on the subway a couple years ago—from multiple angles, I might add."

Larry laughed, "Yeah, I remember that—oh, I guess we better get moving," said Larry as he noticed Smita and Mia motioning impatiently.

They all started floating toward the stairway, talking as they went.

"It could have been worse though," said Marty, continuing her previous thought. "Imagine that situation if I lived just at the beginning of this century, or even back in the twentieth century. Just displaying female sexuality at all would have been bad enough, but to be gay on top of that—oh the outrage. Really, the female part has only been halfway acceptable the past couple decades. If a woman dared to even openly admit that she was a sexual being, it was just the end of the fucking world for some people—the ridiculous fucking gender roles—oh the moral outrage, all those evil sluts—how dare they! Yet it's all right for the guys. However, it was insulting for them, too, when you think about it. Being thought of as mindless beasts, unable to control their actions, driven to do all sorts of things at the briefest glimpse of female flesh. Evil temptresses and mindless automatons—how very anti-human! But what do you expect from the sexual attitudes of these fucking recovering puritans and all their Post-Victorian bullshit?"

"Tell us how you really feel, Marty," said Larry, smiling at her.

"Preach, Sister!" said Brian approvingly.

"I don't know if I would put it in those words, but I agree wholeheartedly," said Mia.

"Yes, indeed, a little harsh, but well said," added Smita.

When they got back up to the main deck, most of the people had gone to their rooms, but a few were still in the common areas. Marty took Mia by the hand and they floated back to their room.

✳ ✳ ✳ ✳ ✳ ✳

After getting all their stuff secured and getting their bed ready, Marty and Mia stripped down to their panties. Marty zipped the bedding part of the way up, while Mia put on a nightshirt. When Mia had positioned herself in the bed, Marty zipped it up to their shoulders and tightened it enough so that they would not float around.

"This is nice and cozy being wrapped up in here with you," said Mia.

"This is perfect. I feel like I could just stay here forever—oh wait, just one thing left," said Marty scrunching down and pulling her panties off.

"There, now it is perfect." She tossed her panties up in the air and snickered.

Mia giggled a little too as Marty's red, lacey underwear floated above them. "That's one of the things I like about you."

Marty pulled Mia close, wrapping her arms around her.

"And that's another one," whispered Mia, putting her arms around Marty.

"Here I am," said Marty, "wrapped up in some cocoon-like blankets, completely weightless, snuggling up to a beautiful woman, waiting to pull out of Earth's orbit and into the blackness of space, off on an adventure, to a place that has only appeared to me as a bright reddish star, moving across the heavens. How lucky am I?"

"Oh, you do have a romantic side, Marty. I thought so. I think there's a tender heart in there," said Mia, rubbing a finger lightly over Marty's chest.

"Only if you know how to access it—and even I'm not sure how that is done. You seem to know the secret though."

"Just like you know about my secret birthmark."

"Maybe I'll see it again tonight," Marty teased.

"Oh, I'm counting on it."

At that moment, the announcement came over the com system that they would soon be under way and everyone needed to be ready for acceleration.

They held each other for a few minutes, waiting for the feeling of g-force. Then suddenly, Marty's panties started gradually sinking and came to rest on Mia's face. They both started laughing as they felt themselves pressing more and more against the bed. Mia pulled the panties over Marty's head and they both laughed harder.

Marty pulled them off and gave them a light toss. Instead of the arc they would travel in on earth, they just kept going on the same trajectory, until they snagged on the door handle. They laughed even harder, starting to get punch-drunk and silly now.

After a couple more minutes, there was another announcement that the target acceleration rate had been reached and they could move around as desired.

Marty and Mia unwrapped themselves and stood up on the bedding, feeling the strange sensation of having weight again after a few hours without. It was also weird to feel so light. Mia, who was not athletic at all, found it easy to do a handstand.

The nightshirt fell down over her head and Marty couldn't help but reach down and cup Mia's large breasts. Mia made a soft "mmmm" sound, indicating her enjoyment. Marty held Mia's legs, opening her thighs a little. She brought her face down to Mia's crotch, just barely able to smell her scent through the thin material of her panties. She gently kissed the bottom of the soft mound, then moving back to kiss behind it and finally nuzzling her seat. She moved back to Mia's mound, pressing her lips against it for a few moments, as Mia softly moaned.

They lay back down on the bed, Marty pulling Mia's shirt off over her head. Their lips locked tightly together, tongues exploring mouths, as they caressed each other. They ran their hands over each other's breasts, massaging them, rubbing the nipples.

Mia lay on her back as Marty kissed and suckled her neck. Moving slowly from one spot to the next, she put a hand between Mia's legs. Through the fabric of the underwear, Marty cupped Mia's mound in her hand. She pressed harder, slowly massaging, rhythmically kneading, as Mia breathed heavier. After a minute, her face tensed up as she shuddered in a wave of pleasure.

Smiling and starting to catch her breath, Mia said, "You are so good at that. You made me come so fast—and through my panties too."

Mia slid her panties off as Marty laid next to her, putting a hand between her legs, touching Mia the way she had touched herself the night before. Mia did the same to Marty and they both reached the peak quickly, releasing together.

Marty put her full lips over the lips between Mia's legs, teasing her at first, kissing and licking just the outside. Then Marty lightly dabbed her tongue on Mia's clit until she just couldn't stand it. Marty finally started licking it up and down, Mia enjoying the intensity. The rhythm continued and Mia soon reached orgasm again.

They turned around and Mia put her face between Marty's legs, pressing her tongue between Marty's puffy lips. Marty looked down at Mia, seeing her mouth right on her most tender spot, her round ass visible beyond that. The site of her gorgeous curves and feeling her soft tongue, eagerly licking, quickly brought Marty to orgasm.

"Oh Mia, keep going! Faster!" cried Marty, feeling desire rather than the uncomfortable sensitivity.

Mia kept rubbing her tongue over Marty's clit, up and down, back and forth, until Marty quivered in ecstasy again, further soaking Mia's chin.

Marty got on top of Mia, halfway straddling one leg, pressing their mounds together. She started humping, slowly at first and then increasing speed. They embraced as the grinding intensified until they finally shook in climax, releasing all tension.

They lay there, holding each other, enjoying the pure satisfaction and the joy of just being in each other's arms.

"That was more intense than I thought possible," Mia whispered. "You seem to know all the ways to make me feel good."

"There is plenty more to come and I'll keep showing you," said Marty, pausing briefly. "There is more to it than just what we do though—and I'm just discovering this. It's all better and more intense just because I'm doing it with you."

"Marty, you make me feel good in every possible way."

"There's something about you, Mia—something special. You make me feel something I can't explain, like nothing I've ever felt before."

After a long, tiring day, passionate sex and the relaxation they found holding each other, sleep came suddenly and with great ease.

Chapter Six

After waking and going out to the galley to get something to eat, Marty and Mia were approached by Hiro.

"Hi, I hope I'm not interrupting," said Hiro.

"Not at all, we were just finishing up," said Mia.

"Dr. Bierbrauer, we would be honored if you would come up to the top deck. The Captain and the rest of the crew would very much like to meet you," said Hiro.

Marty and Mia followed Hiro up to the top deck, where Captain Johnson waited, along with the rest of the crew.

"Captain, allow me to present Dr. Bierbrauer and her girlfriend, Miss Barbotti," said Hiro, ushering them forward.

"It's a pleasure to meet you both," said Captain Johnson.

"We really wanted to talk to you last night, but we didn't want to intrude when you were probably tired, Doctor," said Hiro.

"We were excited to have you on board," said Captain Johnson. "We've been looking forward to meeting you since it was announced. The engines in the ship were overhauled early in the year with your design, Dr. Bierbrauer and it's simply amazing."

A short, thin man of African ancestry, around thirty, stepped forward.

"Hi, I'm Walt Smith, the navigator. It's an honor to meet you, Dr. Bierbrauer. Your design is just so elegant and the increase in efficiency and top speed are amazing. To think that once we finish testing at incrementally higher speeds, up to the maximum, that we'll be accelerating at a full g—that you came up with this shortly before your twenty-first birthday—it's just unbelievable."

"Thanks," said Mia. "It was a natural extension of my original design, improving on the 2078 model—which is the design I did my first doctoral thesis on. By any chance are you familiar with the thesis I did last year for the mathematics PHD?" asked Mia.

"Yes, I saw that, it was the one about increased efficiency in fusion reactors and the related equations," said Walt.

"Ah, well recently I created a follow-up to that, which improves it even further. It's a design I think will be implemented sometime next year. Do you have something I can write on?" asked Mia.

"Sure," said Walt, bringing up a three dimensional board.

"Here is the main equation. It's rather simple really—I was surprised nobody else had come up with it. I double-checked though," said Mia, moving her finger over the holographic board.

She kept moving her finger as various numbers, symbols and letters appeared. She went all the way across and then started on another line. After a minute she filled up more than half the board with a massive equation.

"There, that's the main equation the design is based on. As you can see, this is going to be fairly big for energy production," said Mia.

Marty followed the logic of it all right, but she was unfamiliar with many of the symbols used. Walt seemed to have a little trouble following it, but Mia explained the main points. The rest of the crew's eyes were glazing over at this point though. Mia was something of a celebrity among the crew, so they got a full tour of the top deck.

After lunch, they learned about how the difference in the rotational period of Earth and Mars were dealt with, concerning the time of day. The Martian day was just shy of forty minutes longer, so they had a special time zone called MRT, which stands for Mars Rolling Time. The time rolls back a time zone two out of three days. So they might start out on EST, then CST for two days, then MST. They did this by having a special Mars hour every two out of three days. Then every thirty-six days, they skipped a day and that happened the day they rolled over Earth's dateline, on the backward journey through the time zones.

Every one hundred and forty-four days, they did a single day of Mars time, whereas normally they always went in pairs. They spent all afternoon learning the complex patterns of how the 'Mars hour' days fall on the days of the week, the way shifts are run, the social implications—it was an incredibly complicated thing.

✳ ✳ ✳ ✳ ✳ ✳ ✳

Marty and Mia ate dinner in a group with Larry, Smita, Brian, Yev, Jorge and Zahra. They talked about what lay ahead of them on Mars.

"Ultimately, you are going to be heading this up, Mia, as it falls into your area of expertise," said Larry. "Brian and I can help a great deal with the physics though. Feel free to use us like assistants too. We can write out equations for you, or whatever you need. Jorge and Zahra will be at your disposal. You can also enlist the help of Dr. Petersen, who is in charge of the science team. He should have several resources he can assign to you as well."

"I think I can put you all to work," said Mia, smiling. "I'm really excited about getting my hands on this advanced alien tech."

After a while, the conversation died off and it was quiet for a few minutes, until Brian spoke up.

"Was it just me, or was waiting for the ship to get underway the perfect pretext for sex?"

Everyone laughed and all started talking at once.

"I'm glad it wasn't just us. Larry and I were at it for hours," said Smita, laughing.

"Mia and I had quite a night you might say," said Marty.

"Well, it was certainly a steamy night for us," said Brian, smiling at Yev.

"I hope we didn't keep anyone up," said Yev.

"Yeah, we can get a little carried away sometimes," said Brian.

"I just zipped up in the covers and hoped my roommate didn't notice what I was doing," said Zahra snickering. "She was probably hoping I wasn't noticing her too."

"I'm glad I wasn't the only one," said Jorge chuckling.

After sitting around chatting for a while, everyone finally went their separate ways. Marty and Mia went back to their room to spend the evening together.

* * * * * * *

Marty and Mia had gone into their room intending to relax, unwind and just chat about their day. However, upon entering the room, they began kissing hungrily, hands eagerly exploring each other, their clothes quickly ending up on the floor.

After a few minutes of rubbing and sucking on her nipples, Marty had her face between Mia's legs, tongue between her lips, massaging her clit. Mia moaned as Marty sucked the inner lips and clit into her mouth. Mia's most sensitive parts being sucked back and forth between Marty's puckered lips, her tongue rubbing against the exposed tip of Mia's clit. The stimulation was amazingly intense and it took only a minute for Mia to shudder in orgasm.

Marty gently licked and kissed Mia's outer lips, for a minute until she was ready for more. She put a finger on either side of Mia's clit, moving the hood back and forth, faster and faster, licking the tip at the same time. She kept a steady pace until Mia cried out, quivering in waves of pleasures.

Marty was already worked up and throbbing, her wetness covering her inner thighs, when they switched places. Mia went down on Marty, exploring her inner folds with her tongue. It was only moments before Marty reached her peak, tensing up in climax and releasing.

Mia locked her lips over Marty, like a French kiss between her legs. Finally Mia started sucking Marty's clit between her lips, running her tongue over the tip, just as Marty had done to her. Marty squirmed and moaned as Mia kept sucking, with all of Marty's tender inner flesh completely enveloped by Mia's soft, full lips and wet, silky tongue. Marty moaned louder and bucked her hips, enjoying the feel of Mia's mouth, then shaking in another orgasm.

They kissed, each getting their own taste, from the other's mouth.

"Do you like g-spot stimulation?" asked Marty.

"Yes and you?" replied Mia.

Marty nodded and inserted a couple fingers in Mia, pushing upwards and then rhythmically massaging the area. Mia did the same and they soon had short but intense orgasms simultaneously.

"Do you know about the spot all the way in the back?" asked Marty.

"No, what do you mean?" asked Mia.

"Well once you are warmed up and preferably after clitoral and g-spot orgasms, you will enjoy stimulation around the cervix. Let me show you," explained Marty.

Mia laid on her back and Marty stuck her fingers all the way in, finding the little bump at the back, rubbing her fingers over it and then hooking them behind it. Mia cried out with surprise and intense pleasure as Marty did so.

"Oh! Oh, yes!" exclaimed Mia. "Oh, Marty, yes, oh!"

Mia's cries intensified as Marty thrust her fingers in and out. Then Mia grabbed a pillow, putting it over her face to muffle herself, as she screamed and convulsed in the most intense orgasm she had ever felt.

"Oh fuck, Marty, that was incredible! I had no idea about that." said Mia.

"Surprisingly most girls don't know about that. Or so I've noticed anyway."

"So I just put my fingers in you like this?" asked Mia, pushing her fingers inside Marty.

"That's it, Mia. Now hook them behind that little bump and start fucking me."

Marty humped against Mia's hand as she pumped her fingers back and forth. Finally, she muffled her cries with a pillow, as she shook and quivered with an intense orgasm.

After getting each other off like that a couple more times, they felt satisfied and drained. They snuggled up together and just enjoyed the moment.

A little later, Mia started to fidget. She took a deep breath began to speak, and then bit her lip, remaining silent. Clearly, something was on her mind.

"What is it, Mia?" prodded Marty.

"Well, Marty, it's kind of a secret I want to tell you. I'm embarrassed though."

"You can tell me anything," whispered Marty, placing a hand on Mia's shoulder.

"I know...I keep trying to say it and it won't come out."

"It's okay. I know. Just remember, you can tell me whatever is on your mind."

Mia paused for moment and then continued speaking.

"I've always had a fantasy about being spanked."

"That makes sense considering the way calling you 'my naughty girl' got you off, at the hotel. So you like someone to tell you that you have been a bad girl and you need to be punished, held down to the bed and spanked?"

"Oh yes," Mia breathed softly. "That turns me on just hearing you say that."

"Perhaps next time, we can explore that."

"I would really like that."

"Well, you can let me know anytime, if you're my sweet little girlfriend wanting some loving, or if you've been naughty and need a good spanking," said Marty, smiling and staring into Mia's eyes.

"Thank you, Marty," said Mia, squeezing Marty tighter and kissing her.

✳ ✳ ✳ ✳ ✳ ✳ ✳

Marty awoke in the morning, her brain on overdrive. She started talking the moment Mia's eyes opened.

"I have an idea about figuring out who on the ship betrayed us."

"Oh, Marty, it's awful early for that," said Mia as she yawned and stretched.

"All right, well let's get something to eat and then find Larry," said Marty.

In the galley they found Larry sitting with Smita, Brian, Yev, Jorge and Zahra. Marty and Mia sat down with their food at the table.

"I had an idea about how to figure out who on this ship betrayed us," said Marty.

"What did you have in mind?" asked Larry.

"Well, you know me, it involves a little hacking of course," said Marty, in a hushed tone.

"That's what I figured," said Larry.

"If I get a look at people's financial information, that should allow me to see who's had a large payoff from an unknown shell company," said Marty.

"Even just getting the balance would be a good indication that it's Amalgam Global." said Larry.

"That's true," said Marty. "It's not like any of us are wealthy and Amalgam's offer was pretty high. The trick is covering my tracks so I'm not discovered. From the outside it will just look like it came from the ship, but I'm well versed in covering that up. The problem is that from the inside of the ship, it could be traced back to me.

"If I can link directly into a system console, the only evidence will be logs. With direct console access, I will be able to get the rights to remove those entries. The only problem is the engineering rooms are monitored. But when we lose gravity tomorrow, I'll be able to float into the conduits above one of the engineering rooms, from an adjacent cargo area."

"Brilliant," said Larry.

"That'll work," said Yev.

"When you get a name, I can easily point you in the right direction," said Brian.

"All right, we'll bide our time until tomorrow morning," said Marty.

After they finished eating they all logged into terminals to work on the training material. There were various courses they needed to complete during their journey. They could be done at any time though.

The courses included all the information you needed to know, as well as some you didn't. Despite a little trivia here and there, most of the information was relevant, if not important.

The courses that were given the most weight were the ones regarding safety. You had to sign off on those. It turned out that there are multiple ways to explain the concept of not getting yourself sucked out of an airlock.

Apparently, some people needed a reminder that you shouldn't go outside without a spacesuit. It seemed like temperatures much like Antarctica in the dead of winter, along with little atmosphere, which was mostly carbon dioxide and virtually no oxygen, would have been sufficient. The dryness would suck the moisture out of you pretty quick as well. So, after you are asphyxiated, your body would be quickly freeze-dried.

Many of the safety courses had some good tips though. The ones about operating the machinery were particularly helpful. They also went over how everything worked. There was an interesting one about a sort of hovercraft. It was called a glider, for the way it glided across the Martian terrain. Since the dust covering the surface of Mars is magnetic, a magnetic field could be generated underneath the craft, kind of like the maglev, which allows it to hover.

Marty pictured herself on top of a glider, as a wave of excitement cascaded through her body. She could almost feel the exhilaration of speeding along the dusty red surface, as fast as the terrain and the Martian escape velocity would allow her to go.

They didn't have many gliders, as the manufacturing capacity on the base was low. The weight had to be evenly distributed, otherwise the proper amount of lift couldn't be achieved. Therefore, it only worked for people and light cargo. Most of the transport was more conventional. Marty still hoped she would get the chance to pilot a glider though.

There were also courses that gave a virtual tour of the Mars base, showing you where everything was located. The base looked like a series of nine domes starting with a really little one and then getting progressively bigger. They started out arranged in a line, but veered off in a Y shape at the end

Most of it was surprisingly interesting, which made the time fly by. Marty took a few breaks throughout the day and noticed everyone else did the same—all at different random times. Apart from that, they spent the rest of the day completing the courses.

Chapter Seven

Charles Mantis floated above a chair on a small corporate spaceship, having just boarded from a shuttle. Next to him, Francis pulled himself into a chair, preparing to fasten himself in. Charles did the same, as the pilots readied the ship to leave orbit.

Francis Brown was of both Hispanic and African heritage, average height and kind of wiry, with long, thick, black hair, pulled back in a ponytail.

"How are the ribs and ankle holding up," asked Charles.

"Not too bad," said Francis. "Thanks to the increased healing of the nanobots, I'm getting better pretty quickly. Plus it was just a couple cracked ribs and the ankle break wasn't too severe. I'm still going to have to wear this stupid boot for a while though—that fucking bitch—so how is your nose?"

"It still hurts—that's for fucking sure. They had to put me under and cut it open to repair the damage. We're going to take that fucking cunt out if we get the chance," said Charles.

"I hate to admit it, but I'm a little scared," said Francis looking a little embarrassed.

"Only a little?" prodded Charles.

"Okay, a lot. Mr. Griswold is seriously fucking scary."

"I share your fear. I would say that I am a scary guy and I excel at having people feel just as we are feeling now—and with good reason too. But Mr. Griswold...well, that guy is utterly terrifying. He is what the guy everyone fears is afraid of. That's literally true," said Charles pointing to his chest.

"I'd rather not wake up in an airlock, missing various random body parts, with graphic holograms of my dead, dismembered relatives. Being given a little time to experience that and anticipate what comes next, before the outer doors open and I'm sucked outside," said Francis with a shudder.

"—yeah or getting tossed in the grinder, to become fertilizer for the greenhouse. He may just be the president of a business unit, but I'm way more afraid of him than the CEO or the board members. I don't think anyone else is capable of evoking that emotion in me at all," said Charles.

"I hear you on that," said Francis.

One of the pilots popped his head through the hatch above them. He checked to see that they were buckled in before speaking.

"We'll be taking off in a couple minutes. We've completed more testing with the new engine design and it worked well. With the relatively low mass of this ship, we can easily accelerate at a g and a quarter. That is if you can handle spending most of the next two days weighing twenty-five percent more than you do on Earth."

"I'm sure it will get uncomfortable, but I think we can handle it," said Charles.

The hatch closed and shortly after they began to feel themselves sinking into their seats as the ship moved out of orbit.

"It's kind of ironic that this acceleration is only possible because of a design created by a woman who is bumping cunts with the one who did this," said Charles pointing at his nose.

"I wouldn't mind seeing that," said Francis with a grin. "As much as that one bitch pisses me off, she's quite a looker. I saw a picture of the other one and she's hot too."

"I quite agree, Francis. They are indeed a couple lovely young ladies. It wouldn't stop me shooting them both in the face though, given half a chance. However, I would feel a bit like I just defaced a couple priceless masterpieces."

"Yeah it'd be a shame all right, Boss, but what can you do?"

At this point they were feeling quite heavy, just like on Earth. It just kept getting heavier too, as the ship accelerated faster and faster, off toward Mars.

✳ ✳ ✳ ✳ ✳ ✳ ✳

Marty and Mia lounged on their bed, having just finished breakfast. They had eaten it in their room, because all that was available were the zero-g tubes. Everything had been locked down due to the impending cessation of acceleration.

"That was unbelievably hot last night," said Mia. "The way you held me down and spanked me—I don't think I've ever been so turned on."

"It was pretty erotic for me too," said Marty. "I loved spanking your nice, plump, ass and seeing how wet you were. It was starting to run down your thighs. My panties were soaked by the time you pulled them off of me."

They soon felt themselves getting lighter and lighter as the engine power decreased. Within a few minutes they were weightless, floating above the bed.

"I think that's my cue," said Marty, turning to Mia and kissing her on the lips.

"Good luck," said Mia, as Marty waved and pulled herself out the door.

Distracted by their weightlessness, everyone floated around for the sheer novelty of it. Marty slipped past everyone, flipped over the rail and down the stairwell. She looked around, but saw no one. Satisfied she could proceed, she pushed off the wall and let herself glide through the air into one of the cargo rooms.

Once in the cargo room, Marty pulled herself into a conduit over one of the engineering rooms. In the ceiling of the room, Marty connected her mobile device to the console. The network lay exposed before her. *Time to have some fun.* She manipulated the holographic image projected by her mobile device. Her fingers moved with the speed and agility of a familiar task. Logging disabled and source network obfuscated, she made random routes through both QEC and conventional networks. The sessions would all appear to be coming from different places and she rigged them to mimic a balance check by a point of sale machine.

She wrote some code on the fly, incorporating the names of the passengers from the ships records, minus the ones she knew. She had to wait on that to run for about thirty minutes. This also required some manual tweaking to find all the needed information.

Once finished, she plugged those bits of information into another program she had which actually did the balance checks. That would probably take almost an hour to run. So she resigned herself to just waiting. Marty enjoyed the quiet and peace in the cramped little space and floating there weightless, was rather relaxing. She had to stay focused to keep from dozing off.

＊＊＊＊＊＊＊

Alma Cohen, the seventy-two year old administrator of the Mars base, sat in her small office on the second floor of Dome Four. Dome Four was the first to be built with an additional floor. The ground floor. in addition to the three earlier domes had been turned into a sort of Mars museum. The second floor however, was where the administrative staff worked.

She had shoulder length silver hair, which covered only the very top of her dark gray jumpsuit. Her eyes were starting to look a little tired, but still very sharp.

The years were catching up to her and Andrew was even a bit older. She and her husband enjoyed good health and she knew they still had many years left. However, as rewarding as her career was, it would be nice to fill those remaining years with leisure. Her husband had already semi-retired and only worked as her personal assistant at this point.

Just as she thought about making arrangements to retire in another year or so, she saw a message come in from Dr. Petersen. Apparently, the translation process had completed.

Excellent! That is perfect timing with the ship due to arrive two days from now.

She was anxious to see the project completed. The corporations were circling like vultures. She had heard the stories, so she was concerned that violence could break out in the base. She already had to tighten security a lot more than she wanted. She had hoped the alien ship could have been brought back without them finding out. That didn't work of course. They always seem to find out.

✳ ✳ ✳ ✳ ✳ ✳ ✳

Marty, Mia, Larry, Smita, Brian and Yev all gathered in an upper corner of one of the cargo areas. They crowded in as Marty began sharing what she discovered.

"There are two people here that suddenly have a lot of money. They are sharing a room together, which they put in for just a couple days before we left. It's Hilda—"

"Hilda? On my nursing staff!" Smita exclaimed.

"Yes," said Marty. "The other was Rachel, the mechanic. Now keep in mind, they might not have had a choice. There is a good chance they did this under duress. During my ordeal with Amalgam, when I made it clear to them that I wanted no part of their scheme, they pulled a gun on me."

"That's uncharacteristically calm and reasonable of you, Marty, and I quite agree," said Larry.

"Yeah, I guess I do tend to be more high strung most of the time and less understanding. Experiencing something first hand changes everything though," said Marty.

"Indeed it does," said Larry.

"We're going to have to confront them at some point," said Yev.

"I should probably do it tomorrow, alone," said Marty. "If I don't have anyone with me I could more easily intimidate them, after they saw me in action at the maglev station. Waiting for the deceleration phase would be good, as fighting in zero-g seems like it would be quite tricky. Then if it turns out they had been threatened, I can share my experience with them, which should put them more at ease."

"That sounds like a good plan," said Brian.

"I saw one of the crew come down to the cargo area over there," said Mia, pointing. "We should head back up before anyone notices us."

They pulled themselves over to a wall and then pushed off, gliding through the air toward the stairway. They banked off different walls as needed until they were able to pull themselves along the railing and push off to the common room.

✳ ✳ ✳ ✳ ✳ ✳ ✳

Dez Delacroix sat in her top floor penthouse of The Parasol Group Mars Facility. She was the one The Parasol Group board of directors trusted to get things done and she ruthlessly fulfilled those expectations. She would oversee projects on Earth sometimes, but she was stationed on Mars most of the time and she loved it that way. She lived like a figurehead queen on Earth, but on Mars, she was the queen proper—the supreme authority.

Dez was nearly forty, but used everything that money could buy to keep herself looking young and it worked—shaving ten years off her appearance. She was as vain as she was beautiful, frequently admiring her long, thick black hair, dark eyes, silky skin and slender but somewhat busty figure. She had rather strange, gothic tastes in clothing and décor, dressing primarily in dark leather.

Decadence and excess were what she was all about. She would take anything she wanted and would step on anyone who got in the way. She had several men who attended her. They served many different functions, but were selected from elite bodyguards. In addition to security work, they were also personal servants and assistants, attending to all her needs. They were also selected for their looks, all handsome and muscular. They wore nothing but a belt with a gun and baton and a thong. The only reason for the thong was that one tends to feel vulnerable in a fight when ones genitals are flopping about. So, they of course served as her private harem in addition to their other duties. Their nanobots were tweaked in such a way, that they could be ready for her, so to speak, at a moment's notice. This made them finish quickly, but she had several and they recovered well.

She lounged on a couch, with two of her men massaging her, drinking wine from an ornate goblet. There was a large hologram in front of her displaying an intelligence briefing, which she read while sipping wine.

So, Amalgam is preparing a shuttle. They must have a ship due to arrive tonight or tomorrow. No doubt that has something to do with the ship that is going to arrive at the International Mars Base in a couple days and the alien artifact that was retrieved from one of the caverns.

She made a video call to Jon Tucker, her second in command.

"Tucker here," he responded.

"I got your report," said Dez. "I think you're right. Anton Griswold is definitely starting to make a move. That delusional bastard totally underestimates me. It doesn't even occur to him that I would dare try to stop him."

"Well, he's going to be in for a surprise," said Tucker. "His arrogance will be his undoing and work very much in our favor."

"Oh yes," said Dez. "I'm not only going to stop him, I'm going to steal that alien tech right out from under him. He's used to all his little lackeys cowering in fear, but he doesn't scare me."

"What do you think about Chimera?" asked Tucker.

"Chimera is a mixed bag. They aren't willing to do what it takes to get their hands on the goods. Yet their reluctance to use violence at the IMB clearly doesn't apply to stopping us or Amalgam, nor do they seem to have any qualms about their ongoing espionage over at the International Mars Base," said Dez.

"If one corporation gets it, the other two will be left in the dust, so I can understand them wanting to stop us and Amalgam," said Tucker.

"Perhaps we can stir things up and have Chimera and Amalgam at each other's throats. It's still going to be tricky though. Open violence at the public base will cause an international incident that will kill our market share in the affected countries," said Dez.

"I think a little mischief and shifting blame should take care of that. I'll come up with some options for you," said Tucker.

"Sounds good," said Dez, closing the call.

"All right, boys," said Dez, setting her goblet on a small crystal tabletop. "It's time to line up and give Mama some sugar."

✳ ✳ ✳ ✳ ✳ ✳ ✳

Since deceleration had begun early that morning, the galley was serving real food again. Marty and Mia sat down at a table with Larry and Smita. Just as they sat down, they saw Brian and Yev walking over. It wasn't long before the topic of zero-g sex came up.

"Zipping up that bedding worked really well for us," said Marty.

"It was very snug and cozy too," said Mia.

"Indeed," said Larry. "The tensile strength of the material and its slight elasticity worked well applied to Newton's laws of motion, in gravity's stead."

"Oh, Larry, you're so romantic!" said Smita sarcastically, laughing a little.

"Get used to it, Smita," said Yev. "That's how it goes when you're married to a physicist."

"With Yev's mass I thought general relativity would come into play, but I guess he didn't have quite enough mass to noticeably curve space-time," said Brian, laughing.

Yev shook his head and chuckled and everyone else was laughing as well.

After some good food and conversation, Marty saw Hilda and Rachel heading back to their room. She excused herself to take care of business.

Hilda and Rachel were both slim and of average height, Hilda a blonde with blue eyes and Rachel a brown eyed brunette. They were both in their mid-twenties or so.

They appeared more nervous by the second as Marty closed the gap between them. She caught up with them as they were opening the door to their room.

"I think we need to have a little talk," said Marty holding the door open.

Hilda and Rachel were in the doorway, but turned and nervously backed into the room. They held their hands in front of them, with their palms open in a sort of defensive gesture.

"What do you want?" stammered Hilda, her voice cracking a little.

"I think you know," said Marty, stepping into the room and closing the door behind her.

Her voice was quiet, yet stern and her face showed she meant business. Hilda and Rachel backed into the corner together, squatting down with their hands in front of their faces.

"Please don't hurt us!" Rachel exclaimed in a frightened voice.

"I didn't want to do it," said Hilda, starting cry.

Rachel started crying as well, trying to get words out between sobs. "Neither—did I—"

"Then why did you betray us," said Marty, her voice stern. She took a step toward them, and the two girls huddled together, crying, scared out of their minds. Marty could tell, it wasn't an act. They really didn't do it voluntarily. As scary as this encounter would have been for them after seeing her in action at the maglev station, this reaction was way over the top. Clearly, they were already terrified about something else, so they had to have been threatened.

No more intimidation was needed at this point. In fact, Marty was starting to think she had overdone it. She needed to be sure though. Now the two women were starting to get hysterical. Marty wouldn't have been surprised if they wet themselves.

"All right, all right, Hilda, Rachel, let's talk about this," said Marty, her voice softening.

They both managed to mumble "okay" but they were still crying.

"I was approached and they didn't want to take no for an answer, so I understand. I just needed to be sure you were being sincere," said Marty.

"It was this guy from Amalgam Global, called, Charles Mantis," said Rachel.

"He pulled a gun on us. It happened to us separately, we didn't know about each other until later," said Hilda.

"He threatened to shoot me. Later I noticed Hilda was upset about something and we compared stories," said Rachel.

"He told both Rachel and I there would be people of his on the Mars base and if we didn't cooperate, bad things would happen," said Hilda.

"I see," said Marty. "So that's when you guys put in to get a room together instead of the random match. Well, you two dry your eyes and we'll go talk to Yev, the huge Russian guy. He will be head of security on Mars. I'll be watching your back too."

"Please tell as few people as possible," said Rachel.

"Everyone's going to hate us," said Hilda.

"I'll keep it quiet. I think people would understand though. I might have been in that situation myself if I hadn't fought my way out of it."

"How did that go? Did you fight with Charles Mantis?" asked Hilda.

"Oh yeah," said Marty. "Mostly it was his three guys I fought with. However, I did break his fucking nose and knocked him flat on his back too. I bet he needed surgery to fix his nose. I fucking flattened it."

"Good! Serves him right, the bastard," said Rachel.

Hilda nodded in agreement. The three of them left the room, walking back to the common area. Marty directed them to where the rest of the group sat, waiting.

"It's kind of like we figured," said Marty. "Both of them were threatened just like I was. I knocked Charles on his ass before he got to finish making the threat, but according to these two, there are people at the Mars base to carry it out."

"I'll make sure security is tight," said Yev.

"Thank you. This is the best I have felt since this whole nightmare began," said Rachel.

"Same here," said Hilda. "At least I ended up with a close friend."

As she spoke, Hilda looked over at Rachel, who put an arm on her shoulder.

Chapter Eight

It was early morning when Charles and Francis walked into the spaceport on the Amalgam Global Mars Base, after having just shuttled down to the planet's surface. Anton Griswold was already there waiting for them. He was just a little older than Charles—in his mid-fifties or so. His brown hair had mostly turned gray, his hairline receded a little and he had a bald spot on the top of his head. He had cold green eyes, which seemed to look through you, judging everything, and a wide nose, which was a little pitted.

"Welcome to Mars," said Anton, in a voice with forced cheer and an equally fake smile.

"Thank you, Mr. Griswold," said Charles and Francis simultaneously.

"I want you both to rest up today and tomorrow," said Anton. "The day after, you're going to have a lot of work to do. That's the way it's going to be until you bring me what I want."

"Yes sir, we'll both be ready to go then. We'll get a team together and get this taken care of," said Charles.

"Your progress so far has been subpar at best," said Anton with a scowl. "I would be reconsidering my trust in you by now, but your past performance has been pretty good. I don't want to hear any more lame excuses though. Just get the job done."

"As you wish, Mr. Griswold," said Charles.

Once they had put some distance between them and Anton Griswold, they were able to loosen up and speak freely.

"Can you believe that bullshit?" said Charles rhetorically. "He has no idea how difficult this is! He's one sick fuck too. I'll do what I have to in order to get what I want, because I just don't give a shit—sociopathic they say—but that guy—fuck! That sadistic fuck actually enjoys it. I've never seen anyone who takes so much delight in human suffering. Instead of needing a reason to do something, it's almost like he needs a reason not to. If he ever decides we've failed and we're going to die anyway, him before us."

"Absolutely, Boss, him before us," said Francis.

"I'm not saying this should be the plan, but if by chance the opportunity arises for a certain megalomaniac to have a little accident— well, you know," said Charles.

"Oh yeah, I'm right there with you," said Francis.

✳ ✳ ✳ ✳ ✳ ✳ ✳

Marty and Mia were lounging in their room after having decided to spend the evening together just the two of them.

"You never really mention your family, Marty."

"There's not much to tell. We don't really talk much. I told you about our disagreements. Conversation is just limited to small talk. Even though most of the family wasn't involved, they heard all about our disagreements. They're mainly upset about my attitude. However, my attitude is the direct result of how they look at me. They think a little less of me because I'm an atheist and to a lesser extent because I'm gay. Most people could probably get past that, but it really just pissed me off. It still pisses me off. Yeah guys I'm a 'gaytheist', get over it."

Mia laughed "A 'gaytheist'! Well, I guess that's what I am too. I never really thought of it like that. So you do talk to them a little eh?"

"Yes. It's usually only at funerals lately though. The last two of my great-great-grandparents died recently. One died a few years ago and the last one died not quite two years ago. I didn't really know them though. My great-grandparents I know. They're all in good health, but over a hundred. In a way, I'd like to make up with them, but it's not so easy. Time isn't on my side either. Well, I think that's enough of that for now."

"Most of my great-great-grandparents died quite recently. The last one was just at the beginning of this year. She was a hundred and twenty-one. Back when she was young, the oldest people were five years younger than that, now they're twenty years older—oh sorry, I do tend to ramble sometimes."

"That's all right. I enjoy listening to you," reassured Marty.

"Well, that's good. I can keep going and going sometimes. I tend to be like that when I'm not feeling shy."

There was a pause in the conversation at that point. After a couple minutes, Marty pulled Mia close and kissed her. Mia responded and it wasn't long before things started heating up and clothing went flying.

✳ ✳ ✳ ✳ ✳ ✳ ✳

Oscar Perry stood in front of a full-length mirror in the executive level men's room of the Chimera Mars Base. He ran a comb through his light brown hair, giving it a quick touch-up. Next, he straightened his tie and buttoned the jacket of his black suit.

Oscar looked down at his watch.

Two minutes. There is plenty of time to get to the meeting room. I hope Bill keeps it brief. These things can get so tedious and I know he's just going to do a one-on-one with each of us anyway.

Oscar entered the small nondescript meeting room and sat in a plain, black conference chair at an ordinary, rectangular table. All the other people that reported directly to Bill Jeffries were sitting down around the table as well.

Bill Jeffries called the meeting to order and Oscar sat quietly ready to listen, as did the others. Bill was about forty, with messy, longish brown hair and brown eyes. He wore a nice dark suit with a multicolored, striped tie. He was average height, with an athletic build, although that was hard to see in the suit.

Nice suit, Bill, but for fuck sakes comb your hair. Use a little product if it is that unruly.

Bill looked around the table and seemed to be mentally checking attendance. Then he addressed the group.

"Now that I have had a couple weeks to get situated here, I wanted to go ahead and lay out our general plans. The other senior board members and I are very much in agreement about what to do in our current situation.

"This is going to be a multifaceted project and we all need to be on the same page here in order to best leverage everyone's strengths moving forward."

Oscar continued listening, trying not to roll his eyes at the heavy use of corporate meeting buzzwords.

Yeah, let's do a follow-up to go over action items on leveraging team synergy. More bullshit is exactly what we need.

Despite that, Oscar kept his poker face on and listened as Bill continued speaking.

"Allow me to start with the lowest priority piece, as it is the precipitating event. We know that there is a small ship of alien origin over at the International Mars Base. There are operatives in place and we would certainly like to requisition that tech if at all possible. We need to be discrete about it though. Nobody can trace it back to Chimera. Accusations could hurt our business interests in affected countries.

"The use of force, however, is prohibited at the public base. The other senior board members and I don't just want to avoid an extremely business-averse incident either. No, we simply don't feel it's appropriate for our corporate culture. Furthermore, getting the tech is more of a 'nice to have' rather than a mission critical action item. So, all espionage needs to be very discrete and low-risk.

"At the moment Amalgam Global, along with The Parasol Group, to a lesser extent, are trying as hard as they can to get the alien tech. Either of them getting it would be extremely damaging to our business interests. Whoever gets it will leave the rest in the dust. Espionage on the other two corporations here should focus on evidence of wrongdoing. Exposing them will allow us to gain a huge advantage in relations with world leaders and this, in turn, would result in amazing increases in market share.

"Forceful action against the other two corporations is also acceptable. It must remain covert for the moment in order to forestall reprisals though. You will be notified when I meet with the senior board members to approve the open use of force. The other two corporations seem to have no problem with murder committed against our employees, affiliates and business interests, or the largely innocent general public over at The International Mars Base. Therefore, the other senior board members and I feel that terminating them is acceptable and does not violate our corporate culture, which normally frowns on killing people.

"As always, be mindful of how far down the chain anything shady is disseminated. Is there anything that anyone feels should be brought before the group?"

Oscar and the others looked around but said nothing. Oscar didn't expect anyone would speak up. It was all straight forward and they would have to discuss it with Bill soon enough anyway.

After pausing a moment, Bill continued. "Very well, I'll expect a report from each of you in a couple days and I'll schedule a one-on-one where we can discuss it. My assistant should have the meeting minutes sent out shortly. Thank you."

Good. He kept it fairly brief. I should head down to the ground level and see what's going to be served for lunch.

Everyone pushed in their chairs and filed out of the room, quickly heading off in different directions. Oscar was one of the last out and headed for the lift.

* * * * * * *

Deceleration was almost complete and Mia had easily talked the crew into letting her and Marty come up to the top deck. They followed Hiro onto the flight deck. They couldn't see anything but space outside because they weren't facing the planet. They could see it on a display though, which showed a feed from a camera near the engines. Mars was getting very close.

After a few minutes, they heard one of the crew make the announcement to prepare for weightlessness. After giving it a minute, Captain Johnson slowly reduced power on the engines. They continued to feel lighter and lighter until finally, the engines cut out and they were at zero-g.

The crew maneuvered the ship around with thrusters and slowly Mars started coming into view as the ship oriented itself. After a while Mars was centered and already taking up almost their entire field of vision. It continued to get larger as they approached.

At one point, they could see nothing but the planet. At that time, they were reaching the gravitational field of Mars and the crew maneuvered the ship to go into orbit. Finally, half the display was part of the surface of Mars and the other half was space. They were now essentially falling to the planet's surface.

Marty and Mia floated there, taking in the amazing view. The ship would continue circling in toward the planet, until it finally settles into a low orbit. After getting their fill of the view, they headed back down to prepare for when the shuttle docks.

Chapter Nine

Marty and Mia got out of bed in their quarters on the Mars base. Their quarters were a lot like a small motel room. It was very small and bare, with a tiny, adjoining bathroom. It was nearly twice as big as the room on the ship if you counted the bathroom and the cupboard-like thing that served as a closet. Gray seemed to be the color there, everything dull and boring. The comfortable bed would be an improvement though and they didn't have to worry about shared bathrooms or zero-g toilets anymore.

The previous night had been a bit of a blur. Their weariness after getting off the shuttle was overwhelming. Marty remembered coming out of the shuttle into a tube similar to the ramps used at airports, but it was airtight and pressurized. Then they were in the part of the base that served as a spaceport, Dome Five. They walked through different areas, through some corridors and then into what seemed like a massive hotel with small, crappy rooms.

They had gone to sleep soon after entering the room last night. It was the first night they hadn't done anything sexual since they hooked up. They just got in bed and fell asleep.

Now Marty and Mia were getting dressed as a tour of the base was about to begin. Luckily it included breakfast. That was the most awesome thing ever as far as Marty was concerned. She was absolutely starving. Just as she thought that, she heard Mia's stomach growl.

"I hear you with that. I'm hungry too," said Marty.

"I hope we get to the eating part quickly—I can't believe how fast I fell asleep last night. I was so tired," said Mia.

They left the room, walked down the hall and took a lift down to the ground floor. The place where everyone was meeting was just past the other lifts.

People quickly gathered around and there was a man there who must be from the Mars Base staff, as Marty didn't recognize him. The rather tall and lanky man looked about fifty years old, almost completely bald, with a thin face and a sort of half frown. His frown was belied by the hint of a humorous twinkle in his eye, just as his baldness was interrupted by a patch of graying brown hair around the back and sides.

When everyone was there, the man spoke. "Morning. I'm Samuel Bradshaw, one of the Mars base administrative managers," He said in a rather deadpan voice, with an English accent which was more of the working class, East End kind rather than the posh variety—not quite Cockney though. "I never say 'good morning' though. Nope. Just plain old morning. It's way too damn early to be cheery about anything. Besides everyone secretly wants to punch the sodding git who's all chirpy in the morning."

As he continued his deadpan voice became more expressive and he spoke in such a way that his level of seriousness was a little ambiguous at first. There was the frown, but also that look in his eye.

"The first thing to see on the tour is gray walls, followed by more gray walls, both in rooms and in corridors. There is the more exciting bit outside, but then the weather isn't exactly nice, now is it. Well, let's get some breakfast first. I plan on boring you all to death, not starving you. All kidding aside, there is actually a lot of interesting stuff to see here. It's just the colorless, minimalist décor that's so dreadfully boring."

People chuckled a little throughout this speech, which seemed to be a good ice-breaker. They continued walking through Dome Seven, down a corridor to Dome Six. There were a few different places you could eat, all of them in Dome Six.

They walked to one of places that looked like an office or school cafeteria. This one was fairly close to the corridor from which they had emerged. They all went through the line, loading up trays with the variety of foods laid out like a buffet. When they reached the end, there was a large area full of tables and chairs. It was mostly big, long tables with cheaply made folding chairs. There were also a few smaller circular tables around.

When they all had sat down with something to eat, Samuel continued.

"There we go. The morning is not so bad when you get a little food in you and some coffee of course," he said between bites.

Marty thought the food was surprisingly good, especially compared to what they had on the ship. She could see Mia enjoying hers as well.

"The ninth dome we won't bother with," said Samuel. "Many of you have clearance for it, but you'll also be working there, so you'll get to see that tomorrow. It's all scientific research and some manufacturing."

After a while, they all got up and the tour continued. "We won't bother with Dome Eight either. The entire thing is residential and we have you all in Dome Seven. You're not missing anything though. I live there and I can tell you it looks just like the residential areas in seven, but older."

They went back through the corridor to Dome Seven, as Samuel told them more about it. "Dome Eight has been all residential since it was finished back in the sixties. All the research and manufacturing were moved to nine a few years ago, leaving most of seven empty. It was renovated and turned into additional housing. It's probably not quite a year and half since they finished. It's the same crappy, little rooms as eight, just newer, that's all."

Samuel pointed out where the corridor to Dome Eight was and then the one that led to Dome Nine. He explained the room numbering system, so they could find their way back home if they got lost. He also mentioned that if you take the lift down to the basement level, the medical facility and laundry are down there, in addition to some other resident services.

After they walked back through to Dome Six, Samuel said, "By now you should know your way around seven well enough and particularly how to get to six. That's especially important as most of the stuff you'll need on a daily basis is in six."

He showed them the dining areas, the main airlock, the corridors leading to four of the other domes and the lifts. He explained that in the upper floors were lounges, recreation areas, shops and supply areas. Most things were provided to them, although there were some extra things that were sold. They also sold to employees of the three corporations, who would sometimes come there to get things they wanted, which were not provided at the corporate bases.

They walked down a corridor to Dome Five, which looked very familiar. It turned out to be the spaceport, where they had originally entered the base. It was kind of like a couple airport terminals, plus a garage, where mechanics performed maintenance on shuttles and land vehicles. The lifts seemed to have been redone to make them wider. Samuel explained that this was because all mechanical supplies were on the two floors above, kind of like a warehouse.

They walked through a boarding area, which was a lot like the one they came through from the shuttle. It might have even been the same one. They emerged into what looked like the top deck of a boat enclosed in transparent alumina with an inner layer of aerogel, reinforced with carbon nanotubes. It was the same material used to make the transparent parts of the domes. There were just enough seats for everyone and as they sat down, Samuel closed the door on the walkway tube. While that door was opaque, the door on the glider was mostly transparent. The edge around the frame and the edge around the door were both opaque, as were some of the mechanical parts in the release mechanism. After closing the door, Samuel activated the magnetic seal. With the glider airtight, he was able to release the magnetic lock holding it on the walkway tube.

There was an amazing view. Marty gazed in wonder upon a barren, rocky landscape as far as the eye could see in every direction. All the dust and most of the rocks were reddish, although some rocks had browns of different hues mixed in. The burnt orange colored sky played host to the smaller and dimmer looking sun. It looked like a somewhat cloudy day on Earth. Hills, valleys and even some craters dotted the uneven terrain.

Samuel sat at the controls and soon had the glider lifting off the ground with a hum. He then activated a speaker system so he could be heard in the back.

"This is the larger of our two sealed gliders. The other gliders are much smaller and require a spacesuit as they are not sealed. They are too small for a life support system. It's the same with the trucks and the little carts as well.

"We're just going to go out to the Curiosity Two and Colony Rover landing sites," said Samuel, as the glider began moving.

The glider kept accelerating and Samuel continued. "There are trips to the Exomars and Insight landing sites every now and then. There are also trips out to Gale crater sometimes, which is where Curiosity One landed. The other landing sites are too far. The only time anyone went to those was when they retrieved the lander or rover that was there."

They soon reached an area with a flag and Samuel pointed out where Curiosity Two had landed and the different places it went. Then they drove back toward the base. They could see the edge of Gale crater on the way back. And when they returned they drove to a different side of the base over by the small Dome One. There was a flag maybe a mile from the base.

"That is where the Colony Rover landed," said Samuel. "That was the last one we sent before finally sending people here."

He pointed out some interesting things about the landscape and then they headed back. As they drove toward the base, Samuel pointed out the sites where the temporary bases had been on the two missions before Dome One was built.

Once they were all back inside the base, Samuel led them over to Dome Four.

"I'll tell you more about these early domes on the way back through here," said Samuel. "Right now I'm going to concentrate on the exhibits here. In this dome we have all the earlier landers and rovers, as well as replicas of a couple of the rockets used to launch them. Well, I guess I should say the intact landers. Mars Two we knew would be in tiny pieces so we didn't bother. Mars Six was all crunched up. It was the same thing with the Polar Lander. We do have Mars Three and the two Viking landers though."

They walked through and looked at the exhibits, which featured the lander or rover and a little information about its mission. Spirit and Opportunity were sitting next to each other, with corresponding information on either side. The last thing they came to before reaching the door leading to Dome Three was the Curiosity One rover.

The domes got progressively smaller, as the rovers and landers got bigger. So, the last four were enough to fill Dome Three. They saw the Exomars, Insight, Curiosity Two and then finally the Colony Rover.

In the second dome were exhibits of the temporary bases used in the first two missions. This included replicas of both the exterior and interior. There were also pictures and bios of the members of both missions.

The best part was in Dome One. It had been restored to its original configuration. It was set up exactly the way it had been from twenty-nine to well into the thirties. Marty pictured the doorway leading back to Dome Two as an airlock, which is how it would have been the first two years before the expansion. They also went into the original greenhouse, which had visual demonstrations of how it was initially used.

As they walked back through the domes Samuel told them about the history of the base expansions, how they were changed and upgraded over the years and then finally turned into a museum when they were too relatively small to be of practical value.

When they walked back into Dome Four, Samuel said, "This is the first dome to have an additional floor. It's a museum down here, but upstairs is where the administrative offices are which is where I work most of the time."

Samuel showed them where the corridor was that led directly to Dome Six, so they didn't have to walk through the spaceport and garage areas in Dome Five. Once they were there, he advised that they explore Dome Six on their own and then bid them good day saying, "Don't forget to check out the fitness area. Even with a myostatin inhibitor, resistance training is still vital in preventing atrophy in this weak gravity."

Marty and Mia decided to do as Samuel advised and headed over to the lifts in Dome Six, so they could explore the upper levels. Larry, Smita, Brian, Yev, Rachel and Hilda walked with them. They took the lift up a floor at a time, exploring each as they went. There were four additional floors above the ground level. They got a little smaller as you went up, but they were all close to the size of the ground floor. This was due to the rather flat shape of the dome, which looked like the very top sliver of an enormous ball from the outside. This was the reason the first three domes had no additional floors. They simply lacked the height.

Pretty much anything you wanted could be found on the five levels of Dome Six. It was like a cross between the interior of a cruise ship and a shopping mall. There were many stores scattered throughout. They were all at least equipped to charge money, however most things were provided free if you were a resident of the base.

Support personnel, such as Smita, Yev, Rachel, Hilda and all the folks working in Dome Six actually made up the majority on the base. Industrial and science employees who did the things that the base was there for were in the minority.

Rachel and Hilda mostly just interacted with each other and not so much with the rest of the group. They tended to hang back a little from the others, however, they were never far from either Marty or Yev.

Many parts of the outer walls of the dome were transparent, made of the same material that encased the glider. The rest had been constructed with black carbon nanotubes. This contrasted a lot from the interior which was very gray. They paused from time to time to gaze out and marvel at the Martian landscape.

Once they had explored, they went back down to the second floor to where the fitness center was located. The fitness center was large, taking up a lot more space than anything else on the second floor. It might even be more than all the rest combined. It did appear to occupy about half the level.

The weights were quite bulky due to the low gravity. They were all made there at the base from the Martian iron. It felt like being super hero lifting bars with such large iron plates. They also found they could jump incredibly high—almost three times as high as on Earth. Even Mia, who is not very athletic, was able to do pull-ups with one hand. Throwing things was also amazing. Marty and Yev ended up sparing, hurling each other across the tumbling mat with ease.

Larry had been checking out the other stuff with everyone, but his attention soon turned back to the weights. He wasn't very athletic other than doing some amateur bodybuilding. He was fairly sedentary for the most part, except for a couple hours a week he spent lifting weights. Marty and Yev soon joined him and the three of them walked around planning their workouts around the available equipment.

Once they had finished in the fitness center, they all went down to get some dinner. They ran into Jorge as he came out of a shop, having the same idea they did. Then when they got out of the lift, Zahra was walking by, also on her way to get some dinner. The ten of them walked to one of the cafeterias all in one big group.

Chapter Ten

Marty walked down the corridor to meet up with Larry. The two of them hadn't spent much time together with everything going on—him getting married and her having a new girlfriend. She was really starting to miss him. They had seen each other almost every day, but they weren't able to spend any quality time together. She could tell he was missing her too when he invited her to come have a drink with him. Larry had brought some nice bottles of scotch with him and was planning on sharing with Alistair McDermott, the cryptography expert.

When Marty walked by Larry's quarters, he was coming out with two bags full of clinking bottles.

"Here, take this," said Larry handing one of the bags to Marty. "I told Al I was bringing some goodies, but he's going to flip when he sees these."

"Wow, Larry, what is this, a month's salary worth of the finest scotch?" asked Marty.

"Yes, it probably is now that you mention it. It's not like I bought them all at the same time though. If you notice I've sampled all of them too," said Larry.

"It's been too long, Larry."

"I know, we haven't really hung out since the weekend before I got married. It's about time we got together."

When they got to his quarters, Dr. Alistair McDermott answered the door. "Hello, Larry!"

"Al, this is my friend, Marty. Marty, Al," said Larry, making introductions.

"That's an interesting name for a girl," said Al.

"Yeah, it's kind of unusual. It's short for Martina. It just kind of happened that way. I probably could just as easily have ended up being called 'Tina'. It would be less confusing for people and they wouldn't be expecting a guy when they meet me. It just doesn't sound right to me though. Usually in professional circumstances I just go by 'Martina' to keep it easy."

"Wait 'til you see what I've got," said Larry.

"Aye, come in you two, let's see what you brought," said Al.

Al was short, stocky and muscular, with a large frame. He had light reddish brown hair and a mustache of the same color. He looked to be well into his forties, or perhaps fifty.

"Well, look at all of that," said Al, in awe, as Larry and Marty finished laying out the scotch before him. "There's so much to choose from. Larry, you're a fucking saint! This looks great."

"I brought one of everything, but I have some extras back in my quarters," said Larry.

Al set out three of the cheap, recyclable cups, which were ubiquitous on the base and put ice in them. While he was doing that, they all decided on a scotch to sample. Al poured the drinks and then they all sat down and proceeded to have a taste. Marty thought it was quite smooth, with a warm sensation, a little bit of a woody flavor and only very slightly smoky.

They just chatted at first, as they sipped their scotch. Later they listened to music and played a holographic card game. By the end of the evening Marty was feeling moderately drunk. She was still able to walk without stumbling as she carried one of the bags, walking back to Larry's quarters. It had been a fun evening, very nice hanging out with Larry again.

On the way back to her own quarters she thought of Mia. She had only been out for the evening, but couldn't wait to get back to her. She was anxious to look into Mia's beautiful eyes, hold her tight in her arms and kiss her soft, warm lips. She had been in a lot of relationships, but there was something different about Mia, something very special.

✳ ✳ ✳ ✳ ✳ ✳ ✳

Mia had enjoyed a relaxing evening lying in bed reading. She was a little tired from the day's activities. She was glad Marty and Larry got to spend some time together, but hoped Marty would be back soon. Marty had shown her a whole new world of love and sex and it was wonderful. She was tough and strong, making Mia feel safe and secure. The tough exterior seemed to hide a big heart within, which she was able to see more and more of.

She felt her heart jump in her chest as she heard the door open. She was so ready for Marty to come home and glad she hadn't stayed out too late. She saw Marty's stunning dark eyes meet hers, as they seemed to fill with warmth, her full, red lips curling up in a big smile. She could tell Marty was glad to see her too.

It felt so good as Marty climbed into bed with her. She didn't even mind the scotch breath. She eagerly kissed Marty's lips and helped her out of her clothes. This was the perfect way to end their first day on Mars.

✳ ✳ ✳ ✳ ✳ ✳ ✳

Marty and Mia met up with Larry, Smita, Brian, Yev, Jorge and Zahra on the way over to Dome Nine. The ninth and final dome was by far the largest. The ground floor was almost double the surface area of Dome Seven and fifty percent larger than Dome Eight. It had fifteen levels in total, with ten above the ground floor and four below. Only the first basement level goes all the way across though. The middle two extend only halfway, while the bottom level is half standard height and half triple height.

Marty, Smita and Yev weren't actually going to be working there, but they really wanted to get a look at the alien ship. At the security checkpoint leading to Dome Nine, the guards seemed to recognize Yev.

"Hey, it's the new boss," said one of the guards to the other. Then turning to Yev he said, "Hello, sir, welcome to Mars."

"Ah, so you recognize me then?"

"Yes, Evgeny Petrov, new head of security. I still have to see your badge though and everyone else's too."

Everyone displayed their new badges and submitted to the scan, which checked retina pattern, fingerprints, DNA and other data from the nanobots. They had to state their names as well for the voice print. The badges were created upon arrival, which was unfortunate as everyone looked terrible in their pictures. They were all quite tired and bedraggled when they arrived.

"Sir," said the guard to Yev. "You will have to escort Dr. Patel, or assign someone to do so. Medical doctors are allowed all access, but it's more of a restricted access."

"Yes, of course," said Yev. "I'll remain with her. Dr. Patel, Martina and I will not be staying long."

They ran into an additional checkpoint by the lift at the fourth basement level, then another when they entered the half that took up three floors. Restrictions varied there. Some of the industrial machines required a high level of access and some didn't. There were no low level employees there, just machine operators. Robots did the menial tasks.

Most of the research areas were on the other floors. There was just one area in that section of the base. It was where the most secret work was done and where prototypes were made.

They proceeded through another security checkpoint and then they were in. The cavernous room, filled with every piece of scientific equipment you could imagine, otherwise looked the same as anywhere else in the base, with its gray walls. Only the thirty foot ceiling gave it contrast.

As they looked around, an average sized man of about sixty, with long, thick, white hair draped over his shoulders, approached them. His lengthy beard and bushy eyebrows were white as new fallen snow. Marty pictured him wearing a robe and a pointy wizard hat, because that is exactly how he looked.

Larry and Brian both knew him and introduced him as Dr. Magnus Petersen.

"This is Dr. Mia Bierbrauer, who will be working on the big project," said Larry.

"Ah, I see. It's very nice to meet you, Dr. Bierbrauer," said Dr. Petersen, in his thick Danish accent.

"I think you're at least familiar with everyone else," said Larry.

"Ah yes, your two assistants, your wife and this must be your friend, Martina," he said looking at Marty.

"I look forward to working with you, Dr. Petersen," said Mia.

"Let me show you the alien ship," said Dr. Petersen.

The ship actually looked kind of fake. But they knew it was the real deal.

"It looks like a shuttlecraft from an early twenty-first century science fiction movie," said Marty.

"I suppose it does. Well, at least it doesn't look like a shuttlecraft from the original Star Trek series," said Dr. Petersen with a chuckle.

After inspecting the alien craft, Marty, Yev and Smita headed back toward the lift leaving the others there to begin their work.

After returning to the ground floor, they headed back toward Dome Seven. A number of people walked past them in the corridors and public areas. The moderate crowd had grown in number and activity since the early morning hours. In Dome Seven they walked across to where the lift above the medical facility and the corridor leading to Dome Six were located.

"Well, I think this is my stop," said Smita, as they reached the lift which led down to the medical facility.

Marty and Yev bid her good day and continued on to the corridor leading to Dome Six. It was actually right above the front of the medical facility.

As they entered Dome Six Yev said, "You should come up to the security office with me. I think some areas of our work will be overlapping."

They had to walk across Dome Six to reach the security office. It was in between the entrance to Dome Five and the little corridor leading over to Dome Four. In the office they walked past the guards who all came over to greet their new boss. Afterward, they were able to duck into a tiny room in the back. Yev, the head of security, was the only one with his own private office, but that office was extremely small.

The gray closet-sized room contained a small desk. A chair sat behind it and another in front of it, off to the side in the corner. The furniture seemed to match the sterile, functional look of the other parts of the base—no real thought given to aesthetics.

Yev sat behind his new desk, which looked a little comical given his size. Marty held back a laugh, stifled her smile and sat in the other chair.

"I'm going to make sure physical security is tight and get a rotation together to keep an eye on Rachel and Hilda. We need to know who we can trust though. Try to gather that information as quickly as you can," said Yev.

"I'll be heading over to the technology office. I'll get them started on securing the network here and then try some exploits on the corporations. That should allow me to gather some intel. As I secure the network, we'll see if we can find any communication going out to any of the corporations. That should allow us to round up the spies. After all that is done, we really need to stop people from the corporations from entering the base," said Marty.

"I wish we could do that," said Yev. "Alma Cohen and her staff are kind of stubborn from what I understand. At least according to the research I did on the way here. Locking the place down had occurred to me, but as I investigated I soon discovered it would take a major incident for that to happen."

When their plans were all lined out, Marty left the security office and headed for the technology office. It was pretty close by. She went into Dome Five and it was right there by the entranceway.

The staff in the technology office was expecting Marty. Apparently Larry had already made arrangements prior to their arrival. It took some time to survey what they had, but once complete, she quickly came up with a plan for security. What they had in place wasn't bad and she hadn't detected any signs of intrusion. Hardening the current security was still a good idea though.

The tech staff was pretty knowledgeable, so they had no problem implementing her plan. While they did that, she was free to dig around for information. Now that she had access to their systems, she would be able to work remotely. She headed back to her quarters to begin the task of exposing whoever was helping the corporations.

✳ ✳ ✳ ✳ ✳ ✳ ✳

Mia felt a great deal of excitement knowing she would soon be learning the secrets of an alien species, seeing how their technology worked. She could see from their faces that Larry and Brian shared her feelings. Dr. Petersen began filling them in on all the discoveries.

"The translation was difficult and is certainly far from perfect. There were several words for which we didn't have corresponding words. So we just described it in place of the name. It's rather like calling a car a 'horseless carriage' or a space shuttle an 'airplane that goes to space'. We also had a lot of trouble with units of measurement, like distance, time, mass and so on. Luckily, there were references to known constants, so we were able to extrapolate.

"It was the same thing with the mathematics. First, we had to figure out the symbols they used for numbers and then match them up to the words, as well as determine the sequence so we could know which number was which. They aren't on base ten either. They use octal. Their machines use binary like ours though.

"Some of their technology is on par with ours, but some of it is much more advanced. It would probably take two or three centuries for us to advance to this level on our own."

Mia, Larry and Brian all read through the translation of the computer data. Mia read the more general parts and skimmed the details. The first thing she wanted to do was make a mental note of all things that could be adapted to human technology and as a secondary goal divide the list into things that could be quickly implemented and things that would require more work, either due to complexity or to prerequisites.

✳ ✳ ✳ ✳ ✳ ✳ ✳

Marty flopped down on the bed in her cramped quarters. The room may be small and boring in its simplistic, gray design but it was actually rather cozy and the bed was pretty comfortable. She flipped on her mobile device and it projected a hologram in front of her. She manipulated it with her fingers as she lounged on the bed, connecting to the Mars base network.

She started a data-mining program and while that was running, gathering information she needed from the local systems, she started locating the networks of the three corporations on Mars. After she mapped out the entry points of the corporate networks, she started working on finding exploits. There were bound to be some vulnerabilities that would let her in.

* * * * * * *

At the end of the day, after reading through the alien data, Mia sat down with Larry, Brian and Dr. Petersen. Jorge and Zahra also gathered around to hear what was said.

"Let's compare notes," said Mia. "Here is what I got from reading through these documents. Some of their technologies, detailed here, are quite similar to ours. The computer and quantum communication technologies are nearly identical to ours, so we can put that aside. Their x-ray laser and hydrogen fuel cell design are also quite similar to ours. None of these things is much more advanced than our own either.

"Next we have the fusion technology. The reactors are fairly different from ours, but not much better. The generators and engines they have are also quite different. The generator isn't much more efficient than our current ones and neither are the engines. So, these can be set aside as well.

"The things to focus on are the antimatter generators, the warp field unit and that machine that converts energy to matter. Those are not so far beyond us or difficult to produce that they couldn't immediately be worked on.

"Using a microscopic black hole for energy is going to take time though. The gamma ray lasers needed to make it aren't too far beyond us, but their size would make them time-consuming to manufacture."

"That's my assessment as well," said Larry. "I didn't try to wade through the specifics on the fusion technology though."

Brian and Dr. Petersen nodded their agreement.

"I'm going to need a little help with some of the physics," said Mia. "The engineering and design stuff will be no problem though."

"We'll give you all the help we can," said Brian.

"The science team is at your disposal," said Dr. Petersen.

"It's going to be amazing when we are done with this," said Larry. "Especially for space travel. How about that device that creates the warp field? It's just unbelievable. Being able to go up to twelve light years in about an hour. Simply amazing. Even without the black hole thing, just running it from the antimatter generator, it can still travel up to a light year an hour. Being able to curve space-time to get artificial gravity. To think it comes from the same device too."

After Larry had made the introduction, Marty began telling the base administrator, Alma Cohen, about her findings.

"All data I could find pointed to the same six people, two from each corporation. Two were getting big payouts from a company I could trace back to Amalgam, two from a company traced back to Parasol and two from a company traced back to Chimera. There was evidence of communication on the base network, between the six people and the corporations paying them. I was also able to find data on each corporate network, detailing information from their two operatives.

"They all know about the ship. They also know it is alien in origin, it contains advanced technology, it is roughly a billion years old and base personnel found it in one of the caverns to the south. They don't know any specifics though. None of the six people had much security clearance.

"Yev is removing some of their clearance so they can't learn any more information. We would like to keep this quiet though. We may be able to feed them misinformation, which could prove to be useful in the future."

"Larry told me you'd have it sorted out quickly. Thanks, Marty. I like your plan. It sounds like a very good idea. Keep me informed about how this goes."

✳✳✳✳✳✳✳

Mia was lying on the bed reading a holographic book when Marty returned home from her meeting with Alma Cohen. She was eager to tell Mia about her day, as well as hear the details about the alien ship. Marty could see that Mia shared the excitement and curiosity, emotional cocktail she was experiencing.

Marty shared the details of the day's events first. She told Mia about what she discovered, as well as the technological tricks she used to do it. Then she listened with wide-eyed wonder as Mia told her all about what she learned regarding the alien ship. The details of the technologies involved had her imagination swimming. It was a thrilling and fascinating thing with which to be involved.

During the course of conversation, Marty had removed all her clothes and slid into bed next to Mia. As they finished discussing the implications of the advanced alien technology, Marty pulled Mia closer. Mia responded by putting her arms around Marty and holding onto her tightly. They were soon kissing, each woman's hands gliding over the other. It was going to be another hot and steamy night on the cold, red planet.

Chapter Eleven

Charles Mantis had finished assembling his team and fine-tuning his plan. Francis stood by his side, while his team of five stood to his rear. Behind the team was a clear section of the outer wall of their base, showing the rust-colored, dusty Martian landscape. A few feet in front of Charles, centered in the middle of the gray interior wall, was a black door. It opened as Anton Griswold walked through.

"As you can see, I have the team assembled, Mr. Griswold," said Charles.

"Right on schedule. What is your plan?"

"We'll send the team over to the base with the other folks who are going to trade with the merchants there. However, they will travel separately in one of our pressurized gliders and go around to an airlock on Dome Seven, right next to where it connects to Dome Nine. I gave them an exploit that will allow them to enter undetected. They will grab one of people working on the alien tech project, preferably Dr. Mia Bierbrauer. They'll use her to get past the security protecting the area with the secret projects if they can. Whether that ends up being possible or not, they will bring her back here so we can find out everything she knows."

"Yes!" said Mr. Griswold with an evil grin. "You will bring her back to me and we will torture every detail out of her. I'll be looking forward to it."

"Well, sir," said Charles. "We're going to threaten her some and rough her up a little, but no torture. It won't take much to make her talk."

"No, the torture will make sure we get everything and it will be quite entertaining as well."

"Maybe do that after we are done. We want to make sure all the information is accurate—"

"Don't contradict me, you spineless little bitch! Bring that fucking cunt here and we are going to do things my way. You'll do what you're told and you'll like it."

"Yes, sir," said Charles, with an expressionless face.

After Anton Griswold left, Charles dismissed the men and then turned to Francis.

"As much as that really pissed me off, I'm actually quite pleased. If this works, I get a good portion of the credit. If it fails, it looks very bad for Mr. Griswold. I think the CEO and board of directors could be convinced we need to, 'let him go', so to speak. Without the need for a cover-up I can just casually shoot him in the face right in front of everyone and have his body thrown in the grinder for compost. That makes it all so easy."

"I trust that your forthcoming promotion would mean I'd be up for one as well," said Francis.

"Of course. I'll see to it that you always report directly to me. So when I move up a spot, so do you."

"That's what I like to hear, Boss. You understand my motivations very well."

"Indeed. Mine are much like yours, so I find it very easy to understand. Mr. Griswold seems to understand that the stick is a good way to control people through fear. However, he doesn't seem to understand that only the carrot gives you true loyalty and sometimes that's exactly what you need."

"You always know when to use the stick and when to use the carrot. Regardless of which it is you always make it a big one."

"I think he also fails to see the value of bribery, Francis. I always prefer to try that first, myself. It's so much easier and more cost-effective in the end. But if it fails, well that's what I have you for."

✳ ✳ ✳ ✳ ✳ ✳ ✳

Dez sat on a couch casually massaging the buttocks of one of her men, who stood in front of her wearing the typical uniform, which was essentially just a thong. Jon Tucker entered the room at her invitation.

"Ah, Tucker, nice of you to join me. So how are things coming along with our plan?"

"It's progressing nicely," said Tucker. "We have stolen some mining supplies from both Amalgam and Chimera. It's not enough for either to notice though. But we can use them to cause an explosion at each base. I have some guys adding to the explosives, from our own stock, so that we have enough to do the job. It's only raw chemicals though, so it can't be traced back to us. I'm going to destroy the labeling and alter the chemical composition a little. That will make it difficult to figure out where it came from, but if we don't do that, they'll never believe it was the other corporation that did it. They might even suspect us. I'm sure they are smart enough to figure out the tampering though."

"Nice work, Tucker," said Dez, who had pulled down the thong of the man in front of her and turned him around. She had been cupping his balls with one hand, gently rubbing his erect cock with the other. This sort of thing no longer got any reaction from Tucker, which spoiled her fun just a little. She still enjoyed playing with the sexy man and his beautiful cock anyway though.

"Let me know when everything is ready," continued Dez. "I want to have that plan staged so I can implement it later when the time is right."

"Will do," said Tucker, as he turned and left.

Dez got the attention of one of her men on the other side of the couch. "Come around here."

"That's it," purred Dez. "Now suck on this," she said indicating what she held in her hand. One man sucked on the other, as Dez watched with delight. She liked seeing two men together sometimes. She also got some perverse pleasure out of the fact that her men didn't seem to enjoy it. She was nice to them the vast majority of the time, but every now and then she liked to be a little mean.

After a couple minutes, the man on the receiving end tensed up and grunted a little. The man on his knees, doing the giving, made a bit of a face as he kept going.

"Now open your mouth and show me what you have," ordered Dez.

When she had seen enough she told him to swallow and he did so.

"You've been a very good boy," purred Dez. "Get your cock out, I'm in the mood to give you a little reward."

She kissed him, tasting the other man in his mouth. Then she knelt down in front of him, teasing him with her fingers and tongue. Tasting the other man got her excited and then seeing this handsome man look down at her with desire increased the arousal further.

Dez knew that after she finished this bit of fun, it would be time to have the other guys line up to take care of the need she felt growing more and more urgent within her.

✳ ✳ ✳ ✳ ✳ ✳ ✳

Oscar Perry walked into the small, gray office of Bill Jeffries feeling eager to report his good news. Bill looked like he needed some good news. He appeared to be a little stressed, not his usual relaxed self.

"I have some good news to report," said Oscar.

"I was hoping you would say that," said Bill. "There has been a lot of pressure because of this situation, especially in regard to stifling our competitors."

"We have positive ID on the two Amalgam Global operatives in the International Mars Base. With that complete, work has begun on investigating Parasol."

"Excellent! See to it that the Amalgam operatives are eliminated."

"It will be arranged," said Oscar turning to leave.

"Oh and Oscar, make sure it's done discretely."

"Of course," said Oscar turning his head as he walked out.

Oscar walked down the hall considering whom he should send. He also needed to decide which method would be the best. It needed to be quiet since the discovery of bodies was going to cause a big enough stir, as it was, no need to make things worse.

✳ ✳ ✳ ✳ ✳ ✳ ✳

Curtis O'Brien piloted the pressurized glider across the Martian landscape, the other four members of his team sitting behind him. He wished Francis had come to lead this, as he didn't really want to be a leader. It would be nice to have a more legitimate job too, but the shady stuff he had always done paid so much more and required less work. It might end badly for him, but that's what they always predicted. All the people who dealt with him growing up never thought he'd reach adulthood. They may have been right about the course of his life, but for more than a decade, he'd proven their morbid cynicism wrong. The prediction had come close once when he let his guard down. The big scar across the side of his face was a reminder of that.

The dusty, rust-colored plains went by in a blur as they glided along on an invisible magnetic wave. The International Mars Base came into view and got larger and larger as they sped toward it. They pulled up next to the airlock on Dome Seven, right by the connection to Dome Nine.

Once the glider's hatch sealed around the airlock, Curtis connected to the airlock computer and ran the exploit. As the airlock opened, he opened the hatch on the glider. All five of them stepped out of the glider, into the airlock. He wished they could have brought guns, but Francis insisted that stealth was critically important.

Curtis looked through the window of the inner door, trying to figure out what to do next. Just then, he saw someone walking by. It was the person he had most hoped to find.

* * * * * * *

Mia entered Dome Seven, coming from Dome Nine. She was meeting Marty for lunch and she was running late. She walked quickly and decided to avoid the crowd in the main corridors. So, she went along the outer wall, looking out at the rocky, dust-covered plains of the red planet. After she walked past the airlock, she heard it open behind her, which was rather strange.

Suddenly Mia felt hands grabbing her. One big hand wrapped around her throat, choking her, pulling her backward. Another hand pressed against her mouth, as her chest tightened and her heart thumped ever faster. She felt dread washing over her making it hard to move, her legs becoming rubbery, her body not responding to her commands. The strong, rough hand choked her, constricting around her throat like a snake subduing its prey.

"You're going to come with us, or you die right here, right now," said a voice directly behind her.

Mia stopped resisting and stepped back and to the side, going where her abductors led. She felt the hand loosen a little on her throat, but it still held her very tightly.

"If you scream, I'll twist your head right off," said the ominous voice behind her.

Her captors flipped her around just in time to see three men ambush the guard at the entrance to Dome Nine. They jumped him and slammed his head against the wall. The guard fell to the ground and lay there motionless.

With Mia under their control, the intruders were able to get into Dome Nine. They looked around a little to get their bearings and then headed down the side looking for a lift in an out of the way area. Mia knew they must be after the alien ship. She wanted to stop them from getting in there, but she was too scared to think and her body still wouldn't obey her.

"There are too many people around, even by the lifts over there. Anywhere we can go there are two or three guards and they'll see us coming," said one of the men behind her.

"We don't stand a chance, Curtis," said another voice.

"I really wanted to get a firsthand look," said the voice directly behind Mia. "We'll have to settle for taking her back with us though."

Mia freaked out when she heard that. She had already been scared but now she felt a surge of panic. The hand around her throat just gripped tighter as she struggled. The man dragged her along and she could no longer breathe, as her throat closed under pressure.

$$* * * * * * *$$

Marty finally grew tired of waiting for Mia. She wondered what was taking so long. Had she gotten lost? They hadn't even been there a whole week yet, but they walked around all over the base many times. Mia could get distracted and be absent-minded though. So, Marty decided to go look for her.

She checked some of the other corridors in Dome Seven, but no sign of Mia. After a few minutes, her search took her around toward Dome Nine. She looked in the other direction first to see if Mia was there and then headed for Dome Nine.

When Marty saw the guard, she thought it must be a medical problem. On closer examination there seemed to be signs of a struggle. She called over to the security office to raise the alarm and the guards said they would tell Yev and then run over there.

As Marty walked into Dome Nine, she saw a group of five men. She felt herself ignite with rage. One of them had Mia by the throat, dragging her along with them. Her fury burned as her jaw tightened and fists clenched. She took off running at them full speed. It was more bounding leaps than running in the low gravity though. She bounced up with each step, almost hitting her head on the ceiling.

The men were all dressed in black jumpsuits. They were muscular and athletic, but also lean and agile. The man holding Mia had a big scar on his face and the biggest of the men stood next to him. The other three lunged forward to intercept Marty.

The tallest of them reached her first. Marty dodged to one side and then the other to avoid his fists. She spun around and kicked him hard in the gut. In the low gravity, he flew backward and slammed against the wall, then bounced off almost landing on his face. He was able to catch himself enough to keep from eating a big floor sandwich, but he was clearly hurt and getting up slowly.

One man attempted to grab her and she shoved him into the other. The one in the back flew back a couple feet and hit the floor. Mr. Grabby bounced off him and used the momentum to lunge forward. Marty saw his arm pull back to wind up for a punch. She countered extremely fast, feeling so light from the low gravity. She drove the heel of her palm into his nose, making a sickening crunch and a spray of blood. Grabby flew back almost hitting his comrade again. The blond man behind him dodged though and he hit the floor.

The blond fellow was fast, slamming Marty sideways into the wall of the corridor. He punched her hard in the mouth and then strangled her with his other hand. Marty, dazed for a second, felt blood dripping from her lip down the side of her chin. She wiggled out of his grasp and as he tried to regain his hold on her, she pulled his arm back and pushed on his shoulder at the same time. It made a loud pop as it came out of the shoulder socket and she wrapped her arm around to gain leverage.

She punched him hard in the face, keeping him from flying back with the grip she had on his dislocated shoulder. She rotated to the side as he tried to grab at her with his other arm and then swung back, using the momentum to drive her fist even harder into his face. She punched him several times before the tall guy was back for more. She threw Blondy at him, but he dodged out of the way. Blondy's head landed right where the wall met the floor, taking most of his weight and bending in an unnatural way.

Scarface and the big guy both had Mia and were heading for Dome Seven. Scarface still had her by the mouth and throat, while the big guy grabbed her legs. Mia struggled but it did no good as they easily dragged her away.

Marty tried to go after them, but the tall guy held her back. She positioned herself so that he was unable to hit her or throw her into the wall. She was unable to escape his grasp though. The other two had disappeared with Mia into the corridor to Dome Seven.

The guards in Dome Nine arrived at that time. One of them apprehended Grabby, who was struggling to get up, blood running down his face. The other two pulled the tall guy off of Marty and she quickly spun and punched him in the gut and then drove her knee into his groin. He was no longer able to put up much of a fight and the guards easily dragged him away.

As soon as her knee was out of the tall guy's groin, Marty quickly turned and ran for Dome Seven. She had to catch them before they got away with Mia. She felt sick and her stomach knotted up with worry.

Marty ran for the nearest airlock. She saw Scarface there dragging Mia inside. On the other side of the airlock, Yev grappled with the big guy. Size is definitely relative though. While the man she thought of as "the big guy" was a little bigger than the other men who were with him, he was a little on the small side compared to Yev. Very few people are bigger than The Russian Giant.

Marty lunged at Scarface, forcing him to loosen his grip on Mia. Mia wriggled free and soon Scarface needed his hands to grapple with Marty. They struggled in the airlock and then back out in the corridor. Scarface was backing Marty up, until she tried to trip him. He jumped back and then lunged forward taking a swing at her. Marty quickly evaded and then kicked him into the airlock.

Before Marty, Yev, or the security guards who came running could do anything, Scarface closed himself in the airlock and then opened the outer door. They were unable to get in while the outer door was open. By the time it would open again, he would have the glider detached and be ready to go.

At that point, Marty didn't care. She had Mia back and that's all that mattered. She took the trembling Mia in her arms and held her close. Marty could see the bruising starting to darken on Mia's neck. She ran her fingers gently through Mia's hair, trying to calm her, let her know everything would be all right.

"Mia, are you okay?"

"I'm scared, Marty. My neck really hurts too. Please just hold me. Don't let go."

"I've got you," said Marty, picking Mia up in her arms.

Yev had his men take the intruders to a holding cell. Then he went to catch up with Marty, who was walking to the medical facility carrying Mia.

On the way to the medical facility, they met up with Larry and Brian who had come to see what was going on. Yev filled them in on what happened while Marty was quiet. She just held Mia tight, like a precious baby she was afraid she would drop.

"We have to do something about this. I don't think I can bear to even let you out of my sight, Brian," said Yev half hugging Brian and half picking him up.

"I'll be fine, with my big strong man here," said Brian.

Brian and Yev looked into each other's eyes for a moment and then kissed.

Marty carried Mia all the way to the medical facility, not wanting to let go. Mia got an ice pack for her swollen neck and some drugs for the pain. Marty had to ice her lip too. It had long since quit bleeding, but it was getting swollen and puffy.

Marty finally had time to think about what happened. She was relieved to have Mia back, but it was all very unsettling. Then she thought about the way the blond guy landed. He might be dead. She had just meant to throw him at the tall guy, but he dodged and this is the result. She never killed anyone before and she didn't want it to be true. It was unintentional, but it still weighed heavily on her.

Hilda set Grabby's nose and then got to work on the rest of his injuries. Then a couple guys carried in a stretcher with a sheet over it. Marty knew it was the blond guy, he was definitely dead. Marty felt sick. It was probably good that she hadn't made it to lunch. Death wasn't a punishment, or revenge, or retribution. It was an ending. It was the final end. All those concepts became meaningless. The person in question simply ceased to exist.

"Marty, it was an accident," said Yev. "Don't let it get to you like that. You did what you had to do to protect Mia and accidents happen. I know how you feel though. I've had to do it in the line of duty a few times. You were there the last time it happened, there at the maglev station."

"I know, Yev. Thank you. I'll be all right in a little while."

Pointing to Grabby, Yev said, "This guy and the other two in the holding cell have refused to talk from what my men tell me. They know that if they don't talk, all we can do is send them back to Earth."

"Let's do some brainstorming tomorrow and come up with some ideas to prevent this sort of thing in the future," said Marty.

Larry walked over. "Is there anything I can do, Marty?"

"I'll be all right, Larry. I just need to get Mia home and take it easy for a while."

"Let me know if you need anything," said Larry.

With their treatment complete, Marty and Mia headed back to their quarters. They were both in desperate need of some quiet time.

Chapter Twelve

Charles Mantis walked through the Amalgam Global base deep in thought. He heard about the mission failure from Francis a little earlier. That was very bad, considering Anton Griswold being on the warpath lately. His mood was bad enough at the best of times and this made his behavior even more unpredictable than usual.

As Charles paced around, he saw activity over by the entrance to the greenhouse. Amalgam Global had an expansive greenhouse where certain foods were grown, just like the other three bases on Mars. A disturbing thought occurred to him regarding the fate of Curtis O'Brien and Mr. Griswold's propensity for sadism and pointless destruction.

As he walked by the entrance to the greenhouse, Charles could hear the grinder. At first, the engine seemed to be idling. Then he heard a sudden cacophony of loud and terrible sounds. The scream of a man, hysterical, first in terror and then in pain, mixed with the revving of the grinder engine as well as the crunching and grinding as it chewed up what it was being fed with its mechanical teeth. Over this horrible din came the worst noise of all. It was the maniacal, cackling laughter of Anton Griswold.

It sounded like Mr. Griswold was having the time of his life. These are the cackles of glee consistent with the ongoing progression toward the satiety of Mr. Griswold's bloodlust. Very little bothered Charles Mantis, but this was just sick and twisted enough to make him feel uneasy. With the unease, he felt hints of revulsion, maybe a sort of disgust as well. The feeling didn't just come from the act itself, he also felt this sort of revulsion even in regard to the purely moral aspect of it.

That was something he had only felt a couple times before. He surmised that this is like a mild version of what people usually feel about things they consider unethical or morally wrong. He could understand the moral rightness or wrongness of an action, but there was no feeling with it. The ethical consideration simply didn't matter in his mind. It took something truly horrific to elicit this emotion in him.

Charles also didn't understand people doing things that wouldn't benefit them in some way. Doing what society deemed to be evil acts seemed fine to him, when done to advance one's goals. Doing them just to do them and taking joy in the activity was just silly. Whether you did one of these acts or didn't was simply irrelevant. The important part is what you gain from doing it. He could maybe get a sense of satisfaction from revenge, but usually the act was beneficial at least in some small way. So it didn't really compare to the pleasure Mr. Griswold took in the pointless things he did.

Charles had been walking away from the greenhouse as he pondered the situation. The sight of Francis approaching, with a look of worry, pulled him from his contemplation, abruptly interrupting his thoughts.

"I have bad news, Francis."

"I figured as much. Did you get any details?"

"I walked by the greenhouse and I heard what was going on, but I didn't care to go have a look."

"The grinder?"

"Yeah. Curtis is compost now."

"All right, well I need to go get some rest," said Francis, looking depressed.

Just then, an explosion rocked the base. Charles ran to where the noise came from, Francis following close behind. It looked like a tornado hit one of the mining areas outside the base. There was nothing burning, which seemed unusual. However that's the way it is on Mars. With barely any oxygen at all, things can't catch fire.

Sabotage was not unheard of, but this was more extreme than usual. Charles thought one of the other corporations might be trying to distract them. Conflict could definitely slow the progress of acquiring the alien ship and its secrets. Perhaps the other two may be a threat after all. A little attention may have to be diverted that way. He hoped this wouldn't be at the expense of the main project though.

After a while, he saw men in space suits running out to the scattered debris. A casualty or two was expected. There was nearly always someone out at the site, keeping an eye on the machinery. The space suits could protect you from a lot, but not something like this. The helmets, made out of the same stuff as the bases, could easily stop a bullet. However, most of the suit had to be flexible. Woven airtight with carbon nanotube fibers, it was nearly impossible to puncture. However, it provided no protection from blunt force.

"What do you think?" asked Francis. "Parasol Group or Chimera?"

"It could be either. We'll have to see the results of the forensic evidence to determine that. It has to be one of them though," said Charles.

Charles went back to pacing around. His thoughts returned to Anton Griswold. He decided that should any future plan go wrong in any way, Mr. Griswold would die. He still needed to figure out the details, like covering it up. Staging some sort of accident would probably be the best thing.

✻ ✻ ✻ ✻ ✻ ✻ ✻

Oscar Perry was about to head back to his quarters. It was quite late and he really needed to get some sleep. He heard a rumbling sound and ran in the direction from which it emanated. He reached the transparent outer wall and looked out to see a bunch of debris strewn about, down below on the Martian surface. It was right where one of their mining facilities had been.

This was a strange turn of events. He wasn't expecting The Parasol Group, or Amalgam Global to attack. Well, unless they knew about the espionage. The hit on the Amalgam Global spies hadn't happened yet, so it couldn't be that. Besides, they would assume the International Mars Base security forces caught them.

It occurred to Oscar that the corporations would most likely realize their goal if they were willing to work together and split the prize. That was never going to happen though. Their greed would see to that. Instead of going for an almost certain and extremely large prize, they would go for it all and probably end up with nothing.

Even if he could convince Bill Jeffries of the folly of this, Anton Griswold and Dez Delacroix certainly wouldn't listen. Charles Mantis would probably listen, but he's a very dangerous, devious man. Oscar soon returned to his original plan of getting some sleep.

* * * * * * *

Marty awoke in the morning with Mia snuggled up next to her. Marty held her in her arms as she peacefully slept. The events of the previous day continued to replay in her mind. The man landing on his head, the way his neck bent, the covered stretcher, it all seemed to be haunting her. It was an accident, but it still happened, it was during a struggle, but for the purpose of defending herself and Mia.

Marty learned in recent days that two of the men she fought on the way back to the Newark subway, Charles and Francis, were here on Mars. She also learned of Anton Griswold. The stories she uncovered about him also weighed on her mind. His greatest pleasure was the pain of others, his joy derived from the sorrow of his fellow man.

Her thoughts then turned to Mia, the woman for whom she had developed feelings. Those feelings got stronger and stronger all the time. She wanted to keep Mia safe more than anything, during the incident of the previous day. What mattered more than anything was keeping Mia there with her, just as she was now. She cared about Mia quite a lot. It felt good knowing Mia had strong feelings for her too.

Was this love?

She would find out in time. She was at least open to the possibility and in fact, it seemed an inevitable conclusion.

* * * * * * *

Mia slowly opened her eyes, as the veil of sleep lifted. She could see Marty was awake already. She was holding her and it felt so good. She felt so safe and secure in Marty's arms, as if nothing could ever happen. Her neck still hurt and it was probably time for another dose of pain medication.

Look at Marty's poor lip. It's still swollen.

The stuff she learned the past few days was amazing. It was well worth the danger to learn from an alien species through that recovered artifact. From a billion years in the past comes technology that would take decades, or in some cases centuries to develop independently.

The best part of all was being there with Marty. She was tough and sexy, but so sweet on the inside. She felt special seeing that tender, hidden side of Marty. She made Mia feel so comfortable too, as if she could tell her anything. In fact, she had. All the secret fantasies she thought she would never reveal to anyone were now known to Marty. Marty even helped make them come true.

The sex was fantastic. She had no idea it could be so good. Marty would make love to her all tender and sweet, or if she wanted, hold her down and spank her. She loved the master and slave games they would play. She liked to be a naughty slave so that she had to be punished. The thought of it was getting her exited. She got that tight feeling in her stomach and started to throb down below.

She had always wanted to meet someone and fall in love, some day. Was that starting to happen now? Maybe she was starting to fall in love with Marty. Whatever it was, she never wanted it to end.

Dez felt light and almost giddy. The morning report was all good news. Last night's activities happened just as she hoped they would. The large explosions at Amalgam and Chimera certainly must have caused a great deal of chaos. No doubt, their forensic teams would be hard at work trying to figure out what happened.

Would they suspect each other?

Perhaps they might suspect her. It was unlikely but you never know. The tightened security would deal with that though. She hoped they would tighten theirs and then launch attacks against each other. With their forces tied up, both bases would be vulnerable. Stealing corporate secrets, planting spy equipment and performing some strategic sabotage would go a long way toward advancing her goals.

This was a situation where sexism could work in her favor. Everyone will likely continue to underestimate her, the people at the public base, Chimera and especially Amalgam Global. They would likely assume a woman was not ruthless enough or smart enough to carry out the attacks, frame the other corporations and then capitalize on the situation. Sexist sentiment may be too weak to blind them completely to her power and ambition, but it would be enough to create that seed of doubt.

The failed kidnapping attempted by Amalgam played right into her hand. She had just learned of that this morning as well. If the IMB security personnel, already stretched a little thin by the tightened defensive measures, could be dragged into some sort of conflict, they would be strained to the breaking point. Their involvement would also further sap the resources of the other two corporations.

Dez sipped her coffee as she pondered this. She gazed first at her men, who were mostly standing around talking to each other. Then she turned her gaze to the transparent section of the outer wall. She always enjoyed the view from above, looking down on the barren, dusty surface of Mars. It was cold and inhospitable, but it was her kingdom.

✳ ✳ ✳ ✳ ✳ ✳ ✳

Marty walked through the entrance to Dome Four, heading to the meeting, with Mia by her side. They desperately needed this after the incident yesterday. When they reached the lift Marty pressed the button and the doors opened. There was only one button on the inside, other than the door and communicator controls. With only two floors, the lift had only two places it could be. So pressing the button simply moved it to the other place. Mia pressed the small, white, unlabeled button and they moved up to the top floor.

The upper floor of Dome Four was mostly just a bunch of cubicles. There was also an office, a meeting room and a couple other small areas, which were sectioned off. Most of the floor was wide open with the exception of cubicle walls though.

They went back to the meeting room, which contained a long table and chairs, which looked like they might have been stolen from one of the dining areas. Alma Cohen, the base administrator, sat on one end of the table while Yev sat at the other. Larry, Brian and Dr. Petersen occupied the seats on the far side of the table, while two of the three chairs in front of them were empty. An old man sat in the chair nearest to Alma Cohen. Marty sat down next to him, while Mia took the chair to her left.

"Everyone is here, so we'll go ahead and start early," said Alma. "This is my husband, Andrew. He'll be taking notes for us. He's retired now, so he just works part-time as my unofficial assistant."

"Hello," said Andrew, waving. "I'm just hanging out until she joins me in retirement. Until then I'm part secretary and part Mars Base First Lady."

Andrew laughed a little, as did everyone else. He was definitely in his seventies, wrinkled and mostly bald, with just little hints of black in his gray hair.

Alma continued, "We are going to address what happened to Mia yesterday, but first Yev has some breaking news to share."

"One of my guys called me a little while ago. They discovered two bodies today. They both had a single, small puncture wound on the neck. Initial scans showed they died from some sort of neurotoxin. The crazy thing is they are the two identified as Amalgam Global spies. It looks like one of the corporations wants to reduce the competition. We may need to put the other four we had identified on the next ship going back to Earth."

"Thank you," said Alma. "I'll sign the order approving those four being sent back to Earth."

As the meeting continued, Yev made several proposals for tightening security. He knew better than to ask for total removal of access for all corporate employees. Instead, he pressed Alma to agree to require all nonresidents to have their corporate badges, which would identify them and the company for which they worked.

Yev also laid out a plan for increasing the number of locations where guards were posted. They would pay special attention to Dome Nine and all who worked there. The people leading their most secret project would get the most intense focus. This primarily meant Mia, Larry, Brian and Dr. Petersen.

Marty offered to patch the airlock systems, as well as the other systems on the base. That should prevent any more of these nasty surprises.

With their plans all figured out, everyone got up to leave. Yev made his way to the security office, while everyone else headed back to their quarters. Marty planned to start working on the airlock patch, but preferred to do so from the comfort of her bed.

✳ ✳ ✳ ✳ ✳ ✳ ✳

Back in their quarters, Marty reclined on the bed, propped up by some pillows, about halfway between sitting and lying down. She was wearing only her pants, which she had worn to the meeting. Her shirt and bra hung haphazardly off one corner of the bed. She manipulated a hologram in front of her, which came from the small mobile device on her lap.

Mia, feeling playful, stood up, took off her remaining clothes and then flopped back down on the bed next to Marty, completely naked. She rolled around a little, making cutesy faces at Marty and then lay partially over Marty's legs.

Marty found it a little annoying, but also rather endearing. It was definitely distracting her from the task at hand. Mia was so cute, with a child-like innocence, at least on one level. Then there was the genius side of her, which seemed incongruous, but gave her so much depth. She had a kinky, sexual side too, which Marty had awakened and fueled.

Realizing she would soon have no choice but to take a break, Marty worked on getting herself to a good stopping point. This kept her attention focused for a couple minutes. Just as she was finishing, she saw movement of light and shadows in her peripheral vision. When she looked over, Mia's huge breasts were jiggling back and forth mere inches from her face. Marty chuckled a bit and Mia put a breast on either side of Marty's face, pressing them together.

"I caught you in my booby-trap!" said Mia, laughing.

It was cute, funny and sexy all at the same time. Marty was beginning to enjoy and welcome this distraction.

"All right, let me close out of this," said Marty, as her face emerged from Mia's cleavage.

As Marty worked on saving and exiting, Mia began playfully fondling Marty's breasts.

"jiggly jiggly jiggly," said Mia, as she bounced Marty's breasts up and down by pushing up with her hands from underneath them. "Jiggly jiggly jiggly-boobs!" she said, continuing to play with Marty's breasts.

Marty Shut off her mobile device and was putting it on a stand next to the bed and noticed Mia had quit playing with her breasts. She had to lean over to reach the stand. As she moved back and turned her head at the same time, she ended up with her face pressed against the crack of Mia's butt. Marty pulled back a little, as she was surprised. Mia laughed at having surprised Marty in such a way.

"Mia, you little bitch!" said Marty playfully, slapping Mia's big, soft buns.

"Oh you know you like it," said Mia, continuing to laugh.

"I guess I do," said Marty, putting her face right back where it had been, squeezing Mia's cheeks with her hands.

Marty took off the rest of her clothes, as Mia moved to the middle of the bed, taking up as much space as possible and then smiling up at Marty.

"Very cute, Mia."

Marty pretended to push Mia over and Mia wouldn't budge. Marty turned and sat right on Mia's face.

As she smiled about the amusing situation, she could hear Mia's muffled giggling coming from underneath her. The way she sat placed her vulva right on Mia's mouth. Mia stuck out her tongue licking Marty.

"That feels good," said Marty.

After a minute, Marty got off Mia and then lay down next to her. They put their arms around each other, as their lips met, locking together. The work she had been preoccupied with was now the furthest thing from Marty's mind. Mia turned an ordinary day into the time of her life. Marty got lost in the moment, loving every second and every inch of Mia. This is what life is all about.

Chapter Thirteen

After finishing the airlock patching and all the other things she did around the base, Marty was able to talk Alma Cohen into letting her pilot a glider. *This was going to be awesome.* She saw Rachel working on a truck as she walked through Dome Five. She leaned over the front, standing on a small platform. She saw Marty and set her tools aside as she stepped down from the short platform.

"How are you doing, Rachel?"

"I'm all right, just finishing up with that truck there. How about you? Taking your first solo ride on a glider?"

"Yes, I am really stoked! I've wanted to do this since we got here, so well over a week now. I see your security detail is looking on."

"Thanks for getting that taken care of. You and Yev have really been great about that. Hilda and I have really felt safe. Plus, look at the guard who is assigned to me during the day while I'm working. Is he hot or what—well I guess you wouldn't think that, but I sure do."

"I may not find men attractive, but I can tell when a guy is particularly handsome. He certainly is."

"Darren is really sweet too. We're kind of seeing each now. He's so tall and muscular and I love that long thick black hair."

"He's really got you turned on, hasn't he?"

"Oh yes, I feel so naughty too. I just want to rip that uniform right off of him. I know I shouldn't. Not this early."

"There's nothing wrong with getting you some. Go ahead and grab a piece of that."

"Oh, Marty you are so bad," said Rachel, blushing a little.

"I'm glad things are going well for you."

"Well, I guess I should get back to work and I'm sure you're anxious to get on with your ride."

"Well, you have fun with Darren," said Marty placing her helmet on and fastening it to her gray spacesuit.

When the airlock opened, Marty stepped out onto the dusty surface. This was only her second time walking outside the base, the first time being her morning training session with the vehicle. She sat in the glider and powered it on. It made a humming noise and then lifted off the ground when she activated the magnetic field.

At first Marty just took the glider around the base, starting slow and then speeding up. Soon she was moving away from the base, going as fast as she could without it getting too bumpy. She decided to stop accelerating when going over bumps and craters began jostling her around.

She sped along, rocks and craters going by in a blur, heading northwest toward Gale Crater. *This is just as amazing as I thought it would be. I'll have to take Mia out here sometime. She probably wouldn't want to go quite this fast though.*

When Marty got to the crater, she slowed down and went in. She could see the flag marking the landing site of Curiosity One, which landed there seventy years ago. She planned to look around there for a while and then head back to the base.

✱ ✱ ✱ ✱ ✱ ✱ ✱

Charles Mantis sat in a black executive chair, with a mobile device in his lap. He brought up a hologram from it and worked on orders to increase security. That should keep the other corporations at bay and allow their mining operations to recommence.

He knew there was little he could do in the near-term and his sights must be set further out. Increasing security around the base was the only good move. The investigation into the incident at the mining facility pointed to Chimera, but perhaps it was Parasol. He wasn't sure Dez had it in her, but worried he may be underestimating her. Perhaps Chimera tried to make it look like Parasol was attempting to frame them. They were the underdog out of the three, so they stand to gain a lot, but so does Parasol.

Workers returning from the International Mars Base confirmed their operatives were dead. That ended the little trickle of information they got from the IMB. To make matters worse, the new security on their network was impregnable.

An incident so soon after the botched abduction of the engineer would lead to the base being sealed off to them altogether. There was also no way the airlock trick would work again. He needed to give it time.

Something more extreme was required too. It just couldn't be traced back to Amalgam.

They were certainly reverse engineering the alien ship. As long as he stole the secrets before transmission, all would be well. He knew they would wait until the project was complete before transmitting, in order to keep their secret.

✳ ✳ ✳ ✳ ✳ ✳ ✳

Mia moved things around on the design program in the hologram in front of her. She worked on connections to the anti-matter intake piece. That would connect to the already completed particle accelerator and anti-matter containment parts. The design for the anti-matter generator progressed very well. The technological leaps had her mind spinning, going off in all directions. When her designs were complete, she could probably spend the rest of her career deriving new technologies from them.

Mia noticed Larry walking by and turned to him. "Thanks for your help on the containment section. That was the final piece I was missing. I have it completed and have moved on to the intake."

"Glad I could help. You are really whizzing through this."

"Only because I have a team of people helping me. It makes it so easy having a team of top scientists which I can just use like assistants."

"So how are things going with Marty? It's been a couple days since I heard from her."

"Well Larry, that's because she was able to pester and guilt Alma Cohen into letting her pilot a glider. It's all she talks about lately. I swear one time it came up while we—uh"

Mia paused as her face reddened a little and then continued. "So anyway, it's going well other than that. She's so sweet and sexy and just makes everything fun. It's better than I thought a relationship could be."

"Yeah, that's Marty. She's quite a girl. Absolutely brilliant and a very loyal friend. She's quite a character too."

"Is she ever! This guy put his hand on my shoulder while trying to hit on me. He quickly removed it when I let him know he was barking up the wrong tree. Marty saw it though. And said something like 'you'll keep your fucking hands to your fucking self, motherfucker, if you want keep all your fucking teeth. What the fucking fuck is this shit?' I think there might have been a couple more 'fucks' in there somewhere."

"Oh yeah, that's her favorite word I think. You wouldn't think the phrase 'shut the fuck up you fucking cocksplat' would have much occasion for use. But she manages to find occasion to use it on a fairly regular basis. As quick as she is to anger, she's very quick to forgive and forget and to apologize when needed. She's quite eager to help people too."

"She makes me feel like a princess."

"She would normally keep girlfriends at arm's length, like a friend you can have sex with. She absolutely adores you though. Well, I guess I should get to it. The sooner we get this done the better."

Mia went back to working on the anti-matter intake connections. As exciting as it was, she couldn't wait to get back to Marty.

✳ ✳ ✳ ✳ ✳ ✳ ✳

Marty sat on the bed, reclining back a little, with the covers pulled up just over her waist. She had her mobile device in her lap, playing a video game on the hologram in front of her. She heard Mia come in, but looked up only when she spoke.

"Marty, are you playing video games in bed completely naked?"

Marty smiled saying "Well I do have the covers on halfway."

"That doesn't count, you smart ass! Is that all you did today or did you take the glider out again?"

"Oh come on, one day I spend half on the glider and half playing video games in bed naked and you act like that's all I ever do. What about all the time I spent patching the airlocks and all the security work before that? Not to mention hacking the corporate networks to get much needed info."

"I know, Marty. I'm sorry. You did work really hard for a long time with those projects. We've been trying to make as much progress on this alien tech as possible. I'm a little tired when I come home I guess."

As Mia spoke, she was taking her clothes off and had stripped down to her panties.

"That's all right, Mia. You're doing a little strip tease for me, so that more than makes up for it."

"Oh Marty, of course you would say that!" said Mia in a playfully disapproving voice. "Well, here."

With that, she danced over to Marty, turned around, wiggled her hips and then bent over seductively. When she stood upright she continued wiggling her hips as she turned back to face Marty. She then leaned over the bed putting her breasts in Marty's face.

Marty was enjoying the show. Mia was so very beautiful, so very sexy and sensual. She felt tightness and tension in her stomach, her nipples tingled and the ache and throb, which began between her legs grew intense and urgent.

Mia pointed at her nipples saying, "I think someone is enjoying that."

Marty paused the game and moved the device from her lap. Mia pulled back the covers and put a hand between Marty's legs.

Marty let out a quiet gasp and felt as if she was going to reach orgasm just from that.

Mia giggled softly. "Oh my, you are very excited, Marty. You got all wet for me didn't you?"

"Oh yeah, baby. It sure wasn't the video game. I was completely dry before you came in, as far as I know."

Mia left her hand where it was, wiggling her fingers faster and faster. Marty felt her breathing get heavier as Mia expertly stimulated her. It took only a couple minutes as Mia's fingers moved ever faster, for Marty to reach orgasm. After the final shudders of her orgasm subsided, Mia moved her hand away. Then she got in Marty's face and licked her dripping fingers. She took each on in her mouth sucking them off.

Marty felt her arousal going up again. "Mia, you just keep getting naughtier. That was really hot."

"Well that's all you get for now. You have to pleasure me first."

With that, Mia removed her panties and flopped down on the bed. Marty kissed her and rubbed her hands all over Mia's body. She rubbed and sucked her nipples and stroked the inside of her thighs. She then put her mouth between Mia's legs, smelling her musky scent, hearing the sweet gasp escape her lips.

She sucked and licked Mia's most tender parts. She brought Mia to climax after climax. Then she inserted her fingers, continuing to bring

Mia to orgasm, each more intense than the last. Then finally, Mia screamed as she tensed up and released in the biggest yet, her grand finale.

"Thank you, Marty. I feel much better now," said Mia, in a tired, shaky voice, as she lay nearly motionless on the bed.

"It was my pleasure. The smell and taste of you is pure delight."

Mia rolled over pushing Marty onto her back, surprising her. She kissed Marty between her breasts and then continued slowly kissing her way down Marty's stomach as she pinched her nipples. Finally, she made it all the way down and Marty squirmed when she felt Mia kiss her between the legs. She felt more soft kisses there making her throb even more. When she felt Mia part her lips and touch her clit with the tip of her tongue, it brought Marty right to the edge.

Marty squirmed as Mia pulled her tongue back, teetering right on the edge. Then Mia suddenly pressed her tongue against Marty's clit and just held it there. That sent electricity through her body, with Mia's tongue pressed there, it took two seconds for her to climax very hard. Mia withdrew her tongue only as her orgasm subsided.

Mia buried her face in there again and Marty could feel her clit being sucked and licked. She came again and again. Then with Mia's fingers inserted deep inside her, she had another string of orgasms until she screamed and shook with intensity. Finally, she lay there feeling as if she were in a trance, unable to move, with an amazing sense of sexual satisfaction.

She pulled Mia up into her arms, holding her and then giving her a soft kiss.

"Well my day just got a whole lot better," said Marty smiling at Mia. "How was your day?"

"I just had mind-blowing sex, so pretty good now."

"Yeah, that was amazing. How about before you came home?"

"We made a lot of progress. I have most of the design done for the anti-matter generator. I'm working on the reactor right now, with only the output section left to do."

"That is really fast."

"It's amazing what you can do when you have more resources than you could ever use."

"Well, after doing all that patching, I had some ideas about airlock systems. Therefore, I worked on that most of the day and I figured out a great hack for them. I am confident I can get in any base I want undetected, unless of course someone is walking by. After that, I played games for about an hour until you got home. To be honest though, I've been completely naked since I crawled into bed last night."

"I thought that looked like the remnants of room service there. You told them you weren't feeling well, didn't you?"

"I was hungry and right in the middle of a breakthrough. Plus, Dome Six is so far away. Actually as lazy as I felt, my pants seemed too far away."

Mia just shook her head and then lowered it back down to Marty's shoulder. Marty lay there and enjoyed the feeling of Mia snuggling up in her arms.

✳✳✳✳✳✳✳

Oscar Perry sat at his desk, not sure what to make of the results of the forensic data. Was it Amalgam, or was it Parasol. He figured it had to be Parasol. Amalgam had ignored the other two corporations so far and worked in a single-minded fashion, focusing on the alien tech at the IMB. There was no reason for them to do this even though the evidence pointed that way. Therefore, he thought it must be a frame job perpetrated by Parasol.

Dez was getting quite bold. He would have to talk to Bill about increasing security in order to get mining operations going again.

The apprehension of their agents inside, as well as the increased security on the IMB network meant they were flying blind. That disheartened him. However, he knew Amalgam had been greatly delayed, which would give them breathing room to come up with a plan B.

Oscar got up from the padded black chair, shutting off the device sitting on his small, gray desk. He took it with him and walked down the corridor to have a nice long chat with Bill Jeffries.

✳ ✳ ✳ ✳ ✳ ✳ ✳

Dez sat in a plush, oversized chair, upholstered in soft leather, overlooking the rocky landscape below. She sat alone, drinking her favorite wine, pondering the report she read a little earlier, adding it to what she already knew. She needed time to process it all and then to hatch a plan, which would tip things in her favor.

Ambivalence gripped her now. It mixed a very dissonant emotional cocktail, which flowed in waves to every corner of her mind. It was like life. The facts were that the attacks on the other two corporations were successful and resulted in security changes, which would stretch their resources. However, there was no resulting conflict. She had also lost her operatives in the IMB and could no longer access their network. Did the joy of her success make up for the disappointment and crushing failure? Or, was it the latter which spoiled the former?

Dez didn't like uncertainty. It was just as unsettling as her ambivalence. That was, however, a truth consistent with the realities of life. Nothing could ever be simple, or black and white. Nothing good remained entirely unsullied. No matter how dark and thorny, nothing lacked a silver lining. She had to deal with it. The only option was to see what happened and be ready to pounce. Caution and vigilance would allow her to capitalize on unfolding events.

Chapter Fourteen

Marty sat in one of the common rooms over in Dome Six with Mia on her lap. Marty held her and spoke softly as her mouth was right by Mia's ear. They took time to spend with their friends, but arrived early to have a quiet moment alone. At least it was somewhat quiet. There were a few other people around here and there. It was an internal room and rather out of the way, therefore much less popular than other places. It was very gray, but the furniture was comfortable.

"It's been almost a month since I met you," whispered Marty. "Even if none of the rest of this happened, it would still be the best month of my life."

Marty had trouble getting that out, but she had to do it. It was the truth and Mia needed to know how she felt.

"Oh, Marty, you say the sweetest things! I wasn't sure if you were even keeping track. It's been the best month of my life too. You've shown me things I didn't even know were possible."

"It seems like I just walked into that lounge yesterday, but at the same time it feels like I've known you for years."

"You better watch out Miss Martina. You're going to make me fall in love with you."

Marty wasn't quite ready for that. That was a little scary, but it also sounded wonderful. This was the best thing that ever happened to her. Whatever she did, she couldn't screw it up.

"Well maybe that's not such a bad thing, babe."

Mia turned her head and kissed Marty on the lips. Marty brushed her hand lightly over Mia's face as they kissed. Then she sat there for a little while with Mia on her lap, just enjoying the moment.

"Oh, they're so cute, Larry," said Smita, walking over. "I don't want to disturb them."

Marty and Mia looked up smiling.

"Well, we were expecting you," said Marty.

"I've never seen you like this, Marty. I'm very happy for you," said Larry smiling.

Marty felt self-conscious, but at the same time, she was very proud of having Mia as her girlfriend. Mia was so smart, sexy and beautiful. She felt very fortunate.

Brian and Yev came in next, both pushing carts full of supplies with which they could make drinks. Jorge and Zahra were right behind them carrying a few additional odds and ends.

"I come bearing gifts," said Brian. "It's nice having assistants. Well, two assistants and one husband, which is basically the same thing."

The four of them started getting set up at one of the tables. Then Rachel walked in with Hilda on one side and her new boyfriend, Darren on the other. The three of them seemed to be very tight. Finally, Al walked in with Dr. Petersen, Samuel Bradshaw, who ran the tour, and another man who was about forty with light brown hair and a thick mustache of the same color.

"Hey, Marty, good to see you again," said Al. "That was a hell of a night when you and Larry popped by with all that scotch!"

"Fucking A!" said Marty. "Had a lot of fun and the scotch was fucking amazing."

"Larry!" called Al. "I brought some friends with me. Magnus, who you know, Samuel, who you should remember from the tour and this is Jean Pierre Dubois, who worked on the translation with me."

"Yes, I remember him from the Columbia campus, as well as my short stint studying in Paris. Hello, everyone. It's been a long time, Jean Pierre."

"Yes, indeed it has. Good to see you again," said Jean Pierre in his French accent. "That was a fascinating project. Likely to be the crowning achievement of my linguistics career."

Brian was the mix master, so once everything was set out, he started making drinks for everyone. Marty agreed to try his new vodka martini recipe, as did most of the others. As expected, Mia opted to get some sort of sweet, fruity drink that would normally come with an umbrella in it. She didn't like anything where you could taste the booze. That was probably for the best since she became tipsy after only two of those rather weak cocktails. The night they had drinks in their room, she had three, which got her a little drunk. This in turn made her even more silly and playful than usual. It was a fun night though.

"I'm not usually much of a martini fan, but this is really good, Brian," said Marty after tasting her drink.

Everyone else seemed to like theirs as well, which had Brian smiling wide.

"Very good, I'm glad you're all enjoying them," said Brian as he finished mixing his own drink.

Marty noticed that some people mingled, walking around to different areas of the room, while others remained where they were. Brian stayed with the liquor since he was making the drinks. Jorge and Zahra hung out there with Brian the whole time. They were also quite chummy with Larry, but he was flitting about the room like a manic hummingbird. He had so many friends there it seemed almost like a challenge for him spend time with everyone. Yev hung out with Brian part of the time, but also came and visited with Marty. Over the past month, she had been developing a friendship with Yev. They had a number of things in common, particularly weight lifting, martial arts and security. Hers was more data and network, while his had more to do with physical security though.

Al sat off to one side of the room with Dr. Petersen, who he called Magnus, Jean Pierre, who he called JP, and Samuel. Larry made regular stops there as he moved around the room. Marty found herself over there sometimes, always while talking to Larry or Mia. Mia seemed to have developed a friendship with Dr. Petersen as well. She even called him Magnus.

Off in a corner were Rachel, Hilda and Darren. They were quite preoccupied with each other. There was definitely an interesting dynamic going on there. Hilda and Rachel had become extremely close, but they almost seemed like lovers. They were both straight as an arrow though as far as Marty knew. Darren was hyper-focused on Rachel, which made sense as they were seeing each other. However, he seemed to be doing the same thing with Hilda. Marty had fooled around with enough poly people that she recognized it when she saw it. She was sure that's what was going on. They seemed secretive though, as if they were hiding something. *I bet it just happened spontaneously. Their first foray into polyamory.*

Smita was the only one that really went over there to talk to them. She spent most of her time flitting around with Larry though. Marty went over just to say "hi" briefly. She knew better than to stay over there though. The more she drank the more likely she was to ask them about their situation. She could tell they wouldn't want to talk about it. They needed time to get used to the idea of what had probably just happened. Marty decided to give it at least a week before giving in to her curiosity. She didn't want to be rude and make them feel uncomfortable.

"Another one, Marty?"

"Eh? Oh, yes, please, Brian. Your new recipe is pretty good."

Brian mixed up the cocktail and handed it to Marty.

"You like to observe people too, don't you, Marty?" asked Yev.

"I guess I do a little bit. More at big parties where I don't know most people. Even this is interesting though."

"I'm the same way. People and the things they do are very interesting."

Marty chatted with Yev for a while and then went over to hang out with Mia, who was currently standing in a small circle with Dr. Petersen, Larry and Smita. Al, JP and Samuel had formed another circle just a few feet away.

Mia was getting a little drunk at this point. She even had the occasional misstep. It wasn't quite stumbling though. She still talked expertly on the topic of antimatter too. Marty could relate. On a heavy night of drinking, her ability to walk gave out long before her ability hack into things. Her mind was always working, always thinking about something in the background.

While joking about being able to beat someone at a video game with her hands behind her back, operating the holographic controls with her tongue, she got a bit of food stuck in her teeth. As she worked the bit of peanut out of a back molar with her tongue, she suddenly thought of having a computer hologram in her mouth.

On the way back to their quarters, Marty told Mia about what she thought of.

"Marty, you wouldn't be able to see a hologram in your mouth."

"Yeah, I know. It's just light, which wouldn't pass through my body. The thing is the controls would still work. They sense movement through RF signals, which will go through your body."

Mia giggled a little. "That's kind of funny. You wouldn't be able to see what is going on and you would likely end up breaking something."

"Actually, I just had an idea about that. I make a secondary holo-display and when I turn it on, it starts an application, which will be the only thing you can interface with through that hologram. I would have to affix my mobile device to a specific place so it lines up. When I program the application, I set the controls in such a way where you have to make a tiny circle on a particular plane, in a certain spot that will line up with certain things, like my teeth for example. So, if I circle my tongue around one tooth, it executes a specific function. Each function I program like a hotkey. It's like when you push something and it launches a program. I set each hotkey to launch a different script. So by circling my tongue over my left maxillary first premolar I execute one script and circling the right mandibular second premolar executes another."

"Did you consider dentistry before becoming a freelance consultant?" asked Mia, laughing.

"No, but one time when I had a cleaning I was in a room that had a diagram of human teeth."

"You mean you just looked at a diagram on the wall one time when you got your teeth cleaned and you remember all that?"

"Yeah, that's how my brain works. For most things I just have to read it once to understand."

"I learn fast, but that's amazing. You could have a collection of PHDs if you had tried."

"Maybe. I hated school though. Nothing I ever wanted to do required anything like that either. I got just what I needed. If ever I need a certification in order to charge higher rates for my services, I just download the books, read them and then go take the exams. I learned everything I know by reading about it, someone explaining it to me, or just figuring it out on my own through experimentation. Like the last time I learned a new programming language. I read a comprehensive book on the topic and then I just played with it until I had it figured out. I can also apply what I know about one thing to something completely different. It's like a mental shortcut."

"Now that I understand. That's how I figure out the alien tech I'm working with. It's one of the secrets to reverse engineering something."

"That's how I reverse engineer stuff too. It's useful for hacking."

"Oh I see. I guess it is kind of similar."

"Yep, you're hacking that ship. But instead of looking for vulnerabilities to exploit, you're looking for ways to adapt it to our current technology."

At that point, they reached their quarters and went inside. They both busied themselves with taking their clothes off. Mia stripped down to her panties and then rummaged through her stuff to find a nightshirt. Marty got completely naked and flopped down on the bed.

Mia put on her nightshirt and lay on the bed next to Marty asking, "So, was school really that bad?"

Absolutely! Oh Mia, where do I even begin?

"Yeah, it was. The teachers really didn't get me. Well, most of them anyway. It was horribly boring too. Advancing me might have helped the boredom, but they didn't want to do that because my maturity level was barely average. In fact, it was below average the first few years. The teachers and I would usually come to some sort of an understanding eventually. They got the message that their jobs would go easier if they let me be and I aced all exams, so they didn't have to worry about me flunking.

"I wasn't always very nice, but they had it coming. It was all tit for tat. Well actually, I do feel bad about one situation. It was when I got kicked out of Catholic school."

"I thought you would have felt happy about that."

"Yeah, that kind of came out wrong. I was ten at the time. I hated Catholic school the most and I was thrilled about being kicked out. I still think that is one of the best things that happened back then. It's how it happened that I regret. I had this nun as a teacher."

"Really, a nun? There are almost none now—"

"Oh, Mia!" Marty groaned. "That was a horrible pun."

Mia laughed, saying, "Yes, I know. I'm sorry. I really couldn't resist. Seriously, though, there aren't even a hundred of them left in the whole world and they are all very old. Even back then there couldn't have been many."

"Yeah, true enough. There were very few then and they were all at least somewhat old. There were two or three of them where I went, or at least that's how many that weren't in the retirement home. When they let women become priests, that took a big bite out of their numbers. Only the totally old fashioned holy rollers became nuns then. Plus, religion had been on a major decline for decades. Even priests could be hard to come by. So while there are even less now, they were still rare back in the sixties, when I was a kid."

"Okay, so it's you and a nun, at a Catholic elementary school in 2066."

"Sorry, I went off on a tangent. You're the one that distracted me though."

"Usually I'm the one that does that. I think I must be rubbing off on you."

"Yeah, I think so. You had better watch out, or I'll be influencing you too. Before you know it 'fuck' will be prominently featured in your daily speech."

"Get the fuck on with it!" said Mia laughing.

"It was the end of fourth grade and I had barely put up with this nun all year. She was well into her eighties at the time and should have been long retired. She would always forget stuff and sometimes seemed confused. She could also be such a bitch. She got to be a bigger and bigger bitch as time went on.

"One day she had been real bitchy and had been going on and on about what ladies do and how ladies behave. 'A proper lady does this and a lady does that,' it was total bullshit. Plus, I was getting so sick of all the extra religion crap. It was way more than the regular teachers.

"I started talking back to her and she started yelling. It was mostly religious platitudes. I just happened to feel a lot of gas right at that moment. So, I said, 'Here's what I think of that,' and then I spun around and pushed. I was hoping it would be loud, but it was even louder than I expected. I totally farted on her and she looked at me all disgusted and shocked. But, without skipping a beat she started in about proper behavior for ladies. So, I just screamed at her, 'I may be female, but I ain't a fucking lady!' Then I started talking about her life being a waste and how god was her imaginary friend. I felt pretty justified after the way she had been treating me and the other kids all year. I was sent home, which was fine with me, although my parents were furious.

"The school contacted my parents the next week and said that I did well enough to move on to fifth grade without having to make up any work, but that I could not go back there. My parents were still forcing me to go to church though, so about a month later I heard that nun finally retired. It had nothing to do with what happened and it was not because of her age either, at least not directly. I found out she had dementia and it had been getting worse."

"Oh, that's terrible!"

"I had heard of that, but didn't know much about it, so I looked it up of course. That's when I discovered that she wasn't purposely being a bitch at all. She couldn't help it. She was ill and had very little control over what she did and said sometimes. It all made sense then. The reason she got worse and why she would be reasonable sometimes. The way those reasonable periods happened less and less. Only the times she was being reasonable did I see her as she really was. The irrational crabbiness and meanness were symptoms of her illness. The same thing with her cognitive problems.

"I felt so bad about that and I still do. I even decided to apologize to her a couple months later. When I talked to her though, she didn't know who I was. The nurse said that I could try coming back another time. Sometimes she remembered everything all right and sometimes she didn't. That's when I found out that the past couple years, she would sometimes walk off after class. People would find her wandering around. Luckily, she couldn't go very far without stopping to rest. When that happened, she would be confused and didn't know where she was or how she got there. She wanted to keep working though and they let her do so until she couldn't stay lucid long enough to do it. Some of the kids had been telling their parents about her becoming confused and forgetting which lesson she was on. I think it was worse than I had noticed, because I just tuned her out if she wasn't talking to me. I never did go back to see her again. It was just too disturbing seeing her like that and it would only get worse."

"That's a very sad story. I was laughing about you farting on her, but it's not funny at all now."

"It was hilarious until I found out what was going on. It's the things I said though that I really regret."

"It couldn't have been a bad experience every year."

"It was never good per se, but some years weren't too bad. Every now and then, I would actually end up with a really good teacher. They seemed to know what to do and would try to work with me as best they could, within the confines of the system. Some of them would see how quickly and easily I would learn stuff—even complicated things and they would get very excited.

"Those teachers were the best. They would just give me access to their lessons as soon as they had them and I could do them whenever I wanted. I didn't have to participate in class. They would even give me things, provided they were educational in some way. Even stuff they had to pay for. Anything educational I wanted. I just had to take the tests and cooperate with their experiments. I didn't mind though. All I had to do was read a few pages of something and then regurgitate it back to them in my own words.

"They could have ended up in big trouble though for teaching me extra stuff during regular class time and not forcing me to follow along with the class during lessons. Really they were supposed to make me participate and only teach me interesting stuff after class."

"That sounds pretty cool."

"Yeah, but I still had to be there all day and sometimes I had to make it look like I was doing the lessons with the rest of the class because the principal was watching. Most of the teachers were total ball busters too. It was just the odd one that was cool like that.

"I think my favorite one was this older guy I had in middle school. Some of the kids thought he was crazy. He might have been a little. He certainly was very odd. I could call him eccentric and unconventional, but that is understating it a lot. He was awesome though, it would have been a good year if I could have been in his class the whole day. He noticed I was different right away.

"He said to me, 'You know, they want me to teach you this stuff right along with everyone else. The hell with that! That would be an utterly disgraceful waste of time, not to mention your talents. It's bullshit and I refuse to do it. I'll let you read over this silly stuff at your leisure. I want to know what you want to learn.'

"I remember he would frequently mention how all this 'cookie-cutter crap' is 'foolishness,' as he would say. Something about them throwing out the best and brightest like a bunch of old rubbish, just because they're too dimwitted to know what to do with them. I didn't understand all of that at first, but I fucking loved the way he ripped on the school board, administrators and even other teachers, who he considered lazy, or timid. 'They just go through the motions, like robots on an assembly line. We're supposed to be educating young people, not building a bunch of damn blasted storage shelves,' he used to say.

"He knew of a few colleagues, who thought the same way he did. So the rest of my time in school, I always had at least one period, sometimes two, where I got a brief respite from the usual 'cookie-cutter crap,' as he called it."

"I had it much easier. The only thing I had to contend with was my demanding parents. I went to the best schools though and I didn't have any behavioral or maturity issues, so there wasn't any problem advancing me early. Thirteen might have been a little young for college though. I don't think I ever got much of a chance to just be a kid."

"I at least got the chance to be a kid. I didn't really take it though. I was more like a very immature adult than a kid. I didn't like college either. After I met Larry though, I discovered that many universities actually did have courses with people like me in mind. I came from a very poor community though. We didn't have the resources that the people in the nicer neighborhoods did."

"Look at you now though."

"I know. I don't exactly put a lot of effort into my business. However, I developed a reputation that makes me a comfortable living even working part time hours. In a typical year, I'll work a month of full time, about eight months of part time and then three months of time off. It's all mixed up though."

Marty and Mia snuggled up together and started to get sleepy. They had settled in quite nicely there at the International Mars Base. Marty felt quite pleased. She got a lot accomplished, but still had time for fun. She came up with some brilliant ideas too. Best of all, everything was going great with Mia. With Mia there in her arms, it felt like something that had been missing for so very long was finally back. She felt complete for the first time in her life. *What was happening?* All she knew is that it was something wonderful and she couldn't wait for it to continue to unfold.

Chapter Fifteen

Mia sat in her lab at the end of a long day. She mentally took stock of her progress as she organized her virtual objects on the hologram in front of her.

I made a lot of progress in six weeks. The entire anti-matter generator design is done, as is the design for the warp device. Next will be designing the machine that converts energy to matter and then the gamma ray laser, which should be the easiest. The black hole part of this is where things will get tricky.

After thinking about how to draw energy from the black hole containment field, her thoughts turned to Marty. Everything about the entire situation was like a dream come true. She couldn't wish for better. Marty was like her guide and protector, helping her navigate with ease, a world she dared not explore, save for a small fraction. She stepped out of her little shelter, into wide-open spaces, without fear of danger, or of losing her way. She always knew she could achieve any intellectual feat, but through Marty she learned she could handle whatever came her way.

Fun and pleasure were part of her exploration, catalyzed by the assistance of her friend and lover. She learned to let loose, to enjoy, to discover herself and to learn acceptance. There really was more to life than work and studies. That is the reality in which she now lived.

She made a lot of progress with Marty as well. Marty had the biggest, most pure heart of gold, but like any precious treasure, was hidden away under heavy guard. It was something Marty didn't share, a place nobody could enter. However, it was a light that shined on all at least a little, like sunlight through the cracks of a wall. Mia became the exception. She alone got to see Marty as she was, her whole being. Only she saw all of Marty's vulnerability and the heart within.

Recently she realized she had fallen in love with Marty and just now, that Marty was in love with her too. It would all be hard for Marty to come to terms with, but she had to tell her. It was time for her to know.

✳ ✳ ✳ ✳ ✳ ✳ ✳

Marty reclined on her bed, leaning against pillows. She casually looked through compiled feeds of data organized on the hologram in front of her. She felt quite pleased and satisfied with herself.

This is fucking awesome! I have all the networks and systems here locked down tight, other than that one site of course. It's so amusing when they get into that, thinking they are getting to something real, when actually they are being infected with a nasty little program I made. Thanks to that, I only had to do half the hacking required to get all this lovely data. The other half they did to themselves! Then there is my airlock hack—oh and I can't forget the hologram with the controls keyed to areas of my mouth. Linking it to the hologram lock feature was a stroke of genius as well.

Marty smiled as she thought about that, almost laughing when she imagined people at the corporations accessing her dummy site. She hadn't yet managed to crack the nanobot security, even though she had known how to connect to them for some time now. She did have this feeling that she was right on the verge of a breakthrough. It may or may not turn out to be useful, but she was sure it would be fascinating.

Then of course, there was Mia. That was by far the best part of all. Mia was so sexy, cute, fun to be around and had this strange, incongruous combination of innocence and naughtiness, which just drove Marty wild. Once she got Mia out of her shell, there was no stopping her. She was brilliant too.

Mia was so very special. Marty knew she could tell her anything. She was intelligent enough to understand, as trustworthy as any person could be. Anything Marty didn't say, she at least wanted to. The entire problem was getting her mouth to say it, not any reservations about Mia hearing it.

At the same time, it was scary to care about someone so much. It was hard to let someone in like that. However, it was impossible not to, with someone like Mia, because deep down, that's what her heart desired. Mia felt like a part of her.

This was the best thing that ever happened to her. It was like a whole new dimension, added to something familiar. A path she had walked so many times, suddenly leading to new and exciting places she never knew existed.

Marty heard the door opening and moved the device from her lap to welcome Mia home.

"Hey, babe how was your day?" asked Marty, as she slid her legs over, planting her feet on the floor.

"It was good. We're really making a lot of progress," said Mia, smiling at Marty.

As Marty stood up, Mia was already taking her clothes off. Marty stood behind Mia and unhooked her bra. She rubbed her hand from Mia's neck to her shoulders, pushing the straps aside. She massaged her shoulders as the bra fell to the floor and Mia relaxed. The tension drained from her as she rubbed her shoulders and then gently kissed her neck.

"Oh, that feels so good, Marty."

"I'm happy to see you. I was thinking about you, hoping you'd be home soon."

Mia turned around after a few minutes as the two embraced. Then they sat down on the bed together.

"Marty, I'm so glad you walked into that lounge. I can't imagine my life without you."

"Having a look around the hotel was the best decision I ever made. I've met a lot of people, but no one like you."

"Marty, I love you."

I thought so and I love you too, Mia. I need to say it. It's too scary. No, don't screw this up.

"I know. I," Marty stammered.

Mia's smile faded and she started to look away.

No, Marty, no! Fuck! Don't ruin the best thing that's ever happened to you. Don't hurt the dearest, sweetest woman you've ever met. You've taken many steps you've never taken before, don't you dare miss the final one.

"Mia, wait," said Marty getting down on her knees in front of her, looking into her eyes. "It's just—well, you know me. I want to say it though! Because I really mean it."

"I know," said Mia, her smile returning.

"Mia, I love you. I love you so much it scares me. I've never felt like this about anyone."

Tears came to their eyes as Marty said that and they put their arms around each other. Marty rotated back onto the bed next to Mia and they lay back. They held each other, enjoying the moment, wishing it would never end.

✱ ✱ ✱ ✱ ✱ ✱ ✱

Marty lounged on the bed in her quarters, feeling quite pleased with herself, as she manipulated the hologram in front of her. She felt like she was on a roll. She was able to accept how she felt and even express that to Mia. It was the sort of thing at which she never was any good. It went very well though and now her relationship with Mia was better than ever. This was a whole new level, which she had never experienced. As if that wasn't enough, now she had managed to hack into her nanobots.

Marty worked on reverse engineering the code on which the nanobots ran. She wanted to know what she could get them to do and be able to script things if needed. Everyone had nanobots and medical equipment wasn't restricted in any way, however the software was proprietary. There were multiple companies in the business, but due to regulations, they had to maintain standards for compatibility with their competitors' equipment. The software would have been a closely guarded secret anyway, but the forced cooperation made them all the more touchy about it. They were all very strongly opposed to sharing with any upstarts as well.

It was then that she got a message from Yev. Larry had gone missing. Those words felt like a hard kick in the crotch. She ran out the door and headed over to the security office.

When Marty arrived at the security office, she saw Yev, Smita and Samuel Bradshaw standing out in front. Yev and Samuel were talking, with a look of concern on their faces. Smita had been crying, her red, puffy eyes peering out from a face awash with tears and running makeup.

"Hey, Marty," said Yev. "I wanted to let you know about this right away since you and Larry have been such close friends for several years. In addition, your skills would be useful in the investigation. I'll let Samuel explain."

Marty put her arm around Smita, who clearly needed comforting. She embraced Marty, resting her forehead against Marty's shoulder.

"I took Larry out in a small glider over to Gale Crater. We were just doing some sightseeing, checking out the different land formations. Next thing I know, Larry is nowhere to be seen. I look around and all I see is this other glider heading out of the crater. It had a Parasol Group logo on it. I thought it was strange, but wasn't concerned at that moment. After looking around for a while though, I realized that Larry wasn't there, see. I went up to high ground and could see he definitely wasn't there. That's when I realized he may have been taken."

"I want to see if you can snoop around and find out if Parasol has him," said Yev. "If they do, we can ban anyone from Parasol entering the base and put pressure on them."

"What the fuck are you talking about? We need to go get him," said Marty.

"Well it's not like we can go over there and storm the base. Just find some evidence so we can take action."

Marty turned her gaze to Samuel, "How did you not notice anyway?"

"Well, I was looking at these rocks what were strewn about kind of funny, see. He was going round the other side of that big rocky mound thing in there. You know how he is. Walks fast when he gets excited, he does. I followed after a minute or two, but he'd already buggered off. I saw him disappearing round the bend just as I was starting after him."

"Yeah, that's Larry all right."

Marty put her hands on Smita's shoulders, looking her in the eyes. "Don't worry. One way or another, we're going to get him back."

Smita nodded and Marty turned to Yev. "I'm going to go dig around a little. I'll let you know what I find out."

With that, Marty went back to her quarters to confirm her suspicions.

They have another think coming if they think I'm not going right over there, once I confirm this. Then again, only Smita knows me well enough to understand that and she's too traumatized for reasoning at the moment. Whoever has Larry is going to be getting to know me. They're not going to like it either.

✳ ✳ ✳ ✳ ✳ ✳

Confirming where The Parasol Group took Larry was easy. Convincing Mia everything was going to be okay was hard. Marty had to tell her all her plans in detail and still it was difficult. Mia did finally agree though, albeit reluctantly. Marty didn't want to leave without telling her though.

Marty went into an airlock that was kind of out of the way. She closed herself in and suited up. Once she was ready, she set it to operate without sending notice that it was in operation. Once it was depressurized, she exited.

Marty walked around the base for a while until she got to where the gliders were. Nobody was around, so she climbed up on one and powered it up. It quickly came alive, lifting off the dusty, reddish ground. She turned it toward The Parasol Group's base and sped away.

As she rapidly glided across the landscape of Mars, her anger and determination grew. The showdown with Dez Delacroix would be interesting, judging by the few reports she had read and the many rumors, not to mention her pictures. She was beautiful in a dark, gothic way and also very flashy and eccentric. Marty found the rumors that Dez was borderline insane at least somewhat believable. She would definitely be unpredictable, at least to a certain extent. A formidable woman to be sure, but Marty wasn't too concerned.

All she could think of on the ride over was getting Larry out of there. She had known Larry for more than eight years now, which was her entire adult life. They had been very close for most of that time. They had been through a lot together too, over the years.

They were both in a time of great transition when they met. She had just recently struck out on her own as a freelance consultant, left her family home to live on her own and support herself. She had also just ended things with her final boyfriend and come to terms with her sexuality. It was a hard time.

Larry had spent literally half of his life attending university. He finally graduated with two PHDs and had just taken a job there as a professor. It wasn't quite as turbulent for him, as he just went from student and part-time lab assistant, to professor at the same university, on the very same campus. It was still a big change though.

Chapter Sixteen

After his abduction by a group of thugs, Larry found himself in a large penthouse atop The Parasol Group's base. This lavish but gothic place very much matched its owner. The strangely dressed woman looked like a cross between a dominatrix and a pimp, or maybe a sort of warrior queen. She was quite attractive though. All the men up there, including the ones guarding him, were nearly naked. Many of them hovered around their mistress, like pets.

The dark, unusual woman approached. She had cold, piercing eyes, which just stared right through you. Her gaze remained fixed on Larry, as she stopped just a couple feet in front of him. She was nice enough, but spoke in a way that would strike fear into most. It hinted that her demeanor could change instantly and not for the better. A sort of masked evil was in there somewhere, just waiting to emerge.

"Ah, the esteemed professor, Lawrence Wellington. I'm Dez Delacroix. Welcome to my little corner of Mars. I do hope you've been well treated, or as well as possible under the circumstances. After all, you're going to be my guest for a while."

"Keeping me prisoner here will do you no good."

"A prisoner? You're more of an involuntary guest. You definitely have some information I want. You likely have access to some valuable data as well. I'm also hoping your little friend comes for you."

Larry was surprised. This woman had an awful lot of information. Her response really caught him off guard.

"Oh, don't look so surprised. I know a lot more than you think, including a certain friend of yours. She's made things very difficult for me. I'm going to persuade her to do a couple little tasks for me."

"Nobody is coming for me. But if someone was, I guarantee you will not like the outcome."

"I'm ready and waiting, so we'll see about that. Right now though, I'd like to hear more about that alien ship."

Larry just stared her down, not saying a word.

"The silent treatment will only buy you a small amount of time. We're going to have a nice long talk later and I'm going to be very persuasive."

✱ ✱ ✱ ✱ ✱ ✱ ✱

Smita paced nervously waiting to see what Yev and Alma Cohen were going to do. She knew exactly how these things went. Jurisdiction could be a problem on Mars. As long as the person in question was released alive and well, nothing really happened. Even enduring some amount of torture didn't change this. A death would trigger an investigation, but frequently it could be covered up, made to look like an accident, or blamed on some rogue employee, usually one who was recently deceased.

Finally, after what seemed like an eternity, Yev emerged from an office and walked toward her.

"Yev, what's the plan?"

"I have to create a report to file with the authorities. We can also consult a lawyer. Threats of legal action in civil court can sometimes expedite things."

"All right, thanks. Just please hurry! Oh and what about access for Parasol Group employees?"

"Yes, I will try to do this as fast as possible. Now on the other issue, I can give you some good news. Alma Cohen has agreed to bar all Parasol employees. The badge requirement went in a while back and that helped. Now everyone not residing here must have a badge from either Amalgam Global, or Chimera. All others will be left outside, or if they have nowhere to go, kept in a holding cell until they can be shipped back to Earth."

"That is good news. I wish we could ban them all though, or at least Amalgam."

"It can be tricky. Banning people from any public places, including here, requires reasons for doing so. It's very different from private property. The placement of security restrictions allows us to regulate it though."

"Yes, I understand," said Smita pausing for a moment. "Just please bring my Larry back to me."

"We'll get him back as soon as we can."

Smita walked absently back to her quarters, in a very surreal state, unsure what to do with herself. Every second seemed like an eternity.

※ ※ ※ ※ ※ ※ ※

Mia walked down a gray interior hallway over to one of the common areas in Dome Six. She really needed to get her mind off everything that happened. When she walked in, there were not many people in there and as she looked around the room, she spotted Brian. He sat at one of the little tables, sipping on a cocktail and playing a 3D solitaire game.

"Hey, Brian. So you needed to keep your mind off all this too, eh?"

"Hi, Mia. Yeah, this is driving me nuts. Larry and I have been working together for quite some time now. Really ever since I moved to New York from San Diego to work at the university."

"I bet the change in climate was a shock to your system."

"Yes, it certainly was," said Brian, nodding. "I lived my whole life in the San Diego area, so I was not used to it getting cold, ever. It's even bred into me. My mother's side of the family has been in southern California for more than two centuries, some since the civil war era. My father's side of the family comes from southeastern China, which has a similar climate. I think that's why my grandparents decided on California when they moved."

"My family has been in New York since before I was born, so I'm used to it and then being half Russian too. From one of the cold parts, as you can see from my coloring," said Mia, holding up her arm. "I go through a lot of sunblock if I have to be outside for more than a few minutes."

"I know how that is. Yev practically has to bathe in it if we're going to be outside. Going to the beach when we visit my family is quite an ordeal. I have a case of it shipped over to my parent's house whenever we go. That man has quite a lot of surface area."

Mia and Brian started working on a two-person variation of solitaire, which was as much a puzzle as it was a card game. It was nice to be able to just chat with Brian and keep her mind occupied playing the game. Her mind kept going back to thoughts of Marty and Larry, but she kept fighting it. It wouldn't do anyone any good to sit there and stew about it.

"So, did your father teach you Chinese?"

"He originally wanted to, because he learned English, Mandarin and Cantonese as a kid. That didn't even last long enough for me to remember him speaking anything but English, well except for occasionally when talking to my grandparents. I think it's because my mother spoke only English. He also got out of the habit because he was born in California too. My grandmother was actually pregnant when they moved. The joke was that he was born in the USA, but with a 'made in China' label," said Brian laughing.

Mia laughed too. "It was similar in my family. My mother knew a little Russian she picked up from her mother, but never spoke it. My father knew English, German and Russian and taught me when I was little, but I barely remember it. He kept at it longer than your father did, but probably not much. I can speak them a little, but I was probably seven before I knew which words were Russian and which were German."

"Yev tried to teach me Russian. Language is not my strong suit. That's why I'm a physicist. Science I understand, it just makes perfect sense to me. I don't know how Yev did it. He barely spoke English at all when we met. He slips back into bad habits when he gets excited, but he has a larger vocabulary than many people who spoke English all their lives."

Brian made himself another cocktail as Mia started up a new game for them.

✳ ✳ ✳ ✳ ✳ ✳ ✳

Marty could see the large oblong dome that housed The Parasol Group Mars operation off in the distance. The tall building protruded from the ground like a giant bullet. It appeared larger and larger as she drew closer.

She thought they might be waiting for her and if they caught her, they would take her right to Larry. That might prove easier than sneaking around. She pulled up fairly close to the dome, but left the glider in a small, shallow crater.

She walked over to the dome, changing course a little, as she spotted an airlock. It was not quite opposite the main doors, but it was close to the back. She could feel a thrill and the quickening of her heartbeat. It was a little scary, but mostly it was exciting.

She had set the interface for her device so that she could start the airlock hack with her mouth. After a few seconds, she could hear the airlock depressurizing. It was set to silent mode too. Everything was going according to plan.

Once the depressurization completed, the door slid open. She hesitated for just a quick moment before stepping in. she closed the door with the control panel inside the airlock, started pressurization and set it to return to its normal mode in five minutes. When pressurization was complete, she cautiously looked out through the transparent section of the inner door.

Seeing no one there, she opened the door and peered out into the gray corridor. Seeing nothing, she quickly removed the transparent helmet and attached it to a hook on the side of her belt.

Remembering the schematics of the base, which she had previously studied, she walked cautiously down the corridor. If people passed by without looking at her closely they likely wouldn't think anything of it, as the Parasol spacesuit is similar. However, if someone were to lock directly at her, it would be obvious she wasn't supposed to be there.

As she moved along, she got the feeling something was going on. The place was strangely deserted. Suddenly she heard doors opening and others closing. Within seconds, she was completely surrounded by Parasol security.

Marty just went with it. This way had its advantages. After a scan for weapons, they led her into a lift, which took her to the top floor. They had her remove her spacesuit, which they confiscated along with her mobile device. It wasn't the device that mattered though. She almost laughed when she saw the three guys, into whose custody she was being delivered. She quickly remembered what she read about Dez. They were handsome though. This would probably be quite pleasant if she was straight, or so she imagined—these were the sort of men society expected girls to like anyway. Guns drawn and her things in tow, they led her into the penthouse.

There were plenty more men around, all wearing the same scant bit of fabric, with a uniform placement strategy. Then she saw Dez across the room. Just like in the images, she saw earlier, Dez was sexy. She looked like a demon princess. Well, hot or not, she would be one of two things. She could choose to be cooperative, or she could choose to be sorry.

"Well, look at what we have here. I thought you would show up eventually, Martina, but I had no idea it would be so quick. They were just getting set up, expecting a long wait and then you just come walking right in."

"You must be Dez. I really don't know why you know who I am, or why you are expecting me. I know who you are, but you're the face of The Parasol Group's operations on Mars. I'm more obscure."

"Oh, I hear things. Or at least I did. Once I knew who was over there, it wasn't hard to learn more about you. You're fairly well known in certain industries, particularly with small to medium size organizations. I would have found your profile arrogant and suspected some reviews of your services as being forged. However, you kept the best I could find out of the network in your charge. Therefore, I knew it was true and it was the reason I went digging in the first place. Then I discovered you have a reputation for other things as well."

"So this is about me?"

"No, not really. The professor was worth taking anyway. But you are a nice bonus."

"I want to see Larry."

"And so you shall. I can assure you he has come to no harm. Yet. I am eager to discuss some things with you, as well as continue my conversation with the professor. But that will have to wait. Until I return, you will be held under guard with the professor, so you will have an opportunity to see he's all right. My men can provide you both with food and drink. If you fancy one of them, I'm sure they would be quite willing to entertain you in private. You can have anything but your freedom. For now anyway."

The last sentence came out harsh and threatening, in stark contrast to the pleasant tone of the rest of her speech.

"Thanks. Refreshments are always appreciated. These guys aren't really my type though, you might say. But let me tell you, if I wasn't in a serious relationship and the circumstances were different, I wouldn't mind having a go with you."

"Oh, I see what you mean. Well, never mind the entertainment then. Make the most of your time. It will be the only part of this visit one would describe as 'pleasant'."

Turning to her men, Dez said, "Take her to the professor and feed them. Keep a very close eye on her at all times."

As Dez turned to leave, her men motioned for Marty to go with them. She turned and walked in the direction they indicated, leading further into the penthouse.

$$* * * * * * *$$

Mia walked back to her quarters, deep in thought about the current situation. Just then, Yev seemed to appear out of nowhere.

"Oh sorry, Mia. I didn't mean to startle you."

"That's all right. I'm just distracted right now."

"Marty went down there, didn't she?"

"Yes, she did. She does have a pretty good plan though. Let me see what time it is."

Mia paused briefly to check the time.

"You should have a message from her in about five minutes, Yev. It will explain it all. I think she will be fine, but I'm still nervous."

"It's probably the only way to get Larry back any time soon."

"Smita can use some good news right about now. I'm still getting messages from Marty indicating all is well and she is still preventing the message indicating trouble from sending."

"I'll go with you. That was going to be my next stop anyway."

Smita looked tired and worn out when she let them in. Her face was furrowed with worry and she looked like she had aged ten years. She spoke softly in a weak, shaky voice.

"Is there any news?"

"Well, I was going to tell you we were doing all we can," said Yev. "I'll let Mia tell you what's going on."

"Marty came up with a plan and went over to the Parasol base. I was going to try to stop her at first, but I think she can do it."

Smita smiled and shook her head before finally replying.

"Oh, I should have guessed she would go out there. You wouldn't have been able to stop her, Mia, even if you wanted to. I quickly learned never to doubt her. She always has a plan and even when things don't go her way, she still gets it done in the end. I'm still worried though. I keep feeling like I'm about to be sick."

"I'm going to read that message and take care of a couple things at the security office," said Yev turning to go.

"I'll keep you posted if things change," said Mia, turning her head. Then looking back at Smita, "Do you want some company, or maybe to get out for a while?"

"No, I think I need to get some sleep. I'm going to take a sedative and try to relax. Worrying isn't going to bring Larry back."

"That sounds like a good idea. Let me know if you need anything."

Mia went over to Dome Six to force herself to eat. It wouldn't be easy, as she struggled with her own anxiety over the situation. She had always been a little anxious anyway. She could always project calm and confidence, even as she masked her inner feelings of unease.

While walking through Dome Six, she was approached by Rachel. The greetings and small talk quickly gave way, as Mia thought they would. Rachel's expression of concern, curiosity and general puzzlement were plain to see.

"What's going on Mia? I can see it's something big, but I'm just getting bits and pieces. Then at one point, I thought I saw Marty walking by out of the corner of my eye, but then she was gone. Later I noticed a glider was missing."

"Well, Larry was abducted by The Parasol Group and Marty went to go get him back. That's the short of it."

Rachel had many questions and Mia answered with as much detail as she could. They wanted to keep things as quiet as possible though to prevent panic. It was like living in a small town though. Everyone knew everyone, so things got around. If it wasn't top secret, it got around eventually. After her chat with Rachel, Mia picked up some food and brought it back to her quarters. She really needed some quiet time and a little rest.

Chapter Seventeen

After the nearly naked men led her through the penthouse, Marty felt quite relieved finally to see Larry. She saw just a hint of something register, but he maintained his poker face with the guards nearby.

"How are you, Larry?" asked Marty.

"Not bad, all things considered," said Larry in a guarded tone.

They kept the chat like that for a couple minutes, until the men who escorted Marty backed off a little. They maintained watch, with weapons drawn, but were back far enough that Marty and Larry could whisper without being heard. Being in a little alcove in one corner of the room, Marty and Larry had no way to evade. Their captors, however, stayed further back in order to be able to pick them off no matter which way they tried to run.

They were left with a tray filled with a variety of different foods, as well as ice, soft drinks, tea and fresh water. It looked like catering from somewhere far fancier than Marty had ever been. They dug in, as they began whispering freely to each other.

"Are you all right, Larry? Did they hurt you at all?"

"I'm fine. Other than a little rough handling when they grabbed me, Dez has been quite nice. She hinted that things were about to change for the worse though. But enough of that. What are you doing here?"

"I came here for you of course. There was no other way really."

"Well thanks, but I don't see how getting yourself captured is going to help."

"Larry, I have a plan. Trust me. Things are well under control. I don't want to say any more, other than you need to be ready for anything."

"I know that face and tone of voice. I learned not to doubt a long time ago. Betting against you is the longest of longshots."

"Good. That's what I like to hear. So what happened?"

"Well, I was walking around in Gale crater with Samuel, I went around this big mound and suddenly I'm being grabbed. They had ahold of me before I saw anything."

"This has all gone too far. At least they are going to be banning Parasol Group employees from the base though. I wish we could ban everyone, but apparently, Alma Cohen has to have some sort of justification to overrule the inevitable whining. Last I heard, it was looking likely that everyone would be forced to stay in the base. No more outings. Or at least that's what I got from skimming the latest security update right after I arrived here.

"The same political bullshit surrounds this situation. We had to go through Earth authorities to secure your release. That's just too slow and not acceptable. That fucking bitch is starting some shit. One way or another I'm going to fucking finish it."

"Yeah, I was worried I might be in for an extended stay. Smita is probably a wreck right now too."

"She was. I wasn't much better, at first. But that just makes me all the more determined."

They talked for a while until there was finally a pause. A minute later Marty could hear something going on. It sounded like Dez had returned.

✳ ✳ ✳ ✳ ✳ ✳ ✳

Oscar Perry walked into the office of Bill Jeffries at the Chimera Mars base. It was a fairly large office and one wall overlooked the Martian landscape ten stories below. The furnishings were the same typical office pieces found in all parts of the base. Bill motioned for him to take a seat and he did so.

"Well, I guess we should begin with the news you were telling me about, Oscar."

"It's pretty crazy, Bill. Apparently, Dez has something planned. Parasol Group personnel captured a professor from the IMB. It was one of the lead people on the alien project. Secondhand reports state they just grabbed him while he was on some sort of field trip out at Gale crater."

"Wow, she is getting daring. So did they find something over there?"

"No, supposedly it was a recreational outing. Keep in mind, he hasn't been on Mars very long and this is his first time coming here."

"Oh I see. Yeah, it is pretty exciting initially. I remember going on a few outings myself."

"That, in addition to other things, is why I think we need to reevaluate strategy."

"All right, Oscar, I'm willing to listen to suggestions."

"I think our secondary objective is holding us back and it has become extremely unlikely. With no more operatives in the base and no way into their network, we are shit out of luck. Unless we want to get drastic and risk sending an armed team in there, or something like that, we might as well forget it. We need to go all in on stopping Amalgam Global and even The Parasol Group if they end up becoming a threat."

"I think you may be right, Oscar. Going all in may be the only way to ensure the other corporations don't get their hands on the alien tech."

"I think there is even more to be gained here. I'm thinking our endgame secondary goal of gaining favor with governments and bolstering our image can be expanded. We offer our help to the IMB. I mean straight up too. We don't try to trick them, or make a longshot attempt at the alien ship. We ally ourselves and pool resources to stop the other two corporations. That guarantees success of the primary objective and greatly increases the success on our new secondary.

"This improves our opportunity to severely tarnish Amalgam and Parasol and simultaneously gives us a PR jackpot. Between public perception improving our brands and inroads we make with world governments, not to mention the exact opposite happening to our biggest rivals, we stand to gain an incredible amount of market share."

"I knew I had you around for a reason! That's brilliant, Oscar. This will put Chimera on top. The senior board members will be quite pleased. This will mean promotions and a little cut of the profits for us. Granted it won't even be a whole percent, but it'll be a lot more money than either of us have made our entire lives."

"I think information our operatives uncovered about Amalgam's illegal manufacture of plasma weapons will come in handy. I'm sure someone at the IMB is all over the Amalgam network, since we have detected snooping coming from there while doing our own electronic espionage. However, the plasma stuff is all off network. No record of it at all. Having people on the inside is the only way to discover it. Therefore, I'm sure they don't know yet.

"We can also offer to help get their guy back from Parasol. With all that, we may be able to score the majority of research and development contracts and probably the same for manufacturing as well."

"Sounds good, Oscar. I'm sure the board will be very excited. Since this is your baby, how would you like to take point on this?"

"I would love to, Bill. I think I have just the sort of diplomatic skills we need to pull this off."

Oscar walked out of Bill's office feeling quite pleased with himself. He worried Bill might be stubborn, but as it turned out, that was not the case. He decided to take a little time to think this over and come up with the best way to execute the plan. This could end up being amazing. Another five to ten years raking in a share of the profits from the highest growth period and he could retire to some tropical paradise and live like a king—preferably somewhere with many young, attractive, gay men. A swarthy, twenty year old, cabana boy who wiggles his cute little, tan bottom while he walks, would be perfect. For now, focus is the key though.

✳ ✳ ✳ ✳ ✳ ✳ ✳

Marty sat on a small, ornate couch, upholstered mostly in leather, with Larry to her right. Dez sat across from them on a larger, but similar looking couch. She drank wine from a goblet that matched the ostentatious, yet gothic décor that surrounded them.

"Would you care for some wine?" asked Dez, as if she had invited them for a social occasion.

"Yeah, that sounds good," said Marty.

"Yes, Please," said Larry.

Dez snapped her fingers and then made a sort of slight waving gesture, all in one fluid motion. Within seconds they were being handed goblets of wine. Marty sniffed and then sipped. It was a very smooth red, somewhat dry, with a little tartness and a hint of spice to it. It was quite delicious.

"That's some good stuff," said Marty, smiling at the pleasant taste.

"Indeed," said Larry. "Not a surprise though, as the food was quite good as well."

"Good, I'm glad you are enjoying yourselves."

"I assume there is something you want," said Marty.

"Yes, there is. I'm hoping this can be done pleasantly, like old friends having a drink together. No need to get nasty and eventually I could even be persuaded to let you leave."

After pausing for a moment, Dez continued in a harsher tone. "Uncooperative guests don't have such a nice visit, but I still get what I want."

"And what would that be?" Marty asked, looking Dez right in the eye.

"Well, my dear," said Dez with mock politeness. "I want to know all about the alien ship. I want the professor here to tell me everything he knows. I want you to access all the data about it for me. Then I want you to get me into the Amalgam and Chimera networks. My people have got into to those to a certain extent, but I think you have access to it all."

"Most of that isn't going to happen. But, I'll tell you what. Amalgam has made quite an enemy of me. I'll get you into everything they have. Chimera hasn't particularly done anything, but I'd be willing to negotiate. I'd even be willing to do your security for you. But, fuck the rest of that bullshit."

"No, I don't think I would trust you to do the security here."

Dez paused as Marty began laughing very hard. It was a belly laugh, nearing the point of hysteria before it finally subsided. Dez just stared Marty down, waiting for an explanation but refusing to inquire. Marty finally spoke as her laughter subsided.

"Bitch, please! I've had the run of your whole fucking network for over a month now. The only thing that would change is nobody else would be able to get in. It's mainly Chimera by the way, Amalgam doesn't seem to have put much effort in."

Dez ignored her and continued. "Go ahead and get me into Amalgam. We'll start with that since you are willing. Then after that, I'll be a little more, 'persuasive', shall we say."

"After I give you access to everything Amalgam has, it would be in your best interest to just let us go."

"You're not in any position to bargain. You'll do what you're told with a smile on your face, or perhaps a sort of clenched grimace."

"You'd be surprised. With your high expectations, I think you're going to be in for some disappointment no matter what. Whether or not you're in for anything else will be up to you."

"You're actually going to threaten me, here where I control everything? You must have a giant set of solid steel balls on you, bitch."

"Well, you could come put you're fucking face down here and find out," said Marty, spreading her legs, bucking her hips forward and pointing down at her crotch.

Dez clenched her jaw in anger, getting a little red in the face. Larry put his hand over his mouth trying not to laugh.

"Just give me access to Amalgam's network and we'll see what happens after that," said Dez, trying to mask her anger.

With the device, they supplied her and under careful scrutiny, she got into Amalgam's network and then quickly made similar back doors and a script they could use to get them in. It took her all of about twenty minutes. Then she explained what to do.

"All you have to do is execute this script and follow the menu."

"Thank you. That will come in quite handy. Now how about you continue being cooperative."

"Nope, that's all you get."

Looking over at a couple of the guys who were not holding the captives at gunpoint, Dez said, "Teach her the value of being cooperative."

They came around the back of the couch. Marty saw a hand reaching down to grab her. She caught him by the wrist and leaned forward, dodging a blow from the other man. In the same motion, she flung the man at Dez and then spun around kicking the other man in the face. She soon found herself surrounded by men pointing guns at her face, at very close range.

"You are full of surprises. You're not going to fight your way out of here though."

"True, but that isn't exactly what I had in mind. Last chance to let us go."

"Oh, I don't think so. I think things are going to get uncomfortable for both of you. Perhaps we should shoot one of you in the leg."

Marty stared her down coldly, looking very defiant, as countless weapons were leveled in her direction.

Chapter Eighteen

Alma Cohen sat in her office reviewing space flight schedules. It was time to plan for the next period where Mars and the earth are on opposite sides of the Sun. During this time, she got a communication request from Chimera. She put it on video as that was the preference listed. She was tempted just to let him leave a message, but changed her mind, as she grew curious about what he wanted.

"Hello, what can I do for you?"

"Mrs. Cohen, I'm Oscar Perry from Chimera. I work for Bill Jeffries. I wanted to see if you had a few minutes to discuss something."

"Oh yes, I have met Mr. Jeffries. Well, I'm rather busy, Mr. Perry, but I suppose I have a few minutes."

"Thank you very much, ma'am. I heard about the incident with one of your people being held at Parasol. If you need any help, Chimera would be only too happy to assist. We may be able to apply pressure to encourage their cooperation."

"We are working on that, but if you are able to resolve that, it would be appreciated."

"Parasol is only a small problem compared to Amalgam."

"Mr. Perry, your company may be in third place, out of the three that are here, on the problem list. However, you are still on the list. There is the business of a couple operatives who were sent back to earth and I suspect they are the reason the Amalgam operatives were shipped back in bags."

"Yes, I do admit we wanted to get some information about a certain secret project. If you notice though, all we did was a little snooping; we didn't harm any of your people. Our primary objective is to stop Amalgam Global. They cannot be allowed to get their hands on, 'you know what'. The incident with the bodies was in regard to that. We didn't realize you were already on top of it. You want to keep prying eyes away from certain things, so I think we have a major objective in common."

"Yes, I suppose we do, Mr. Perry. It is true that you haven't harmed any of my people, which is more than I can say for the other two. Don't think you're going to get my trust though. I wouldn't trust you any further than I could throw you on Earth. It would be nice to stop them proactively though, rather than waiting for them to do something to justify banning them from the base. It won't take much either as they are already suspected of a certain incident, but I'd rather not wait around for them to try something."

"That's fine, Mrs. Cohen. You don't have to trust us. I just want to work together to stop Amalgam Global. You have someone in your employ, who I think has access to every part of the Amalgam network. We have access to much of it, but not everything. A little assistance in that regard would be nice. In return, we have operatives working at

Amalgam. There are things they are doing which are kept off the network and systems. We have discovered they are producing plasma weapons both for use in their more shady operations, as well as for sale on the black market. We are trying to get solid evidence of this. That should put them on the defensive."

"That's a serious charge. I wouldn't put it past them though. Anton Griswold is the most thoroughly evil person I've ever encountered. Charles Mantis is here now too. He's not exactly a saint either and from what I understand he oversees all of those shady operations you mentioned."

"Great, so we have a deal then?"

"Yes, I suppose we can work together a little. At least until Amalgam Global is stopped."

After the call ended, Alma arranged to have a meeting with key staff members to figure out how much cooperation to give, as well as how to make the most of Chimera's offer. This could help, but she needed to proceed with caution.

❋ ❋ ❋ ❋ ❋ ❋ ❋

Larry felt his heart pound faster and his stomach tie itself in knots. He always had confidence in Marty, but he didn't know how they were going to get out of this. He kept his poker face on though, not letting anyone see what he thought or felt. Why was Marty being so provocative? He saw guns aimed mostly at his dearest friend, who stood at his side, but a couple of them pointed at him as well.

The men all looked determined and ready for action. Marty appeared confident, but it looked like she had something stuck in her teeth, or was trying to get peanut butter out from between her cheek and gum. Just as he looked at Dez, she made a face as if someone snuck up behind her and poked her butt. Larry thought maybe she was about to give the order to open fire. Then suddenly the men lowered their weapons a little and kind of bowed their heads a bit.

Dez started to look a little faint and then her men dropped to their knees. Larry just stood there with his mouth open, as confused as he could be. What is going on here? The men all slumped over struggling to get up, as Dez dropped to her knees. Marty had a wicked, devious smile, her apparent glee growing as she looked around the room. As Dez collapsed, the men all seemed to be unconscious.

Larry grabbed the space suits, helmets and other personal items belonging to both Marty and himself. When he turned back around, Marty had flipped Dez over on her back. Dez seemed weak and could barely move, but still conscious. Everyone else was out cold. Marty glared at Dez with a frightening, crazed look on her face.

"If you or anyone here so much as looks at anyone I know the wrong way, I'm coming after you. You will never know what is going to happen or when. This is one example. Now I'll give you another."

The bewildered Dez, looked more frightened by the second as Marty spoke. Then Marty grabbed her by the throat and lifted her up a little as she squatted down, bringing their faces closer together. Dez looked utterly terrified at this point. Marty squeezed hard and Dez opened her mouth as if struggling in vain to inhale.

"I've never killed anyone intentionally. But things fucking change. If you piss me off, this face is the last fucking thing you will ever see. So don't fuck with me!"

With that, Marty released her and Dez fell back gasping for air.

"We have to fucking move now, Larry. You got everything?"

"It's all here," said Larry, still confused, but just going with it.

"We'll suit up in the lift," said Marty, running for the door.

Larry ran after her, with all of their stuff in tow. It wasn't much more than a minute before they were in the lift. Marty, grabbed her mobile device from Larry, fiddled with it for a minute and then shut it off, as the lift began to go down.

"We're safe for the moment. Nobody can get in and it won't stop until it reaches the ground level. We aren't going to have much time though. '

They both quickly put their suits on as the lift continued down. Larry was still trying to make sense of what was going on.

"Marty, what happened?"

"No time for that right now, Larry. Listen to me. We aren't going to have much time before they come after us. The pep talk I gave Dez will probably keep her away from us later on, but it's not going to delay her raising the alarm for more than a minute or two, once she can get around again. They'll be onto us by the time we reach the airlock. So, we need to get our helmets on and be ready for the outside when I open the lift doors.

"I can secure the airlock, but it won't take them long to override it. I'm talking twenty seconds at most. Once that happens, they can open the inner door, which will prevent the outer door from opening and that can't be overridden. The flip side to that is that when the outer door starts to open, they can't get to us. Chances are we won't have much time for depressurizing. I'm going to have to set it so the outer door opens as soon as they attempt to override. We'll need to lie on the floor near the inner door, just off-center. That way the door will be most of the way open when we get sucked through and that should keep us from getting banged up. Keep your arms over your head just in case."

"All right, I got it," said Larry as he secured his helmet. He could hear Marty's muffled voice again through the helmet, as she lifted her own up to her head.

"You're bigger, so you got the bottom. Sorry, buddy. It's just dust though. I didn't see any rocks in front of it."

The lift stopped at the ground floor as Marty finished securing her helmet. Then she opened the doors and darted out. Larry took off right behind her. They were starting to draw attention to themselves, but the airlock was in sight before anyone seemed to be onto them.

When they reached the airlock, Larry could see people running toward them. Marty secured and closed the door, then pointed to the floor in front of it. Larry lay down on his back, as Marty started the depressurization. He put his arms over his head and Marty quickly lay down on top of him. No sooner had he felt her legs clamp around his and her hands grab tightly onto his upper arms, than the outer door began to open.

The rush of air quickly grew in strength and he felt himself move forward. The movement accelerated rapidly as the pressure differential sucked them out. He partially lifted off the ground just a slight bit. This caused them to glide easily over the dusty surface. As they slowed Marty pulled on him and then let go, kicking her legs back. Larry used the momentum to swing his upper body forward, he landed on his feet, with Marty right in front of him.

Larry stumbled a little from the momentum and Marty almost fell backward. He reached out and grabbed her, helping her stay upright.

"I have a glider over there," said Marty, her voice sounding muffled through their helmets.

She ran toward a small crater and Larry followed. He could see the outer door of the airlock close as he looked back. The crater was still a little ways off, so they ran for a few minutes. When they got there, they slid down into it and then paused for a minute to catch their breath. When Larry looked back, he could see the door opening and people coming out.

Marty got on the glider and he jumped on behind her. It came to life with a quiet hum as it began to lift off the ground. There were people at the Parasol base running off in different directions, presumably looking for transport, while three others were running right at them. They were still a fair distance away as the glider slowly moved forward, out of the crater.

Once they cleared the crater, they quickly accelerated. Marty put some distance between them and the base, as quickly as she could. Larry finally started to feel as if he could relax a little. For the first time since this whole thing began, he felt like he was safe. They continued to speed away, the Parasol base getting smaller as Larry looked back.

✳✳✳✳✳✳✳

Mia ran down the hall toward Smita's quarters. She felt a powerful wave of excitement, relief and happiness, cascading throughout her body. The message from Marty had her on her feet, cheering, dancing and then running for the door. She was almost out of breath when she neared

Smita's quarters. She tried to get it all out at once as soon as the door opened.

"Smita! I've got wonderful news! They're all right! Marty and Larry are out! They are on their way home right now!"

It took a minute for it to register for Smita. She was looking a little confused.

"Mia, hold on. You're going too fast. You got a message from Marty?"

"Yes, she and Larry are coming back."

"Oh! My Larry! Thank you!"

She flung her arms around Mia as tears flowed from her eyes. She was almost hysterical as she put her face on Mia's shoulder, suddenly leaning some of her weight against her.

"Oh Mia! Thank you so much," she said with a sob.

Mia hugged Smita and held onto her.

"I was getting worried too, Smita. Now I'm so excited I don't know what to do!"

"This is such a relief," said Smita finally lifting her head up and starting to wipe her eyes. "There was a time there I thought I might never see him again. What happened? How did they get away?"

"I don't know. The message was a generic premade one. She set it up so it could be sent while she was on the go. We'll have to ask them when they get back."

"She thinks of everything. Doesn't she?"

"Yeah, she is very resourceful. Well I should talk to Brian and Yev. They'll want to know too."

"Okay, thank you again, Mia."

Smita went back inside as Mia went to see Brian and Yev. When she finally got over there and told them the news, they were quite relieved as well. Even after all that, she still felt like she had ants in her pants. So, she went up to the fitness center to burn some of that off.

✳ ✳ ✳ ✳ ✳ ✳

Marty was far from Parasol at this point, but still a long way from home. That was fucking fantastic. Everything went according to plan. She taught that lunatic woman one hell of a lesson. She had her best friend back and was headed home, to the woman with whom she had fallen in love.

"All right, can you tell me what the hell is going on now?" said the muffled voice behind her.

"Yeah, sorry. Hang on. Let me get our communicators synced."

Okay, go ahead and switch on."

After a minute, Marty cycled hers off and on again. "Can you hear me?"

"Loud and clear."

"Let me start at the beginning. I have one of those extra small devices. I set up an extra hologram output for it. I have it projected up to my mouth. While you can't see it, the input still works. You know how you can hot key stuff to certain places on a hologram display?"

"Sure, I set some of that up on mine to use as shortcuts."

"Well, I have it so I can kick off preset things by moving my tongue around in certain ways, in specific areas of my mouth."

"Where did you stash that thing?"

"You don't want to know."

"Oh gross, you stuck in your butt didn't you? I hope you wrapped it."

"Fuck no! I don't like anything bigger than a finger going in there. Let's just say it took up residence in the little pink house next door. And yes, I did wrap it up."

"Marty, when am I going to start taking your advice when you tell me I don't want to know?"

"You're a slow learner, man," said Marty, laughing.

Larry chuckled too. "That may be. But I still don't understand what happened."

"Well, I figured out how to connect to people's nanobots and even hack them. There are a number of interesting things I figured out how to do with them. Basically, I connected to everyone in range, but had it set to exclude us. I made each set of nanobots think the person in which they resided was having a severe hypertensive crisis. I wanted Dez to remain conscious though. Since I knew a little about her, I knew she would be the only female in the room apart from me. So right beforehand, I had it connect to women only and I signaled a certain allergic reaction. Just enough so she got a little adrenaline, but not too much."

"Aha, so that's what that look was about."

"I know. I almost started laughing. It totally looked like someone goosed her."

Larry started laughing hard. "Yes! That is exactly what I was thinking. You really had me worried there for a minute, with all those guns pointed at us. I was so confused when everyone collapsed. I had no idea what was going on."

"Well, I gave her fair warning."

"That you did. I tell you though, I couldn't believe some of the stuff you were telling that woman. Girl, you're almost as crazy as she is."

"Yep, I fucking showed her."

"Thanks for getting me out of there, Marty. You had a plan and everything, but you still risked it all for me. You are the truest friend anyone could ever have."

"I'm just glad to have you back. I was losing it when I heard what happened. I knew I had to get you out of there. I've known you my whole adult life. You were a friend to me when no one else was."

"I was going through a big transition too, back then. Nothing like what you were going through, but a difficult time for me."

"We helped each other through it and things just kind of continued on like that. I think it will for years to come."

"Absolutely, Marty. I can't wait to see Smita again. I bet you can't wait to see Mia."

"Yeah, I miss her already. That's another thing you did Larry. Going with you to Mars was cool enough, but it's also how I met Mia."

"I think you're falling in love with that girl, Marty."

"You're right, Larry. It was probably happening before I was willing to accept it or even realized. I wouldn't be surprised if you knew it before I did. You know me too well."

Soon they could see the Mars base come into view off in the distance. It wasn't going to be long and they would be home.

Chapter Nineteen

Dez walked into the Parasol medical facility with three of her men, as the doctor requested. The nurse ushered them to the back where the doctor planned to examine them. Having just finished getting set up, the doctor turned to meet with them.

"Come this way, Dez. I'll start with you. So you were saying this just happened suddenly and it was just before the commotion earlier."

"Yes, doctor, it was like I was about to faint, my vision faded out like when you've been resting and stand up too quick. Then the next thing I know, I'm on my knees. Shortly after that, I fell over. I could barely move for a few minutes. All my men report being unconscious. About a minute or two before all that, I got this sudden jolt. It's hard to explain, I got this anxious feeling and my heart started beating faster. It's as if I knew something bad was about to happen."

"That's very strange. It sounds more like you were drugged. Let me see what your nanobots say."

The doctor looked at his screen for a few minutes and his brow furrowed from his eyes up to the top of his balding head.

"This is just bizarre. Your nanobots gave you cortisol and a little epinephrine for an allergic reaction. That explains your jolt, but some of the data doesn't jibe with the report of the allergic reaction. It also looks like a food allergy, but you don't have any food allergies. It looks like bogus data."

The doctor studied the screen a little more, looking more puzzled as time went on.

"This next bit makes even less sense. Your blood pressure was normal, but then went up a little after the epinephrine. Then suddenly there are alerts of a severe hypertensive crisis. The nanobots treated you for that. Then I have error messages about conflicting data, alerts for very low blood pressure, then after a diagnostic, you are treated for the low blood pressure. It's as if someone was able to feed the nanobots bogus data."

"It had to have been Marty," said Dez. "But how did she do it? She was just standing there. It's like she can control my nanobots with her mind."

"It's definitely not with her mind. That's quite impossible. But it does seem like someone accessed them somehow, which is almost impossible, but not entirely."

The doctor examined each of the men. It only took a few minutes, but it felt much longer to Dez, as she filled with worry about the implications of all this. The lack of answers made it worse and the answers that did come only raised more questions.

"These three are all the same and nearly the same as you. They all had the same false hypertensive crisis, which they were treated for and the nanobots then ran a diagnostic when blood pressure dropped so low. Then they treated that issue, just as yours did. The difference is the men didn't have the allergic reaction thing before that."

"Of course," said Dez. "She wanted them unconscious, but she had different plans for me. How do we stop this, doctor?"

"Well for now that same trick isn't going to work again. Nanobots run on very sophisticated artificial intelligence software. Later on, it could work again and there are probably other tricks like that. Nothing that could kill you or incapacitate you for very long though. It is possible to disable automatic stuff like that, but that is not advised. The automatic intervention saves a lot of lives. Those early minutes are precious and it can sometimes take time for someone to get to you. There are no reports of something like this incident ever happening before either. The best thing would be to just stay away from that person you mentioned. Nanobots can only be accessed at close range. That reminds me. I need to give you and all your men an injection to resupply the nanobots."

Dez, didn't like that at all. She was going to be relegated to playing defense for the most part. She didn't want to take any chances. She would have to post security at all the airlocks and beef up surveillance a little, so they can expand the range and have all areas in sight at all times. However, Marty did leave her a little gift. The access to Amalgam Global may allow her to steal any secrets they might acquire. It could also assist in preventing them from getting anything patented. She decided to call Tucker when she got back up to the penthouse. This would be a good project for him.

* * * * * * *

Marty mentally prepared herself for a big commotion. Between their approach, putting the glider back and walking to the nearest airlock, they were sure to have been seen by many. She stepped into the airlock when depressurization completed and the door slid open. Larry stepped in right behind her, sealing the outer door. She could see the crowd through the window, so she took a deep breath, as the airlock pressurized.

At least the people that need to be there were right at the front. Mia and Smita were a few feet from the other side of the door. When pressurization was nearly complete, they both took off their helmets.

As the inner door slid open and they stepped out of the airlock, the place erupted in cheers. Quite a crowd had gathered there in Dome Five. Word travels fast at the International Mars Base. Mia was in her arms almost instantly, she could see Larry holding Smita out of the corner of her eye.

They just stood there like that for a couple minutes, during which time the crowd soon quieted down.

"I missed you so much," said Mia, still clinging tightly to Marty. "I was really worried too. I just wanted you to come back safely to me."

At the same time, she could hear Smita saying something similar to Larry.

"Larry I was so scared! I thought I might never see you again. I didn't know what I was going to do. It is such a relief to have your arms around me again."

After a few minutes of hugging, kissing and strong emotions, the outside world finally came back into focus again. People were starting to go about their business again as well. The four of them started walking toward Dome Seven. Once they reached the points where their paths home diverged, Smita addressed them.

"Marty, thank you so much for bringing Larry back to me," she said putting her arms around Marty, hugging her warmly. "I don't think I can ever thank you enough. I'm very grateful Larry has you for a friend."

"No problem. Anything for you two. You've both been such good friends to me."

Smita turned to Mia, embracing her just as she had with Marty. "I want to thank you too, Mia. You helped me through a very difficult time. I don't know what I would have done without you."

"You're quite welcome. I only wish I could have done more."

"Thanks again, Marty," said Larry affectionately putting his arm around Marty's shoulders, giving her a light squeeze.

"You thanked me enough on the way back," said Marty, patting Larry on the back, just between the shoulder blades.

Marty couldn't wait to get home and get out of her clothes. A rest was in order and maybe something to eat as well. It had also been a while since she had a good release and the need had grown as well, especially with Mia looking so incredibly sexy.

Mia told Marty to go ahead and relax when they got back to their quarters. Marty took off her clothes while Mia left to pick up some food. After a couple minutes, she was completely naked, pulling her panties down as she sat on the bed.

She lay back against the pillows at about forty-five degrees. It felt so good to relax in her bed again. She reached a couple fingers inside herself, removing the tiny device. She disposed of the wrapping and put the handy little device away with the rest of her things.

Mia soon returned carrying a tray with food and drink. "Ooh look at that. I seem to have a naked woman in my bed."

"Food being brought to me in bed. It doesn't get any better than that."

"Sure it does, you know better than that," said Mia, licking her lips.

"Ah you're feeling like a naughty girl. Aren't you? Excellent! I'm feeling pretty horny myself."

"We'll start with this," said Mia indicating the food. She quickly stripped down and joined Marty on the bed for a meal.

After eating, Marty felt even more relaxed and tired. Mia turned to her, putting her hands on Marty's legs.

"You just lay back and relax. Let me take care of you."

Mia's hands were warm and soft, sensually rubbing all over her body. Mia was also naked and her large breasts hung down, swaying and jiggling a little as she moved. Eventually she began rubbing Marty's nipples. Mia's fingers working their magic on her nipples making her ache and throb between her legs and her body tingled all over.

Finally, she mounted one of Marty's legs, moving the other to the side. She put her hands there in the creases of Marty's legs. She bent forward, moving her face down there as well. As she moved her hips back and forth, rubbing herself against Marty's leg, she planted a gentle kiss on her puffy lips, sending a shiver through Marty, making her twitch. She could feel Mia's wetness on her leg, as she glided back and forth. She was so ready when Mia spread her open and felt how hot and moist she became.

Mia's tongue soon worked a magic of its own, much like her fingers did earlier. She was so aroused, that it took only seconds of gentle licking before she felt herself quickly building to climax. She came in waves, with Mia's face between her legs, her body shaking with the pleasure of it all.

Mia must have enjoyed it because the intensity of her humping suddenly increased and she moaned and shook to where Marty could almost feel her climax along with her own. There was a sudden rush of lubricating moisture, which Marty could feel all over her leg.

Mia inserted her fingers, which assisted her tongue in bringing Marty to orgasm again and again. She also continued bucking her hips, gliding back and forth over Marty's leg, bringing herself to climax several times.

Eventually, as she closed her eyes, she felt Mia lie down next to her and snuggle up close. That was the last thing to reach her awareness as she drifted off to sleep, feeling as content and satisfied as anyone could.

✳ ✳ ✳ ✳ ✳ ✳ ✳

Charles Mantis sat at his desk, thinking it was probably for the best that the abduction of Dr. Bierbrauer failed. A story was relayed to him that one of his men heard about while visiting the shops at the IMB. Parasol Group abducted someone and it did not go well for them at all. It was Martina Barbotti, who he met at least two months ago. He didn't know what to believe and what not to believe. One thing was a certainty though. That woman was a formidable adversary. She thwarted his plans, even before they were tainted with Mr. Griswold's pointless destruction and lack of self-control. She took out a couple really big guys who were with him and even bested Francis, which he would have thought impossible. In fact, he did think it impossible prior to their meeting.

There was really only one thing for it. He needed to wait until they were a good way through their project and then take the base by force. That would require a number of people to die and plenty of chaos. It had to look natural though. Alternatively, perhaps he could blame it on Mr. Griswold. Nobody would doubt it. Then as long as things didn't reflect too badly on Amalgam Global as a whole, or any lower level employees, everything would be all right. Anton Griswold needed to die eventually anyway. That would make killing him a simple matter. There would be no need for a tedious cover-up job afterward. As soon as that psychotic piece of shit was dead, that would be that. The hard part was going to be waiting and all the while, pretending to be loyal to Mr. Griswold. It would be torture waiting to kill him, like a wickedly annoying itch he could never scratch. This would be maddening. However, it would give him something to look forward to. When one finally does scratch a horrible itch like that, it is so incredibly satisfying.

$$* * * * * * *$$

Larry reclined on his bed, holding Smita, who was clinging to him tightly. He missed her badly during his ordeal at the Parasol base. She must have missed him the same, but had the added stress of not knowing. She didn't know how he was being treated, or if they planned to kill him. It certainly would have driven him out of his mind. At least she had friends here to comfort her. That meant a lot.

Marty coming to his aid meant a lot too, although he felt ambivalent about it. He didn't want her risking her life for him, as it just felt wrong. It always felt wrong. There was no stopping her though. In a way, he was glad, because she really saved his ass. At least this last time she had it under control, although he didn't know that at the time.

The feeling of wrongness was at least mitigated by the knowledge that he had come to her aid before as well. They had been the best of friends for a few years now, which would remain so, evermore as far as he was concerned.

Just holding Smita and having her close seemed to be the best medicine for her. She was still a wreck when he got back, but she was quickly recovering. She was fast asleep now and from what he heard, this was by far the most at peace she had been since the incident began.

Holding her close and having her cling to him, was the best medicine for him as well. After being a prisoner, it was so nice having her there, asleep in his arms. It occurred to him that he hadn't really slept well either. The growing tiredness served as a good reminder of that.

Chapter Twenty

Marty was in Dome Six, thinking about getting something to eat, when she heard a familiar voice behind her.

"Kia ora koe, Marty."

There were only three people on the base who would use that greeting and not many more with a New Zealand accent. It sounded like a kid, so it had to be Nik.

"Kia ora koe, Nik," she said while turning around.

"I was hoping you would remember me."

"Of course I remember you, Nikora Rawiri Kahurangi the third. You and your parents were on the ship with me. We practically lived together for a week. I was surprised I hadn't seen you around. I see your parents occasionally, but just from across the room when they are going somewhere. That's to be expected though, given their jobs. Where have you been hiding out?"

Nik smiled broadly upon hearing his name and knowing she remembered. He was about average height for a boy of ten. He had the typical dark features of the Maori and closely cropped hair. His father, who had the same name, but was called 'Junior', was the facilities director, which incorporated the maintenance, custodial and sanitation departments. His mother, Aria, was the executive chef, in charge of all the food service staff and the running of the kitchens. Nik looked up to Marty after the incident at the maglev station. His parents were always telling him not to pester her. She didn't mind though, he was a good kid and very bright too. She wondered why she never really saw him and then had kind of forgotten about him.

"I had a lot of school work to make up. My parents weren't letting me do hardly anything until I got caught up. I'm all caught up and in the regular class now. I'm doing well too. Because of that, my parents are letting me do what I want now. Well, after I do my homework anyway. Then I heard about Professor Wellington getting captured and about how you got him out. That was cool! I want hear all about it!"

"All right, I don't mind telling you. It's a crazy fucking—well, uh, it's a crazy story."

"No worries, I've heard it all and I fucking say it all too, as long as my parents aren't around."

"That's good, because I definitely have quite a mouth on me."

Marty relayed the story to Nik, who leaned his head forward a little as he listened, with a big smile and wide eyes.

"Whoa, that was a crazy story!" he said when she was finished. Then added, "I saw some of that fight when those guys had Mia. You were really pissed that they were messing with your girlfriend. You totally kicked their asses too. That wasn't as scary and gross as the magelv thing, but it was just as awesome!"

"Yeah, I just lost it those two times. They were both scary for me. I got it done though. So you liked those moves you saw eh?"

"Yeah, that was cool. You are so fast too. I don't know how you move that fast. You're really strong for a girl, even stronger than some men. You have that warrior spirit in you, like my ancestors."

"Thanks, Nik. Moving like that just takes practice. Being strong is from lifting weights a lot. Some of it is genetics too, I suppose."

"Can you teach me how to do that?"

"Yeah, I can do that. It's going to take a lot of practice to get good at it though. We'll set up a time to meet up in the fitness center. The low gravity here might actually be a good way to learn."

"Thanks, Marty," said Nik smiling.

"Well, I need to get moving, but send me a message."

"See you later, Marty."

"See you, Nik," said Marty, as she went on her way.

Marty got herself something to eat and headed over toward some tables. Hilda, Rachel and Darren happened to be there and invited her to sit with them. She wanted to catch up, as she hadn't talked to them since the incident at Parasol. This might be a good time to give in to her curiosity too.

They of course wanted to know all about her recent adventure. So, she recited it all in detail, which kept them quite captivated. Being a nurse, Hilda was familiar with the nanobots, although not from a technical perspective. She was shocked to hear what Marty had figured out. It was something she never considered.

"I've noticed a different dynamic with you three the past few weeks. I didn't want to put you on the spot though. It's a little different than a woman with her man and her best friend."

"Oh, so you noticed right from the beginning eh?" asked Rachel.

"Yeah, I was getting that vibe at Brian's cocktail party a few weeks ago."

"That was right when things, well, evolved, you might say," said Rachel. "It's probably for the best you let it be, we were still figuring things out."

"I thought so."

"This is a new experience for all of us," said Darren.

"For Rachel and I, it is doubly so," said Hilda.

"It sure is," said Rachel. "First it started with us hanging out, not too long after things got physical with Darren and I. Darren and I were flirting and cuddling under a blanket. It wasn't long before he had his hand between my legs, while I rubbed his erection through his pants."

"I noticed what they were doing after a while," said Hilda. "It didn't bother me though. Rachel and I had been living in close quarters for a while. Sometimes you're relieving a little tension and realize you've maybe been noticed. Or you wake up with the bed shaking a little and realize your roomy is working out some tension. It happens."

"She was so cool about it," said Rachel. "So I pulled my pants down just a bit and also got Darren's cock out. We checked with her again to make sure."

"I told them it didn't bother me, if anything I found it hot."

"When she said that, we felt free to continue," said Darren.

"That plus getting worked up eased our inhibitions," said Rachel. "Since she was aroused and the two of us were already pretty open about this sort of thing, I suggested she may as well go ahead and take care of herself while Darren and I were playing."

"I figured I might as well," said Hilda. "We would both masturbate under the covers while the other was there anyway. So I went ahead."

"I ended up pulling back the covers a little when Darren was ready to cum so it didn't get on the blanket. Seeing that really did it for Hilda. So we talked about it and the next night decided to have sex in front of her. It was so hot and since Hilda wasn't seeing anyone, we decided to carry on. That's when I thought maybe Darren could help her out a little."

"It wasn't long before he was having sex with both of us," said Hilda.

"Hilda and I got even closer too. We started to kiss each other, take turns on Darren and maybe fondle each other's breasts a little. That's as far as we care to go though. It's strange. We aren't attracted to girls, but we are just enough to kiss, make out and feel each other up a little."

"It really turned into a three person romance," said Rachel.

"None of us ever did anything like this before," said Darren. "We just kind of discovered that we are polyamorous and this arrangement worked well for the three of us."

"We're going to get family quarters together," said Hilda.

"Congrats, you three!" said Marty, smiling. "I'm really happy for you. I was glad enough before when you two became close friends through the difficult experience you shared, But even more so with it resulting in this relationship."

"We are so grateful to you and Yev for everything," said Rachel.

"Yev is a great boss," said Darren. "He knows how to get stuff done and he always stands up for his people. Life has been incredible the past two months or so."

After finishing her food and finally hearing the full story, Marty headed back to her quarters. She felt strangely eager to share the news with Mia, whom she knew was also curious.

✳ ✳ ✳ ✳ ✳ ✳ ✳

Marty stopped the glider near the main airlock of the Chimera base. She felt a little apprehensive as she walked toward the big, gray, sliding door.

Am I really going to go in there? Bill and Oscar seemed all right when I talked to them, but this makes me nervous.

They noticed her as she approached and the airlock opened in front of her, just as she reached it. She activated the automatic cycle, which they enabled to allow her access. It went through the cycle of closing the outer door, pressurizing and then finally opening the inner door.

Marty had her helmet off as the inner door slid open. There were a couple security personnel there to greet her. One was a blond-haired man about her age with a Vandyke. The other was a woman who was maybe a couple years younger than she was, with beautiful, thick red hair and big, hazel eyes. She was rather attractive.

"Welcome to the Chimera Mars facility," said the man.

"If you'll just come with us, we'll take you up to see Mr. Jeffries and Mr. Perry. They've been expecting you."

"That's cool. You know this place is pretty similar to the International Mars Base."

"Yes, it is," said the man. "We designed it to be a lot like that. We just have the one dome though, other than some greenhouses and the outdoor mining facilities of course. It's about the same as your ninth dome."

When they arrived, the woman contacted Bill Jeffries by communicator. "Sir, I have a Martina Barbotti to see you."

"Thanks, Emma. Go ahead and send her in."

Emma showed her to the door, while turning her head back in the direction of the man. "Aiden, you dropping by the break room for coffee?"

"That's a big affirmative. I'll grab you one, black as your soul."

"Sweet! You da man."

Marty walked in to see Bill and Oscar sitting at a small conference table.

"What? Do you guys shop at the same furniture store as the IMB?" joked Marty, laughing.

Bill and Oscar both started to speak as she said that, but were unable to contain their laughter.

"I think a lot of this stuff is made here, but then many of our offices on earth are much the same," said Bill, as his laughter subsided.

"We get it all at the Cheap Mass Produced Furniture Outlet Mall," said Oscar laughing harder.

Marty and Bill laughed at that as well. They exchanged greetings once everyone regained their composure. Bill and Oscar were actually both nicer than she expected. She assumed this had much to do with the changing situation. She could trust them only because they needed her help. They were desperate to stop Amalgam Global and they wanted to gain favor with world leaders.

"Oscar, go ahead and start with the pictures," said Bill.

Oscar brought some pictures up on a hologram in the middle of the table.

"As you can see, we have some pictures showing plasma weapons. You can see the standard rifle-sized model here as well as the handgun version. There is supposedly a larger, higher wattage version, which can be mounted, but we don't have any pictures of it. We want to get more detailed shots, as well as video. Then it will be undeniable."

"Nice work," said Marty. "That's good information to have. I look forward to seeing more later on."

"I'll send the pictures and some reports over to you," said Oscar as he transmitted the files to her.

"Thanks," said Marty. "I'll get you access to everything on the Amalgam Global network. I can also improve your security in case Amalgam catches on to what you are doing."

"That sounds good," said Bill. "We'll give you a system which you can configure with access to Amalgam. We are prepared to make you a nice offer if you would like to come work for us after your Mars project is wrapped up."

"I've really already done what I came here to do. However, I'm not very corporate. I like being freelance. You might be able to talk me into the occasional project though, but it'll be pricey."

"Fair enough," said Bill. "We'll leave you to it then."

Mia sat at her desk moving some things around in a schematic hologram. She made a lot of progress on the design of this machine, which would make raw materials from energy. It should prove invaluable in manufacturing.

Dr. Magnus Petersen walked by, looking at the hologram.

"It looks like you're close to being finished, Mia. That's very impressive."

"Yeah, Magnus, it should just be a couple more weeks. Then we'll be on to the gamma ray laser, which should be quick and easy. It's the calm before the storm that will be the black hole energy generator."

"As quick as that eh? We really are making good time. The antimatter generator prototype has gone into production and we have a ship in orbit now, which we can use to retrofit stuff. It even has fusion engines based on your latest design."

"Very cool! I love seeing the things I designed become reality. It's like I thought something up, then suddenly it's real. My imagination coming to life."

"I guess it is kind of like that. So Marty went over to the Chimera base eh?"

"Yeah, we're sort of working with them. We don't really trust them. However, we can rely on their instinct for survival and their greed. Marty should be on her way back by now."

"Hey, Mia, I just sent over that data you needed," said Larry from his desk a few meters away. "Brian, Jorge, Zahra and I all put our focus on that and this should be exactly what you need for the next section you were going to work on."

"Thanks, all. You're just in time. I was just wrapping up the last thing I could do without that."

Once Marty had been back long enough to tell Mia how things went at Chimera and to hear about the latest events of her project, she finally felt able to relax. Mia was a very calming influence on her. By this point Marty had her clothes off and it felt so good to be naked. She leaned back against some pillows at the head of the bed and pulled the nice cool sheets up to her waist. Mia put a shirt on and sat next to her on the bed.

"It's nice to be able to relax, Mia. It's been crazy here for at least a couple weeks now."

"I know, Marty, we haven't had much time for us. It's as if the universe couldn't deal with us being happy and in love."

"Well, it's going to have to deal, or I'll be coming after that universe," said Marty smiling and putting an arm across Mia's back.

Mia leaned into her a little bit, looking up into her eyes, smiling back. "I think you would make it sorry, wouldn't you?"

"Nothing is going to separate my girl from me. I'll hold onto you forever," said Marty, as she squeezed Mia tighter.

"I love you so much, Marty."

"I love you too, Mia."

"That was pretty effortless. I think you're getting comfortable with your feelings about that sort of thing."

"Yeah, I really am. It's not scary anymore. Now it's just the way things are. It's all because of you. You have an effect on me like nobody else. Now loving you just seems so normal, like it was always that way. Maybe it's because all my life I was waiting for you, in order for me to feel like this and I just didn't know it yet."

"I don't even know what to say. You are the sweetest person I've ever met. I'm glad that I have been able to help you grow, just like you helped me out of my shell and guided me through the world you introduced me to."

"I like guiding you. Just like this," said Marty, moving her face to Mia's, gently pressing their lips together.

As Marty kissed her, she felt Mia's arms wrap around her and her lips hungrily kissing her in response. Their tongues met, as their lips locked together. After a long kiss, she stared into Mia's beautiful green eyes and could see Mia staring back into hers.

Chapter Twenty-One

Mia walked into the fitness center and found an out-of-the-way place to sit down. She liked to watch Marty training Nik and teaching him new skills. It was absolutely adorable and rather surprising at first. It was something she wouldn't have pictured Marty doing a few months ago.

Marty and Nik both wore a lot of thick padding all over their bodies. Nik was very quick and agile for someone who had only been training for three months. He worked very hard and had a lot of dedication for a ten-year-old boy. Marty turned out to be an excellent teacher.

As Mia watched the display of extreme cuteness before her, her mind began to wander. Things were surprisingly quiet for at least three months now. Everything just got better and better with Marty. Being in love with her and receiving her love in return felt truly amazing.

Thoughts of her work started to creep into her mind. The project preoccupied her quite a lot. Fortunately, with everyone pitching in to help, she made a lot of progress. The only thing she had left to do was iron out some problems with integrating the black hole containment field with the power conversion components.

The black hole generator she was working on, the gamma ray laser and the warp drive were the only items that didn't yet have a complete prototype. The warp drive would be finished soon though. She was particularly looking forward to running that test. She found the thought of creating the gravitational field very exciting.

$$* * * * * * *$$

Marty felt a little tired after a long training session with Nik. She had noticed Mia waiting for her, so she put the equipment away and walked over.

"Hey baby," said Marty. "You watching the training?"

"Yes, I find it very entertaining," said Mia with a big grin.

"That was awesome! It's so much fun I would do it all day if I could. I learned a lot today too. Didn't I?" said Nik.

"You sure did, Nik. I'm impressed with how quickly you pick this up," said Marty. "Being a warrior really is in your blood."

"You're also a good teacher, Marty," said Nik.

"Thanks, Nik. You should probably head for the lift now."

"Oh yeah, I do need to go. My parents are expecting me back soon and I don't want to get in trouble again. See you guys later."

"Later, Nik," said Marty and Mia together.

Mia's eyes were starting to bug out a little and she was antsy with a big silly smile on her face. After Nik left she said, "Oh my goodness, Marty! That is so cute."

Mia had become very animated as she said this.

"You have seen me teaching him stuff how many times now? And it's still that cute?"

Mia giggled a little saying, "It's always going to be totally adorable. It's kind of like kittens. No matter how many times you see kittens, they are always so cute."

"Yeah, that's true. The cuteness never stops. So if Nik and I were sparring with a couple giant, anthropomorphized kittens, your head would be about ready to explode," said Marty Laughing.

Mia laughed. "That would be overload I think. I would never be able to handle extreme cuteness of that magnitude."

"We should probably get going too. I'm sure I could use a shower."

"Maybe I could give you a sponge bath."

"Now you're talking!"

They had a quick kiss and then Marty put her arm around Mia as they walked toward the lift.

✳ ✳ ✳ ✳ ✳ ✳ ✳

As Dez greeted Tucker and told him to come in, it suddenly dawned on her that she had only left her penthouse a handful of times over the past three months. That was somewhat pathetic, but everything she needed was up here.

"Dez, I have nearly finished the project you wanted me to do. I think you are going to like the results. I understand it's important to cover our asses, but other than that, we haven't done anything in months. We are running out of time."

"Tucker, I'm not going to fuck with it. All I want you to do is finish the task I gave you. You can also keep the surveillance going. If things start happening with Amalgam or Chimera, we can move to stop them. We'll worry about that when it happens though."

"Come on, Dez. Snap out of it. You barely ever come down from here anymore."

"Tucker, you just don't get it do you. You don't have a clue what I've been going through."

"All right, Dez. I'm sorry. You're the boss. I'll leave you be."

"Tucker, don't be like that. We've known each other a long time. I'm not trying to pull rank on you. You just don't understand."

"Then, help me understand, Dez. What is going on here?"

"Do you have any idea what it is like to be powerless, to be completely helpless? Do you know what it is like to be so scared you can't even think, to feel like you're about to die?"

Tears came to her eyes as she spoke and she could feel that terror again. It knotted her stomach and constricted her throat making it more difficult to breathe.

"Well, no. I guess I don't really know what that's like."

"Well, it's something you don't just get over or snap out of. I could barely move at all, just lying there on the floor. She had me by the throat and she is so strong. She completely closed off my airway, with the greatest of ease. I couldn't breathe at all. I was already scared, but then I thought I was going to die too. She had plenty of time. She could easily have killed me, but she didn't. For some reason she let me go."

Dez calmed a little and wiped her eyes as she continued.

"I feel safe up here, Tucker. Besides, we can't even get in the International Mars Base anymore. I think she really will kill me if we cross paths again. I could tell by the look in her eye when she threatened me, she meant it. None of that is worth it. We just need to protect the Parasol Group reputation if they decide to relay their story."

"I think I understand now, Dez. I'm sorry. I just wasn't thinking. I got you covered though. I'm almost done putting together a nice little narrative with tons of video footage and the best part is that most of it is true.

"We just say that the professor was grabbed due to a case of mistaken identity. The woman really did break in here and we have proof too. So, no problems there. Then you just say they were fed while they waited for you to attend to their situation. We have plenty of footage of them eating the best food you can get on the entire planet.

"Then you just say you realized the situation with the professor was a mistake and you apologized over a glass of wine. There is of course plenty of footage of you three drinking wine together like old friends. After the wine, you let them leave."

"That sounds perfect, thank you. Let me know when it's finished."

"Sure thing. It won't be much longer now. A couple days or so maybe."

$$* * * * * * *$$

Alma Cohen sat at her desk waiting for her appointment, as Oscar Perry walked through the open door.

"Ah, Mr. Perry, hello. Please make yourself comfortable."

"Hello, Mrs. Cohen," said Oscar sitting down in the conference chair in front of Alma's desk.

"So you were saying you had something for me."

"Yes, Mrs. Cohen, that's right. Here, I'll transfer the files over so you can pull them up on your display."

Oscar turned on the display for his mobile device and quickly moved some virtual objects around in the hologram.

"You should have them now."

"Yes, I see them," said Alma, looking at the hologram in front of her.

"As you can see, there are tons of pictures and videos in there, all of it shot in 3D, with rendered 2D versions. It's at full 64k resolution, so you can zoom in a lot. We used the finest cameras with the highest frame rates, for smooth video and sharp stills. We have everything they are doing recorded in detail too."

"I see. Yes, this is very good," said Alma looking at pictures in her display.

Each time she motioned to the side with her finger, a new image displayed in the hologram in front of her. The pictures clearly showed plasma weapons of different sizes and the Amalgam Global employees producing them.

"As you can see we got everything."

"Yes, you were very thorough, Mr. Perry. We'll submit these with a report to Earth authorities. It'll probably be a couple weeks before they get around to investigating though."

"We could probably arrange for a little accident to happen over there. Not so bad that it wipes out the evidence, but bad enough that they can't use the plasma weapons or produce more."

"I don't know, Mr. Perry. I don't want anyone to get hurt over there."

"We can keep the death toll at zero and keep the injuries as low as possible, but we can't guarantee nobody will get hurt. They will all recover though. Getting caught up in it would be like getting shot by one of those old fashioned electric stun guns. You know which kind I mean?"

Alma laughed a little, "Of course. I'm seventy-two years old, you know. The police still used those when I was a kid."

"No, I thought you were a little younger than that."

"You don't have to butter me up, Mr. Perry. I'm fine with your…accident. A good zap is what they all deserve."

"Excellent. I'll talk this over with Bill Jeffries when I get back to base and we'll get this planned. We could maybe use a little help getting into one of the airlocks near the plasma weapons. Maybe we could get Martina to assist."

"I'm only in charge of her insofar as she lives on the base I'm in charge of. She helps out a lot, but she isn't officially in my employ, so I can't promise anything. You should ask her. I think she would be happy to help with something like this given how she feels about Amalgam Global."

"Yes, of course. I'll give her a call later to arrange it. I think I have her contact info here. Yep, that's it," said Oscar flipping through a collection of miniature people in the hologram in front of him.

"Very good. Now if you'll excuse me, Mr. Perry. I should get to work on that report. The sooner I send it, the sooner we get the ball rolling with Earth."

"Yes, of course. Well, thanks for taking the time to see me," said Oscar getting up to leave.

"Good day, Mr. Perry."

✳ ✳ ✳ ✳ ✳ ✳ ✳

Charles Mantis could barely tolerate being around Anton Griswold now. The man was utterly infuriating. Here he stood though, after answering a summoning call.

"Charles, it seems like you've been doing pretty much nothing for a very long time now. We need to do something, anything."

"Sir, all we could do was wait. We needed to see what opportunities presented themselves."

"Those have been what? Nothing? You need to make an opportunity."

"Well, it's not that simple, but as it happens, the time for waiting is about over. You're right, no opportunities were presented. We had to try though. I didn't want to move on to more drastic plans until we had to."

"Quit being such a big baby, Charles. The drastic plans are the ones that work best."

"They carry too much risk though and the biological agent wasn't ready until just a couple days ago. However, we have no alternative. From conversations we have overheard in IMB common areas, the project is nearing completion. We'll release the new biological agent in the IMB, put a maintenance bubble on one of their domes and then cut our way in with the laser drill. The bubble will keep it pressurized while we mop up the survivors."

"We could use the plasma weapons. That would be rather entertaining."

"No, sir. We can't do that. No plasma weapons and no conventional guns either. We need to use dart guns. The poison will stun almost instantly and kill them over time. This is imperative. That way it looks like they died from the biological agent, which should be assumed to be a natural disease. We must also repair the dome and erase other signs of our presence."

"You're a real buzz kill. I guess we have to do that though. I would like to bring a couple of them back for interrogation though. I love doing that."

"Very well, sir. We can bring a couple back. Even if they get hit by the poison we have the antitoxin."

"Sounds good. There's no time like the present. It had better not fail, Charles. I'm getting sick of your excuses. I have no more patience for you."

"It will work. I'll get the biological agent ready to go now. Someone can take it over on the next trip to the IMB."

Charles was glad to have that conversation over. Perhaps Anton Griswold might come along on their mission to the IMB. Maybe he'd have an unfortunate accident. Charles smiled at the thought of it, as he continued walking toward the lab.

Chapter Twenty-Two

Marty sat at a table in one of the dining areas with Mia on her right and Larry on her left. Smita, Brian, Yev, Jorge and Zahra filled the rest of the seats at the plain, gray, round table.

Larry said, "This is nice having everyone together. We haven't had time to do this much lately."

"We'll have plenty of time in the very near future," said Brian. "We're nearly finished thanks to Mia." Mia blushed a little, saying, "Well, I couldn't have done it without all the help I got from everyone."

"That's my girl," said Marty proudly, as she looked over at Mia and placed a hand on her back. "She's modest and brilliant."

Mia met Marty's gaze and smiled back at her.

As Yev pushed his nearly empty tray away, Brian said, "Did you finally get full?"

"Yes, I did," said Yev smiling. "Hey, I'm very large. I have to eat a lot."

Everyone chuckled a little at that. Yev was always the last one finished. Not because he ate more slowly, but simply due to the volume of food he needed to maintain his 400 lbs. mass.

"Jorge has some news," said Zahra. "Go on, tell them bashful boy."

"Oh yeah, I have a girlfriend now. Maria, who works in the fitness center."

"And you owe it all to who?" said Zahra winking at Jorge.

Jorge laughed, "You, Zahra. She is quite the matchmaker. I need all the help I can get too, considering how shy I am."

"I just had to do something. Poor boy had a crush on Maria and he was too shy to talk to her."

"Well, I just didn't want to get rejected," said Jorge. "She's so beautiful and I'm a little overweight. I was just afraid she wouldn't like me."

"I knew better than that," said Zahra. "I noticed the way she looked at you. When I talked to her I discovered she was nervous about approaching Jorge."

"When Zahra told me, I was shocked," said Jorge. "Apparently she thought I might not want to date her because she is a transgender woman. So, I mustered up all the courage I had and went up there and asked her out. We admitted our worries to each other. I told her I don't care what kind of body a person is born with and she said she likes men who are a little chubby. We both felt silly at that point considering we were all nervous for nothing."

Everyone congratulated Jorge all at once. Maria was really hot and they would make a cute couple. Marty was surprised she had thought that.

Since when did she think couples were cute? Mia must be rubbing off on her.

"How about you, Zahra?" asked Mia. "Did you do any matchmaking for yourself?"

"I'm actually still on the fence about that. It's been almost a year since my bad breakup, but I'm still not sure. That's progress though. I used to be certain I wasn't ready for another relationship. Maybe when I get back to Earth."

"Someone has a birthday coming up," said Marty smiling at Mia.

"Yep, next week," said Mia.

"Aha," said Brian. "See, I knew I was right to save the candles from Marty's birthday. Well, I did lose a few, but I should have enough. A pack of thirty, so three extras, then we lost six, so I even have one to spare."

"Uh oh, Brian's going to be all excited over the next week," said Yev.

"Hey, I like parties, both planning and throwing them. You big party pooper you."

Yev laughed and rubbed Brian's back affectionately.

"Larry is going to be excited too. He'll have an excuse to get out the finest scotch," said Smita, smiling at Larry.

"Nothing like a fine bottle of scotch with good friends," said Larry smiling.

They all chatted for a little while longer and then took their trays over to the dishwasher. The dishwasher had robotic arms that would separate the trash from the dishes and then scrub the dishes with a brush while submerged in soapy water. It then rinsed them and dried them with hot air.

After leaving the common area Marty and Mia walked together toward Dome Seven and their quarters.

"I am so happy for Jorge," said Mia smiling.

"Yes, me too," said Marty. "I think he and Maria are going to be perfect for each other. I didn't even realize they had a mutual crush. I've gotten to know them both quite well, considering how much time I spend in the fitness center."

"Well, I'm glad Zahra noticed."

Marty was quiet for a moment before speaking again, as the conversation reminded her of a part of her past.

"I was seeing a transgender woman a couple years ago."

"Oh yeah?"

"Yep. She was a little different though. She was kind of scared of surgery, so she only did the hormone therapy."

"So she still had a penis?"

"Yeah, she did. It's kind of ironic that one of the most feminine women I ever had sex with had a penis. It's true though."

"So you had intercourse, like with a guy?"

"Intercourse yes, but not like with a guy. Well, I guess it's hard to explain since you haven't been with a guy either. She responded sexually like any woman would. Like she took a little time to warm up and become aroused, she liked having her breasts massaged and sucked—well not all women like that. I think you know what I mean though. I guess the best way to say it is, that the penis in vagina part is the only thing similar. It's like when we use a toy, except it's attached to her body."

"Yes, I understand. That sounds like a nice experience. Very interesting too."

"I consider myself lucky for having had that experience. I talk to her every now and then. We're still friends."

"You know, now that you mention it, it really isn't about genitals. I find people attractive who don't identify as either of the two traditional genders."

"Yes, exactly. My physical attraction is to feminine features and a more female-like body. I'm not stuck on the false dichotomy that is binary gender."

"I agree. It's a very outdated concept. It is, unfortunately, still quite entrenched in our culture to this day, although that does seem to improve slowly over time."

"I even catch myself slipping into that mode of thinking sometimes. It's a bad habit."

At that point, they had arrived at their quarters. Mia had her bra off the instant Marty closed the door. She rubbed the little red indentations that the straps had made.

"Oh that feels so good. I was in that thing way too long."

"That looks like an excellent idea, Mia. I think I'll join you."

With that, Marty quickly removed her shirt and bra and then put her arms around Mia, staring into her sexy green eyes. Mia responded by kissing her passionately. It was good to be home.

✳ ✳ ✳ ✳ ✳ ✳

Marty was in the lift in Dome Six, going down from the fitness center. When the lift reached the ground floor, a biohazard alarm went off across the base. Instead of opening, the lift doors locked and it went up to the second floor.

Marty wasn't sure what was going on. She got out of the lift and she could see a man wearing an Amalgam Global spacesuit running in her direction. When she moved to intercept him, she could see security guards running down the corridor, in the same direction as the fleeing man.

When the man got close, she lunged to the side, right in front of him. She ducked down low and swung her fist at him. His forward movement compounded the force of her punch and as he double over, she moved her arm in an arc, using his momentum to flip him over and throw him behind her. The man landed hard on his back and then turned on his side, balling up into a fetal position, with his hands on his stomach.

The security guards got there a moment later. That was when the alarm stopped and it was announced that the first floor of Dome Six had been sealed off. Marty talked to the guards, as they apprehended the man. She learned that he had thrown a glass vial on the first floor as he was getting into the lift. They thought that was suspicious, so they went after him. The man ran and they chased him around for about five minutes before the alarm went off.

Marty was feeling more and more nervous as they led the man away. She had a terrible, sickening feeling inside her. She got out her mobile device, opened the communications menu and placed a voice call to Mia.

Mia answered after a few seconds, her voice sounded shaky and weak.

"Hello?"

"Mia, it's me! Are you all right? Where are you?"

"Marty, something is wrong. I'm on the first floor of Dome Six and I don't feel well at all. First, my skin started getting clammy and I started feeling weak. That was five to ten minutes ago. Just before you called, my legs gave out and I fell down. Most of my body just feels a little weak, but I can barely move my legs."

"Just hang in there, Mia. I'm going to get Smita to help us."

"There are other people collapsing in here too. I think the medical team will have their hands full for a while."

"We'll get to you somehow. I love you, Mia."

"I love you too, Marty. I'll see you soon."

Marty called Smita who was only able to talk for a minute. She was quite busy. This biohazard could be serious. Marty felt helpless and she couldn't bear the thought of something happening to Mia. She waited, because that is all she could do.

✳ ✳ ✳ ✳ ✳ ✳ ✳

Smita had been in a frenzy since the biohazard alarm went off. She had no idea how much time had passed. Everything seemed surreal and she just worked as fast as she could.

"Dr. Patel, we have enough nanobot reports in for an accurate sample."

"Excellent, I'll view it at my workstation," said Smita sitting down at a desk in the medical facility.

She looked quickly through the data. It appeared to be a virus that acts like a neurotoxin. Patients present with clammy skin and some red spots after five minutes, then after ten minutes, they become weak and it affects the legs much more than the rest of the body.

The data she looked at was very troubling. The virus appeared to be extremely contagious and initially fast acting. It did look like it would slow down as it progressed though. It may end up being fatal, at least for some.

She checked on the medical computer, which was being given highest priority. It was working to find a way to cure it and to stop it from spreading.

It was only about an hour after the biohazard alarm that the computer gave Smita its findings. It was a paralyzing virus, likely manufactured, as it appeared to be designed rather than an organism, which had evolved via natural selection. The immunity section listed something they could easily synthesize and spread through the ventilation system. That would protect the uninfected. It looked like it could kill any of the viruses that ventured out of the nervous system in the infected. This would prevent the disease from spreading, even to people who hadn't been immunized. However, it wouldn't cure the infected.

The counteragent section was listed as unknown, insufficient data. Treatment, likely none, but unknown, also insufficient data. The prognosis filled her with sickening dread. It said five to six days, 100% fatal.

She needed to get her hands on a sample of the biological agent. It had to be pure, not from an infected patient. That would be the only way to stop this virus.

The counteragent was ready, so she released it into the first floor of Dome Six. While this was going on, she posted an ETA of one hour on the end of quarantine and announced it would no longer be able to spread at that point.

After about an hour, the nanobots that reported in and the air analysis showed all was clear. She lifted the quarantine, which unsealed the doors. Then she started organizing her staff and volunteers to deal with the sick.

$$* * * * * * *$$

When the quarantine was over, Marty was one of the first people on the scene. She had also already responded to Smita that she would volunteer. She would find Mia first though.

The place was clearing out as she ran through. Most of the people lying on the floor were around the main lifts. She quickly found Mia and scooped her up in her arms.

"I'm here, Mia. I got you."

"I feel better already, Marty."

"Shit, I don't think we are going to be able to use the medical facility. There are at least fifty people here. I'm going to carry you to one of the common rooms, the big one."

On the way over, Marty saw Smita and the medical team arriving at the scene.

"Smita, there are at least fifty over there. I think we should put them in the big common room."

"Good thinking, Marty," said Smita. Then she turned to a nurse, "Get resident services to bring bedding down here after you get a count."

"Dr. Patel, I count fifty-seven, including the one that was carried away," said a male nurse from the other side of the room.

Yev and some security forces arrived about that time. They helped Marty and the medical team carry people into the common room. Just as they got everyone in there, some people from resident services arrived pushing big carts full of small mattresses, pillows, sheets and blankets.

Everyone grabbed some bedding, set it up and placed a patient in it. They continued until everyone had a bed. When that was done, Marty stood in a circle, talking to Yev, Smita and the other doctors.

Smita said, "Marty, I hate to ask this of you, but you might be the best person to do it. I need a sample of this biological agent. It's probably in the Amalgam Global base, given that is where it came from. It's the only way to find a cure. Without it, these people only have five, maybe six days."

Those words tore up Marty's insides like a grenade going off within her, spraying shrapnel at every part of her. It was a deluge of emotions, sadness, fear, determination and a seething anger that felt as if it would consume her. She pushed it all back down though. This was her trick for staying cool and being in control. She could hold it back for a time, if she had a plan to let it out at her convenience.

"Marty, I'm so sorry. I know how hard this is for you. I need that sample though."

"No problem, Smita. I'll get it one way or another."

Marty walked over to Mia and sat down next to her. She bent down and put her arms around Mia. She felt her eyes water a little, as she spoke.

"Mia, I love you so much. I have to go get a sample of this thing so we can cure it."

"I hope you do, Marty and love you very much as well. I overheard some of what was said. I know I only have a few days without the counteragent. This just isn't fair. I wanted to spend my life with you."

"Just hang on, Mia. I'm going to take care of this one way or another. You're going to live for many years yet and I'll be with you always."

"I don't want you to let go, Marty. I know you have work to do though."

"I wouldn't leave your side for anything except going to find what I need to save your life. So even though I don't want to go, I'm glad I have the chance to do this."

$$* * * * * * *$$

It had been hard to pull herself away from Mia. Marty knew what she had to do though. She called over to Chimera to see about moving up the time for their little sabotage operation.

She brought up a video call and Oscar Perry was in a hologram in front of her.

"Hi, Oscar, we need to talk."

"What's up, Marty?"

"That operation we had been planning. I want to up the timeline. I know it was supposed to be three days from now, but could we go tonight."

"That's rather sudden. Why the rush?"

"Amalgam Global released a virus here. We stopped it from spreading, but it can't be cured without a sample. I need to get in there and find it. I thought our operation would be the perfect distraction."

"Oh I see. They've gotten bold haven't they? I should be able to manage it tonight. Can you be at the Amalgam Global base in about four hours?"

"Fuck yeah, four hours would be perfect."

"Good, I'll send you coordinates and directions. Then I'll get the team together."

When the call ended, Marty knew she had a lot of planning to do. She headed back to her quarters to get ready. She decided to insert her special mobile device. Without knowing what the situation would be, she couldn't set up a nanobot attack. There were certain general things she had scripted, but that would only be useful in very specific situations. She felt it would be good to have it though, just in case. It was also easier to kick off the airlock hacks from there too.

Marty went over to Dome Five and suited up. Then she operated the airlock. She went out through a door near where the vehicles were kept. She didn't have to sneak around this time. This was an official mission, approved by the base commander. Surprisingly, Alma didn't hesitate to approve this, or to ban Amalgam Global from the base—not even one second. She was actually quite eager.

As Marty sped away from the base, it was at the tail end of the long Martian dusk. It was a good two hours after sunset, but the faint violet glow of the diffused sunlight lingered. It would soon be gone though. As beautiful as this was, the cover of darkness is what she really needed.

Chapter Twenty-Three

Jorge met Maria after her shift at the fitness center. They were going to go down to the first floor for drinks and to get to know each other. When he saw her emerge wearing such tight pants, he felt a wave of excitement pulse through his body. They were the pants with the thin stretchy fabric. They were black and practically painted on. Maria was very fit and curvy, with long black hair, dark brown eyes, full lips and the distinctive Mediterranean nose. She had small perky breasts and he could see her nipples poking through her top.

"Hi Maria, you look absolutely beautiful."

"Thank you, Jorge," she said in her thick Italian accent.

"You are so sweet. I've been looking forward to this all day."

"Me too. I could hardly wait to come up here. I was pacing around nervously in my quarters for a while before I came up."

Jorge noticed Maria checking him out too, which made him more excited.

"Come, let's go to the lift my handsome man."

Jorge walked with her to the lift. On the way, he couldn't help but notice her butt. It was so nice and big in those tight pants. A wave of embarrassment washed over him as he felt himself getting an erection. He had been longing for her for a long time, admiring her from afar, thinking he would never get to be with her. This made just being in her presence extremely exciting.

When they got in the lift, Maria said, "It's ok, honey, no need to be embarrassed." Then she leaned against him whispering in his ear with her hot breath, "I'm excited to see you too."

Jorge just smiled nervously and laughed a little.

"Oh dear, you need to relax, boy."

With that, she embraced him and gave him a big passionate kiss. Jorge didn't know what hit him. She pressed herself against him, with her mouth on his. He was exploring her mouth, feeling her soft tongue on his. He knew he was rock hard and pressed against her, but he didn't care. After the kiss he felt calm—more aroused, but definitely calm.

"There that's better. You're relaxed and I got to kiss you the way I've fanaticized about."

"I've had that fantasy too—wait, you mean you fantasized about me?"

"What can I say, you are my type. I found you very sexy since the first day I saw you."

"Oh wow, I can hardly believe it. I could say the same about you."

"That's good," Maria whispered in his ear. Then he felt her hand lightly grasp his erection through his pants. "Let's go talk and get to know each other."

Jorge twitched when she did that, he didn't quite feel he was on the verge of orgasm when she touched him, but it was going that way.

When they got to the ground floor, Maria said, "I think I at least know you well enough to talk in my quarters. I don't have a roommate right now. So we have the place to ourselves."

"Sure, that sounds good to me."

When they got to her quarters, she led him inside.

"Jorge, I think we are both too tense for talking."

She kissed him again and guided his hand between her legs. He could feel her through the thin fabric. Then she rubbed his erection through his pants.

"Oh Maria, you are so sexy."

"Push up harder with your hand, Jorge. Ah, yes, like that."

It only took a couple minutes before he started feeling like he might cum in his pants and then Maria started to twitch and moan. She was having an orgasm. As hers subsided, he felt like his was almost there. She could apparently tell, because she quickly pulled his pants down right then. While gently stroking him with one hand, she reached over and grabbed a facial tissue. Then her stroking increased in speed and intensity. He grunted softly as he felt a wave of pleasure come over him. Maria kept stroking and held up the tissue with her other hand, catching all of his fluid.

Maria laughed softly, "I should have grabbed two or three. Have a seat while I go rinse my hands."

When she returned Jorge said, "I feel much better now."

"I do too," said Maria giggling and sitting down next to him. "I think we are relaxed enough for talking now."

"Yes, I'm very relaxed."

"Jorge, I should be clear about something. Just because we had a little fun, that doesn't mean I'm going to have sex with you today, or even tomorrow."

"Yes, I understand. That's fine with me."

"So tell me where you are from."

"I'm from New York, born and raised. My parents moved there from Mexico before I was born. I just graduated with a bachelor's degree in science and I work as a lab assistant for Larry and Brian, that's Dr. Wellington and Dr. Wong. How about you?"

"I was born in a little village in the south of Italy on the coast of the Mediterranean Sea. My parents moved with me to Naples when I was six. I've always been into physical fitness. I grew up playing sports and I enjoyed lifting weights. I got certified as a personal trainer after high school. A friend of a friend mentioned something about fitness on the Mars base, so I volunteered."

They talked for a long time about their lives and got to know each other very well. It was late by the time their conversation wrapped up. Jorge was getting tired and he could tell Maria looked tired as well. She gave him another passionate kiss after she led him to the door.

✳ ✳ ✳ ✳ ✳ ✳ ✳

As Marty approached the Amalgam Global base, she veered off to the side to meet up with the people from Chimera. It was dark as the only light came from the stars in the sky. She went over to a small crater and the people from Chimera were waiting there for her.

Oscar Perry was there, along with four other guys. Oscar waved and pointed at his helmet. Marty got her communicator to sync up with his.

"Hi Marty," said Oscar. "This is the team. I'm just here to introduce you. I'll be heading back shortly. You get them in and they'll take care of the plasma weapons and make a nice distraction. As soon as they have it set, they are going to head out. You'll be on your own after that. It should give you the time you need though."

"Thanks, Oscar. I appreciate it."

After Oscar left, Marty walked with the four Chimera guys over to the side of the Amalgam Global base. She found an airlock that should be out of the way according to the schematics she saw. She applied the hack and led the men inside.

"I have this thing set on a special override setting. It is in silent mode too. It will remain like this for a couple hours. In order to use it, you must key in this code I am going to give you."

A long number appeared on the display in the airlock. Pointing to it, Marty said, "Let me know when you have it so I can clear the display."

After they indicated they had it, she cleared the display and started pressurization. When it finished, they all removed their helmets, attaching them to their belts.

They crept quietly through a corridor. It was much the same as the other bases. It had dull gray interior walls, with a lot of transparent walls on the outside, providing a view of the Martian landscape.

The guys all had dart guns. One of them held his up saying, "These will stun in about one second. It lasts for three to four hours. We'll make sure you have a path cleared."

Every now and then, they came to a guard at a checkpoint. They hit him with a dart shortly after he noticed them. After repeating that process a few times, they reached a manufacturing and storage area. They cautiously entered and there was someone at the door. He didn't even have time to react before a dart took him down.

Marty watched as the men rigged small devices in strategic points in the area, shooting anyone they came across. When all the devices were in place, they walked out of the room.

"Marty, when you see flashes of light and hear zapping sounds, make for the lab. We'll be heading to the airlock."

"Sounds good, thanks. So this will destroy all the plasma weapons?"

"Oh yeah. They will all be toast in seconds."

After a couple minutes, Marty saw flashes of light and heard the sound of arcing electricity. The Chimera guys went back and she pressed on down a back hallway.

It was definitely causing quite a commotion. Alarms were going off and she could hear people running and yelling off in the distance behind her. The normally out-of-the-way area she was in should be deserted now.

When she got to the lab there was one guy working. He had his back turned. So she snuck up behind him and pounded the underside of her fist into the back of his head, just above the neck. The man fell to the floor unconscious.

She looked around the lab for a while and finally found what she was looking for. There was a clearly labeled transparent carbon nanotube case on the wall. She set up a brute force attack on the digital combination lock and within minutes, the panel opened. She pulled out a small, hard, metal cylinder. It was silver and about six inches long and two inches in diameter. She opened the end and nestled inside, surrounded by padding, was a small glass vial. That was it!

She pushed the vial back down inside and closed the cylinder. She opened up her suit and put the cylinder in an inside pocket just above her waist. She resealed her suit and cautiously walked toward the door.

✳ ✳ ✳ ✳ ✳ ✳ ✳

Mia was surprised to have had so much company, as she lay there in the makeshift hospital ward. Brian, Larry and Magnus she figured would drop by, but not only did they drop by, they stayed there with her. Smita came to sit with her too. She told her that she would never forget all the support Mia gave her when Larry was a prisoner.

Even Nik came to see her. He stayed until his parents dropped by and told him he had to come home and go to bed. He told her that Marty had taught him so much and he was glad to have her as a friend and teacher. Because of that, he wanted to sit there with her all night until Marty came home to her.

Right before Nik left with his parents, he looked her in the eyes, squeezed her hand and said, "Kia Kaha, Mia."

"Thank you, Nik, you are so sweet."

Mia was so touched by all the friends who cared so much for her. They really kept her spirits up, even though she was facing death.

"Larry," said Mia. When Larry looked over at her, she continued. "The project is basically done. It's all there in my personal folder. It's all in pieces though. You just have to put it all together to create the full schematics file for the black hole generator."

"Oh Mia, don't you worry about that at all, honey. You just rest up. We'll get through this."

"I just want to make sure that no matter what happens my designs live on."

"I've known Marty for a long time. She'll come through for you. She always does and besides, she loves you more than I have ever seen her love everyone else combined. Nothing can stop that."

"Thanks, Larry. I needed to hear that."

✳ ✳ ✳ ✳ ✳ ✳ ✳

Alma was having trouble sleeping and it had nothing to do with her husband, Andrew, quietly snoring. The events of the day had been very unsettling. She felt good though. She was tough and banned Amalgam right then and there. She still couldn't believe the audacity of those people.

She had even thought about banning Chimera. They were helping and Oscar Perry was nice enough, but she still didn't trust them. The only reason she felt comfortable working with them, is that she knew they stood to gain a lot from cooperating with her. Their greed would keep them in line. There was no doubt about that.

She hoped Marty was having success. She had fifty-seven people about whom she was very worried. Since the base was like a small town, she knew everyone. It was like having a bunch of deathly ill friends. Please hurry back with it, Marty.

Chapter Twenty-Four

Marty walked out of the lab into the corridor. The place was still deserted. She decided to take a different path toward the airlock. It would mostly be the same way she got there, but with a detour to avoid the commotion in the area that just got zapped.

She couldn't believe what she saw down the corridor. Anton Griswold walked past and through another door. She walked down there as she felt the bottled rage threatening to explode. That guy needed a beating more than anyone.

When she entered the room, Anton was surprised and startled. He wasn't worried though. He just smiled at her.

"Nice to meet you, Martina."

Just then, she saw Francis step out of the shadows to her left. She had beat him once before back in Newark. It was a hard fight though and he was incredibly fast.

"So we meet again," said Francis.

"Yep. How's the ankle? All healed up?"

"Come here and find out."

Anton backed off as Marty and Francis circled in toward each other. It was time for their final showdown. She planned to beat him until he never even wanted to think about her. It wasn't going to be easy though.

Francis attacked first, taking a couple quick swipes at her, which she easily dodged. They circled around and then Marty lunged at him. Francis jumped back and circled around to her side. Marty spun around just in time to dodge and block a flurry of fists coming at her. Then she jumped over a leg sweep and brought her fists down at Francis's face. He dodged and she followed up with her own flurry of punches. He deflected with his wiry arms.

They both landed some glancing blows, but nobody got a good direct hit yet. Their arms entangled as they tried to strike each other, both vying for the upper hand. Francis took a hard swing at Marty. She dodged by turning her side to him, spinning in toward him and jamming her elbow into his mouth. Francis's lips began bleeding as he spun around trying to land a roundhouse kick on her face. She ducked and unleashed a flurry of punches to his gut. He flew back and hit the ground in the low Martian gravity. As soon as he hit, he did a kip up and was back on his feet, swinging at her. Marty dodged one fist, but the other connected, hitting her in the ribs and knocking her down. Her ribs hurt, badly bruised for sure, but not broken.

Francis tried to stomp her. She swung her legs around trying to knock Francis's out from under him. Francis jumped back to dodge. Marty did a kip up and was back on her feet. She saw Francis's hip move like he was going to kick. Sure enough he did. The next time she was ready. She dodged to the side and while his leg was up, kicked him hard, right in the taint. Francis howled in pain, stumbling and almost falling over. Marty followed up with a front kick to his face while he was hunched over. His nose crunched under the force of her foot, blood squirting everywhere.

Francis wasn't done though. He came at her again, moving quickly, fists flying. He caught her on the side of the jaw, lifting her off the ground, almost knocking her over. While she was off balance, he tried to lunge in with a knockout punch like a boxer. She spun around to his side and punched him hard in the ribs. There was a small crunch like one of them cracked. Then in a split second, she drove her other fist into his gut. Then another blow to the ribs, this time with a loud crunch. Then the gut again to finish the quick combo. With each blow, he bounced an inch or two off the floor.

Francis was trying to back up in order to take away Marty's advantage. When he did, Marty gave him a fast spinning kick to the same area on his flank. There was another crunch and he bent over holding his hands up in front of him to fend off her blows.

That slowed him down just enough for Marty to grab his left arm. While pulling back on it, she jammed the heal of her hand into his elbow snapping it back. She then wrapped her right arm around Francis's broken left arm. Then she drove her fist into his right flank, just above his broken ribs again and again and again. Only her tight hold on his arm kept him in place.

Francis finally dropped to his knees, holding himself up with his right arm. Marty knew it was time to finish this. She took a step back, then lunged forward and kicked him in the face like she was kicking a field goal. Francis's jaw snapped and he flew back and up a few feet, in an arc, landing on his back. Marty looked down at him. He was out cold.

When she looked up at Anton Griswold, he looked nervous for only a second. Then he relaxed and finally smiled at her, which filled her with dread. Then she heard a familiar voice behind her.

"Turn around, very slowly."

It was Charles Mantis. When she turned, she saw that he was pointing a gun at her.

"You beat up poor Francis again. That's twice now. I've seen him get his ass kicked on two occasions now. You, both times! I'm kind of wishing you worked for me. I really have a lot of mixed feelings about you. In some ways, I just have to admire you. You've been a real pain in my ass though, so I'd rather like to kill you. You do have the access and information I need though. So I'm really quite conflicted."

"What can I say, I'm a complicated woman."

"You are indeed, my dear."

As they talked Anton moved around to Marty's right forming a sort of triangle with her and Charles.

"Quit wasting time, Charles," said Anton.

"Well, Martina, Mr. Griswold reminds me, I do have quite a hankering to do a little shooting."

Marty was getting nervous staring down the barrel of his gun. His tone was getting increasingly threatening.

Charles continued, "Martina, I'm going to get everything I want from you. Well, in just a minute…"

As Charles trailed off, he casually rotated his arm, shot Anton Griswold in the gut while only looking at him out of the corner of his eye and then pointed the gun back at Marty. The whole thing took maybe two seconds, at most. Anton grunted in pain as he hit the ground and curled up into a fetal position. Charles smiled broadly, still looking at Marty.

"Let me tell you, Martina, I've wanted to do that for quite some time. Tonight is one of those times where I'm really liking my job."

Marty was shocked. She didn't know what to do, or what to think.

Charles, still smiling said, "I'm sorry, did you find that upsetting?"

"No, I'm fine," said Marty, trying to play it cool.

Anton spoke through gritted teeth, "What the fuck, Charles?"

"Good I'm glad to hear that," said Charles, ignoring Anton. Then when Anton yelled his name again, Charles said, "Martina, can you pardon me just a moment? Just stay right there, don't move. I mean that literally. If you move, I'm going to shoot you. But just give me a minute here."

Marty just stood there not sure what to think. She watched as Charles turned his attention to Anton.

"You know, Mr. Griswold. You've been quite a pain in my ass. You are a really shitty boss too. I've been miserable because you are such an insufferable, megalomaniacal, destructive, little sadistic halfwit."

With that, Charles shot Anton in the right thigh. Anton hollered out in pain clutching his thigh.

"Now look what you've driven me to. I'm acting like you. I can't help it though. You have terrorized me, insulted me repeatedly and made my job harder by interfering with my plans. But I feel I must continue, because I really fucking hate you."

With that, Charles shot Anton in the left thigh. Anton cried out in pain again. He was bleeding quite a bit at this point and had rolled over on his back.

Marty just stood there, shocked and horrified watching the events unfold.

"Just a little longer, Martina. I'm almost done here. Then I promise you will have my full undivided attention."

He walked a little closer to Anton, who was starting to look scared.

"Are you scared, Mr. Griswold? You're not used to feeling like that are you? Now, this is going to sound weird considering you are technically my boss, but I just don't think you're right for this company. I'm afraid we're going to have to let you go."

Charles pointed the gun at Anton as he said that. Then as soon as he finished speaking, he shot Anton twice in the head. The first bullet entered right between the eyes, the second just above it, at the bottom of the forehead. His head jerked with each blast as pools of blood drained through the shattered skull fragments of the back of his head, which was pressed against the floor. Only the floor held the brain matter in place.

Marty was horrified seeing that. She hated Anton Griswold, but she didn't want to see that. At the same time, she thought it did kind of serve him right. He was the most thoroughly evil person she had ever encountered—even worse than Charles. Her stomach turned and she felt nauseated seeing so much blood running across the floor. It was probably almost four liters, most of the blood he had.

"Sorry about all the unpleasantness, my dear. Now let me see. Ah yes, you probably came here to get a sample of the biological agent to cure people at the base and you led some other people in here to destroy all the plasma weapons. Well, you know, that's all just fine with me, provided you give me all the data on the alien tech. I'll let you walk out of here and go save your friends. It's just a little business proposition."

"Or what? You do that to me?" asked Marty, pointing at Anton's corpse.

Charles laughed. "No, no, my dear, of course not. No, I wouldn't do that to you. I don't normally do that sort of thing to anyone. He was an exception. He had it coming. No, I'd just shoot you in the face. You'd probably be dead before the pain even registered. Not that I wouldn't put someone through agony to get what I want, but it just isn't necessary. You would be dead and everyone infected would die and I would likely still end up getting what I want."

"It's not going to be as easy as you think."

"You can try to knock my gun away like last time, but I guarantee, even in this gravity, I can shoot you dead before you get anywhere near me."

Marty stared him down, as she used her tongue to kick off a script to make his nanobots think he was going into ventricular fibrillation. This became possible to do on account of him being the only other conscious person in the room with her.

"What's your—ah!"

Charles was interrupted mid-sentence, as he cried out in pain, clutching at his chest. His gun hit the floor with a clank. Marty ran and lunged at him, arriving in front of him just as he recovered and reached down for his gun. She kicked him in the chest and he landed flat on his back. Then she drop kicked him in the face, slamming his head against the ground. She looked down at him and he was out cold.

Marty was rather amused by the idea of Charles being zapped in the heart. His nanobots applied current once to defibrillate. Then they checked for sinus rhythm. His heart was beating normally, so they stopped.

Marty walked to the doorway and cautiously looked out into the corridor. She didn't see anyone so she hurried toward the airlock. She was able to walk through the base undetected. After a few minutes, she could see the airlock. She attached her helmet and sealed it up as she walked. She just had to cross a hall and then another few meters past there to the airlock door. There were people down the hall and she hoped they wouldn't notice her. She walked quietly at a moderate pace, hoping she wouldn't draw attention.

After she crossed, she thought she might get out completely unseen. Then the alarm went off as she was walking into the airlock. She was all suited up, so she quickly sealed the door, entered her override code and started depressurization. She could see people through the airlock window, just as depressurization was finishing. They looked pissed when they discovered they couldn't pressurize it. She opened the outer door and set it to stay open for thirty minutes. They could regain control of it, but that would take longer than it would to go to another airlock. She waved at them and then turned and ran out of the base.

She figured she had plenty of time, but not wanting to take any chances with her precious cargo, she ran all the way to the small crater where her glider was waiting. She looked back, but couldn't tell if anyone was pursuing her. If they were, they were too far away to see in the dim light. The violet glow of the Martian Dawn had just begun on her run back to the glider. The glider came to life with a soft hum when she started it. She slowly moved out of the crater and when she was free, she could see people running toward some vehicles. She smiled, knowing they were too late and sped away from them, heading back to the IMB.

It was several minutes before she really felt comfortable. By then she had put a lot of distance between her and Amalgam Global. It occurred to her that she had been in all four Mars bases. There probably aren't many other people who have been to all four. She continued speeding away as the diffuse, violet glow of dawn grew brighter.

$$* * * * * * *$$

Mia awoke early, noticing she had a message from Marty. She felt a great sense of relief when she saw that it was the automated message indicating that she was on her way back with the sample.

"Yes!" she exclaimed in a sort of loud whisper while pumping a fist in the air.

She noticed Smita stirring next to her. Then she opened her eyes.

"Oh, sorry, Smita. I have good news though, I think you'll want to hear."

"You heard back from Marty?"

"Yes, I got the automated message indicating she is on her way back with the sample."

Smita smiled and woke up Larry, Brian and Magnus—Mia's current entourage. When she told them, it woke up some of the patients sleeping nearby. This set off a chain reaction and after a while, everyone was awake and talking excitedly.

"I should go get the lab set up. That way it's ready to go when Marty gets back," said Smita, as she got up.

Larry said, "I knew she'd come through for you, Mia. She always does."

"I thought she probably would," said Mia. "I'm glad that is exactly what happened."

"Are you hungry, Mia?" asked Brain. "I could bring you some breakfast."

"Yes, please and some water too."

"Sure thing, I'll be right back."

"This isn't so bad," said Mia. "Maybe I can't walk right now, but I do get breakfast in bed."

Larry and Magnus laughed.

✳ ✳ ✳ ✳ ✳ ✳ ✳

Smita gave Alma a wakeup call on her way over to the medical facility. She gave her the full report of everything that had happened and let her know she was going to get the lab set up. Alma was very glad to hear the good news. She thanked Smita for her handling of the situation.

When Smita walked into the medical facility, people were surprised to see her there so early. She explained the situation and then headed over to the lab.

In the lab, she went around getting everything she would need and setting it all out in the proper places. She got the analysis machine ready to go and also started the incinerator. She would need to dispose of the sample after analysis. Then she set up a station for creating the counteragent and preparing the forced air syringe to inject it.

She was feeling quite anxious and keeping busy was actually a relief for her. She was just glad that she could actually do something now. When she finished setting everything up, she headed back down to where the patients were. She wanted to wait with them for Marty to return.

Smita met Yev on the way back. She sent him around to have everyone near the perimeter of the base keep an eye out for Marty. She wanted to know the very instant they saw her approaching. Yev agreed and headed down a side corridor.

When she got down to where the patients were, she could see many of them eating breakfast and chatting with each other. The mood had noticeably improved in the room just in the time she had been gone, which was an hour at most.

"Brian, I sent Yev to go spread the word so everyone is watching for Marty to arrive. I wanted to know as soon as she gets here. He should be back here in twenty minutes or so."

"Oh, I was wondering what was taking so long."

Smita looked over at Mia and noticed her eyes were closing. She looked completely relaxed and it appeared that she was about to fall asleep. She looked so peaceful now, lying there in the makeshift hospital bed.

Sweet dreams, Mia. I'll be able to make you well again very soon.

Chapter Twenty-Five

The violet glow on the horizon to the right was now much brighter, more intense and took up a larger portion of sky. Marty could see the base coming into view in the distance in front of her. A couple minutes later, she could see the first hint of the sun starting to peak over the eastern horizon. It was like a reflection of light on a pool of luminous, lavender-tinged water.

She slowed down as she neared the base. By the time she was got around to where the vehicles were kept, near Dome Five, the top sliver of the sun was shining in the distance. The colorful glow of sunrise still there, surrounding it like an aura.

After she parked the glider, Marty walked to the main airlock in Dome Five. She was surprised to see the door open as she approached. Apparently, they saw her coming and depressurized it in anticipation. When she entered, she could see that Smita was waiting for her.

Very good. That is exactly who I need to see first.

As pressurization neared completion, Marty started removing her helmet. When the inner door opened, Smita greeted her. She was as anxious to receive the sample, as Marty was to give it to her. Suddenly, Smita had a very concerned look on her face.

"Oh, Marty, your face! That's a big bruise on the left side."

"I'm fine. It only hurts a little. You can give me something for the pain later. It's really only going to bother me when I eat."

Marty unfastened her suit at the top in order to reach the internal pocket. Then she pulled out the cylinder.

"Here it is, Smita."

"Thank you. I'm going to start working on this. I'm sure you are anxious to see Mia. I'll bring some meds with me when I come."

"Yeah, I'm heading straight over there now. Better make it about a week's worth on the medication. I took a nasty blow to the ribs as well."

"I'll give you an x-ray scan later too, just in case."

They walked together until they got to Dome Six, then Smita veered off to the medical facility, while Marty continued on to the big common room.

When Marty entered the room, Mia looked up and smiled very broadly upon seeing her. Marty walked hurriedly past the other people. Everything else in the room was just scenery. It didn't even seem real. All she could see was Mia, who she had wanted so badly to come home to. When she got over to Mia, she dropped to her knees and gently put her arms around her. She felt Mia's arms tightly around herself too. Luckily, Mia's arms were over hers, or this could have been very painful. They just stayed there, holding each other, for minutes. Marty wasn't able to gauge the passing of time. She just knew she was where she most wanted to be.

"How are you doing, Mia."

"I'm a little weak, but not too bad yet. I'm feeling a lot better now that you're here with me—Oh, Marty, your poor face. You had to fight, didn't you?"

"Yes, but I'm all right. Don't worry about me."

Marty sat next to Mia and put an arm over her. She planned to stay there until Smita returned.

✱ ✱ ✱ ✱ ✱ ✱ ✱

When Smita got to the lab, she removed the vial from the cylinder and placed it in the machine for analysis. She started the software and then let it run while she attended to other tasks. After twenty minutes or so, the software completed and gave her all the pertinent data. The details of making the counteragent to heal the patients, was relayed over to another machine that made various substances. It could create complex molecules and fold proteins in various ways.

It took only a couple minutes to create it and then a couple more minutes to reach the needed quantity. She had it all inserted into a special vial, which she placed inside a forced air syringe. She put the vial containing the virus into the incinerator and set the timer to shut off in a couple minutes. She took the syringe, some painkillers for Marty and her mobile device, then started walking over to Dome Six.

When she reached the room with the patients, Smita called Hilda over and handed her the forced air syringe as well as the small bottle of pills.

"I have it on the needed setting. Just go around and administer this to each of the patients. Also, give this to Marty."

Hilda took them and headed over to Mia first. She handed the drugs to Marty and then pressed the syringe against Mia's arm for a second. There was a quick hissing sound and then she moved on to the next patient.

Smita addressed the group. "Hilda is going to administer the counteragent to each of you. This will destroy all trace of the virus within a couple of hours. Your clammy skin should go away at that point and your spots should begin to fade. You will continue to feel at least a little weak for another day. So figure on about this time tomorrow morning. Your spots should be gone then and from the hips on up, you should be back to 100%. Your legs will take longer though, which shouldn't surprise you since they are almost completely immobile at this point. It will be an additional day before you will be able to walk at all. Luckily, you are on Mars with much lower gravity, so the day after tomorrow you should be able to get around with a walker. Maintenance will rig some temporary walkers for those who want them. After another day or two, you should be able to make do with a cane. Maintenance can get that for you simply by disassembling the walker. You'll need the cane for an additional day or two. At that point, you should be able to walk unassisted, but it will be a little longer still before you fully recover. It's going to be at least a week before you are at 100% again, possibly eight days."

As Smita finished giving them the details on what to expect, Hilda was attending to the last patient. There was a bit of commotion as grateful people all thanked Smita and Marty almost at once. After receiving their thanks, Smita had Marty open her suit up and gave her right side a quick scan.

"Badly bruised, but all I see is a tiny crack in one rib."

"That's what I was thinking based on how it feels. Thanks, Smita."

Smita left to go to the maintenance area to see about building devices to get people ambulatory during their recovery. She hoped people could stay in bed for a couple days. Wheelchairs aren't so easy to piece together from spare parts and she didn't have nearly enough in the medical facility.

✳ ✳ ✳ ✳ ✳ ✳ ✳

Marty felt much better now that Mia had been treated. She was ready to go back to their room now.

"If you're ready, I'll carry you to our room now."

Mia nodded, so Marty bent down and scooped Mia into her arms. Then she lifted her up and carried her out of the room. She held onto Mia tightly the whole way, like a sort of hug. At times, she kissed Mia on the cheek as she walked along.

On the way to their room, she told Mia everything that happened. Mia listened intently and was surprised when Marty got to the part about Anton Griswold.

When they arrived at their room, Mia opened the door, since Marty had her hands full. Then Marty walked over to the bed and gently lay Mia down on it. She got Mia in comfy clothes and tucked her in under the covers. Finally, with Mia taken care of, she took her suit off and then her clothes. She turned her right side to Mia, after taking off her pants, standing there in just her bra and panties.

"Oh, poor Marty! That bruise is huge! It looks really nasty. You have a bunch of little ones on your arms too and even a couple on your legs."

"It's all right, Mia. I took something for the pain. This will heal."

As Marty spoke, she removed her undergarments and retrieved the small mobile device she had hidden. She unwrapped it and put it away. Marty was tired and it felt so good to be at home, completely naked. She pulled the covers back a little and got into bed with Mia.

"Ooh, come here, naked girl," said Mia, as Marty snuggled up next to her.

"I'm going to stay right here, Mia. I'll take care of you until you're better."

"Thanks, Marty. It could get boring here though since I'm not going to be very mobile for a few days."

"I can come up with a nice lineup of holo-vids for us to watch right here in bed. There are games to play, books to read and music too. Then if we need to go anywhere, I'll just carry you around. Your mass only weighs about sixty pounds on Mars. I can lift more weight than that over my head with one hand. So, I can carry you wherever we need to go. We'll be like a gestalt person. You'll control the arms, since mine will be holding you up and I'll control the legs."

"Marty, that's one of the many reasons why I love you."

They lay there in bed, holding each other. Finally, after a while they drifted off to sleep in each other's arms.

✶ ✶ ✶ ✶ ✶ ✶ ✶

Charles Mantis came to with a couple of his men kneeling over him. His head really hurt and he was having trouble focusing his eyes.

"Sir, are you okay? Are you able to speak?"

"My head is killing me," said Charles. "I think I will be fine though."

"We have the medical team on the way with stretchers for you and Francis. We'll get you both into the medical facility. We'll attend to Mr. Griswold later. What happened here?"

"Martina Barbotti got in and let in that team of guys that caused all the destruction last night. Those guys also shot Anton Griswold. Francis and I tried to stop them. Let's keep this quiet though. We may need to use Anton Griswold for a scapegoat if we have to get rough with the IMB people."

"Sure thing, sir. You're the boss until the board replaces Mr. Griswold."

"That's what I like to hear. Is Francis still out?"

"Yes and he may be for some time yet. He's in bad shape."

"Well, it's probably for the best. He's going to be hurting when he does regain consciousness."

The medical team arrived with stretchers and took Charles and Francis away with them. They carried them all the way to the medical facility and then moved them into beds. Once that was complete, the doctors came to examine them. One attended to Francis, while the other took a look at his head.

"You have some bruising and a concussion, but you should be all right. You're lucky that you haven't suffered any permanent brain damage."

"Something weird happened, doctor. It felt like I got an electric shock inside my chest."

The doctor looked puzzled, but pulled a report from his nanobots. He studied it a while and his puzzled look remained.

"This is weird, there is an alert that you went into cardiac arrest, specifically, ventricular fibrillation. It looks like false data though. Every indication shows that your heart was beating normally. Nevertheless, the nanobots treated you with an electric shock. It's like someone was able to change the reading they got from your heart for just a second or two, which was long enough to trigger an alarm. After a single shock, their data was no longer being altered, so they saw your heart beating normally and assumed the treatment was successful."

"Martina! But, how did she do that? It only incapacitated me for maybe two seconds at most. That was all the time she needed though. What can we do about this?"

"Well, you have to be at close range to connect to them at all and the nanobots are too smart for a trick like this to work again anytime soon. I don't think you have to worry. I'm definitely not going to disable that. Even though you have no history of heart problems, you are in your 50's now. So while a cardiac event like this is highly unlikely, it's very possible. These things can kill in a few minutes too. That's why nanobots are set like that nowadays. There are only certain things that are automatic, it's very few of them and it's all to treat things that could kill you quickly before anyone even knew something was wrong with you."

"I see. I quite agree. Better safe than sorry. Let me know how Francis is doing."

"He's in bad shape, but stable. I know we are going to end up performing surgery, particularly on his face. I'll have the other doctor fill you in on the details later."

Charles lay back in his bed as the doctor left. He needed to relax for now. He also had to make some plans. The assault on the IMB must be done, even if the plan to soften them up failed.

✳ ✳ ✳ ✳ ✳ ✳ ✳

Marty felt better after getting some sleep. Snuggling in bed watching a video with Mia helped too.

After the video was over, Mia asked, "Marty, are you in the mood at all?"

"What kind of mood do you mean?" asked Marty, with mock innocence.

"You know," said Mia, pulling Marty closer.

"I could be persuaded," said Marty, as she pulled back the covers a little.

Marty removed Mia's panties for her, as Mia did the same for her shirt. They kissed passionately and rubbed their hands all over one another.

After a few minutes, Mia said, "Marty, I want you to sit on my face."

"Sounds good to me," said Marty smiling. "This is probably the best way to do things under the circumstances."

Marty swung a leg over to the other side of Mia's head, straddling her. She arched her back and sat in such a way that her vulva was on Mia's mouth. As she felt soft lips kissing her there, she leaned forward placing her face between Mia's legs.

She enjoyed inhaling Mia's musky scent, as she felt a tongue lightly touching her, teasing her. She licked Mia a little and then spread her open, her tongue exploring the folds within. It was becoming difficult to do, as the pleasure increased between her legs. Somehow, she managed to keep going and so did Mia. They both came together in waves, twitching and pulsing with the energy of it. She liked hearing Mia's muffled moans of pleasure and this served to heighten the intensity of her climax.

They added fingers to the mix and kept on going, reaching orgasm again and again. They got out of sync after a while, but they had their final big one at the end together.

As it subsided, Marty turned herself around and lay next to Mia. They kissed and Marty could taste herself on Mia's lips and tongue. It mixed with the delicate taste of Mia, much the way their lives had become intertwined. Marty lay there, just holding Mia, enjoying the bliss of the moment.

Chapter Twenty-Six

Oscar Perry sat down with Bill Jeffries to fill him in on the details of recent events.

"It all started with the virus," said Oscar. "Did I tell you about that?"

"Yes, that was the last thing I heard."

"Because of that, Martina Barbotti wanted to go that same night. So, I brought a team over and introduced them. Our guys did good once she got them inside. They fried all of Amalgam Global's plasma weapons."

"Excellent, that should set them back a little."

"I checked back with Martina to see how things went. She ended up following Anton Griswold into a room somewhere. Then Francis, the guy that always works for Charles Mantis, he happened to be around and went after her. She beat him to a pulp too. Our guys on the inside said he was out for a long time and going to need surgery."

"You mean the mixed guy with the ponytail?"

Oscar sighed. "Multiracial, Bill, but yes, that's him."

"Holy shit, that guy fights like some kind of a ninja."

"The crazy part is, after that, Charles Mantis shoots Anton Griswold. He leaves him there a little while, shoots him a couple more times, tells him how much he fucking hates him, then puts two bullets in his head. He got a little animated when he was telling the guy off, but he shot him as if he was making a sandwich."

"That is pretty crazy. Good riddance to that psychopath. Of course Charles Mantis isn't much better."

"Charles Mantis got his too. Martina said she knocked him over and then drop kicked him in the head. According to our operatives he has a concussion."

"I'm glad we didn't do anything to piss that girl off."

"Yeah, no kidding. Well, that's everything that happened. Amalgam is going to be planning an assault on the IMB. They are planning to move pretty soon."

"That sounds like an opportunity. We could tip off the IMB, have them get their security forces mobilized and then we send in a couple teams behind the Amalgam guys."

"That's exactly what I was thinking. We can stop Amalgam and earn up some major brownie points all in one go. If we have a crazy amount of contracts now that are as good as guaranteed, after that, we'll have more than we even know what to do with."

"Excellent. Well, I'll leave it in your capable hands, Oscar."

✳ ✳ ✳ ✳ ✳ ✳ ✳

Marty walked into Dome Five, seeing Rachel, she walked over to say hello.

"Hi, Marty."

"Hi, Rachel, how are you doing?"

"I'm doing good. How is Mia? I was concerned when I heard about what happened."

"She is mostly better. She still can't walk yet though. That's actually one reason I came down here. I told her I could just carry her around, but she wants a walker that she can use for a couple days."

"No, problem. We can make something that will suit that purpose out of some spare parts. Come with me."

Marty followed Rachel over to where some shelves were. There were various metal tubes and bolts on them.

"Most of this stuff you have to bring down from upstairs. We brought it down already though in anticipation of this."

They continued chatting as Rachel started bolting metal tubes together.

"How is it going with Hilda and Darren?"

"It has been wonderful the past few months. The best months of my life so far. We have the family quarters together and it feels like the three of us were meant to be together."

"That's cool. I'm glad it's working out so well. I figured you all would still be going strong. I remember that last time I talked to you, you mentioned how great the sex was. That always helps."

"It's like there is a party in my bed every night. A lot of times Hilda and I lay on our sides and make out a little. That always turns Darren on. It's the best way to encourage him for sure. He'll lie down behind one of us and then the other. Then sometimes he'll be our amusement park ride.

282 \ D. B. DREW

One of us gets on top of him and the other gets on his face. Then after a while, we switch places. It's a lot of fun."

"That does sound like fun."

Rachel put some rubber pieces on the bottom of the metal tubes she had bolted together and handed it to Marty.

"There you go, that should get Mia up and moving. When she wants to switch to a cane, just bring it back."

"Thanks, Rachel. Tell Darren and Hilda hi for me."

"See you later, Marty."

Marty carried the makeshift mobility device with her and headed back to her quarters.

❋ ❋ ❋ ❋ ❋ ❋ ❋

Dez took the lift down to talk to Jon Tucker. He seemed surprised to see her. She had anticipated that.

"Dez, you finally came down from your penthouse. That's a pleasant surprise."

"Well, I can't stay up there forever. I got your message. That's not surprising about Anton Griswold. There's only enough room for one psycho over there."

"Yeah, I think you're right about that. There is more. I learned that Amalgam is planning some sort of attack against the IMB."

"That figures. Well, we have definitely burned the bridge with the people over there, so we really can't go over to the IMB. Perhaps we can force Amalgam to send some of their guys back though. We can't let them get their hands on the tech. I know! We can send a team over to their base while they are going to the IMB. We attack their patrols, which should be understaffed and then we punch a hole in their dome with the laser drill. That'll have them freaked out."

"I like the sound of that. I think I could make that happen. I just need to figure out the details. We should have at least a couple days though."

✳ ✳ ✳ ✳ ✳ ✳

Marty and Mia walked through Dome Six toward the entrance to Dome Five. They were going rather slow, as Mia's legs were still weak and she had to use a walker.

"You're going to be late to your own party, birthday girl," said Marty.

"I really want to take this thing apart though. My legs have become stronger and I don't really need this anymore. It slows me down in a way. All I need is a cane to steady myself and I should be fine."

"All right, Mia. I understand."

When they got over to the maintenance area, everyone was busy working on stuff. Mia found a chair and sat down.

"Marty, get me an adjustable wrench and a pair of channel locks over there."

"You're going to do it yourself?"

"Well, I am an engineer. I think I can figure out some bolts and metal tubing."

Marty handed Mia the tools and she started unbolting part of it. When she had one leg off, she took a rubber piece from the bottom of another leg and put it on the part she had just unbolted.

"There, that should do it," said Mia, standing up with her new cane.

Mia took a few steps and seemed to be ok, so she asked Marty to put away the tools and place the rest of the stuff by the shelves, which contained the tubing.

Mia was able to walk a little faster. She was doing well just steadying herself with the cane in the low Martian gravity. They took the lift in Dome Six up a couple floors to where they were going to meet the others.

When they walked into the room, which was already full of their friends, Larry said, "Ah, there they are."

"Already using a cane I see. Very good," said Smita.

Everyone else waved hello from across the room. Brian, Yev and Zahra were in the middle with the bar supplies. Jorge was standing near that area as well, chatting with his new girlfriend, Maria. Rachel, Hilda and Darren were off in one corner of the room. Magnus, Al, Samuel and JP were over in another corner.

"Hey, why don't you two come over and have a drink?" said Zahra.

"I'll get you all fixed up," said Brian, holding up a couple bottles.

Marty and Mia walked over and Brian made drinks for them.

"We'll sit here, near the drink station," said Mia indicating some nearby chairs. "I designate this: handicapped seating."

Marty laughed as she helped Mia get situated and then took a seat next to her. After they were seated, Jorge and Maria walked over.

"Mia, I want you to meet my new girlfriend, Maria. Maria, this is my friend and colleague, Mia. She works with Larry and Brian. She is also Marty's girlfriend."

"Hi, Maria," said Mia.

"Hello. Good to see you again, Maria," said Marty.

"Hello, Marty. It's nice to meet you, Mia and Happy Birthday," said Maria in her thick Italian accent.

"So you're dating a paesano, eh, Jorge? You better watch out. We're trouble you know," said Marty, smiling. "She's even from the home country."

Marty turned to Maria, "I've been meaning to ask you about that accent. It's a little different than what I usually hear."

"I was born in the far south by the Mediterranean Sea, but lived most of my life in Naples. We have a little different dialect in the south. You look like you are from the south too, but you sound like east coast America. New York maybe?"

"Close. I'm from New Jersey. I've never even been to Italy, but everyone in my family is full-blooded Italian. Most of them came over from Italy nearly two hundred years ago, but more recent arrivals have married into the family. You see, some towns there, just about everyone is Italian and mostly Catholic too. That pretty much describes all the neighborhoods in which I have lived."

"Oh yes of course. One of my friends back in Naples has relatives over in the states. I think that's where most of them live too. But also some in Staten Island."

Rachel, Hilda and Darren came by next. They wanted to wish Mia a happy birthday too. It was almost like a line forming. Magnus, Al, Samuel and JP came by with their birthday wishes as well.

After a while, Brian pulled a flat rectangular box out from under the table. When he opened it, there was a big, beautiful cake inside. It must have been about thirty inches in length by about eighteen inches or so in width and double stacked, at least six inches high with the frosting. It was very nicely decorated too and said "Happy Birthday Mia!" in fancy lettering.

Mia was shocked and said, "Brian, how did you get a cake like that here?"

"I didn't have to do anything," said Brian. "Aria, the executive chef gave it to me. She thinks very highly of you and Marty. She said you have both been excellent mentors to her son. So, she wanted you to have a nice cake on your birthday. She made it extra big because she didn't know about Marty's birthday until a couple days afterward."

"Oh, she is so sweet," said Mia.

After placing all twenty-three candles, Brian turned to Yev. "As head of security, I will leave the fire safety violations up to you."

"I make the rules and I break the rules," said Yev laughing. "In all seriousness, as soon as I light these, you need to blow them out, Mia. This room isn't technically cleared for open flame."

Yev quickly lit them and as soon as he finished, Mia blew them out. Everyone sang "Happy Birthday" afterward. The cake was very good, rich and sweet, but not excessively so. Everyone had their fill and a good time was had by all.

✳ ✳ ✳ ✳ ✳ ✳ ✳

Charles Mantis walked through the medical facility. He wanted to see how Francis was doing, since he had just had surgery the day before. He saw Francis in bed near where they had been just a few days ago. His face was all bandaged up.

"Hello, Francis. I wanted to come by and see how you were."

"Not so good, boss. I feel like shit. I think I'm going to have to call in   sick."

Charles laughed a little and said, "That's quite understandable. I think you can be excused for the foreseeable future."

"I can't believe I got my ass kicked by a girl. Again."

"It's not quite that simple, my friend."

"I know. She is very fast and very strong."

"I wanted to learn more about her, so I did some digging around. Back in 2078, she was the new up and coming youngster on the women's mixed martial arts circuit, expected to quickly win the championship in her class and remain there for years to come. She won the few matches she was in handily. Her last match, she weighed in after eating a meal so she could go up a weight class. She did that to fight a woman two weight classes above her. Just because she wanted to. That was her hardest fight, but she still won quickly. She quit not long after that, just out of the blue. The women's MMA archive I was looking at said that the reason she gave was simply that the prize money is way too low.

"She continued practicing and sparing though, so I have a feeling she's better now than she was back then. I discovered that she also placed third in the 2082 New Jersey state women's powerlifting championship. So she has a lot of strength to work with and this allows her to hit like a truck."

"I feel like I got hit by a truck."

"You look like it too."

"What are you going to do about getting the alien tech? We're almost out of time."

"I'm afraid it's time for desperate measures. I'm going to send almost everyone I have down there. They will stick two maintenance bubbles on the dome, one inside the other. It will function rather like an airlock after we punch a hole in the dome with the laser drill.

"I'm going to get what I want one way or another. I don't care if they have to shoot every man, woman and child in the IMB. I will have that ship. Then I just blame it on Mr. Griswold and anyone else who dies along the way. Neat and tidy."

Charles left the medical facility with a big smile on his face. He had a great plan he was about to put into action. It was a shame that most, if not all of the people at the IMB were going to die. However, if they wanted to live so badly, then they should have given up the ship. They must not understand the natural order of things. Power gives you more power and a large corporation is many bits of power combined. The fools won't understand until it is far too late.

Chapter Twenty-Seven

Marty was drying off after a shower when Mia came home from work. She had worked out at the fitness center earlier and ended up rather sweaty.

"Hey, babe, how did you do walking without a cane today?"

"I did all right. My legs are still a little wobbly, but I managed. It will be nice to have my legs back to normal. That's probably going to be a couple more days though," said Mia, as she changed her clothes.

"That's good. Sounds like you're making progress," said Marty, as she discarded the towel and flopped down on the bed.

"I'm excited for other reasons though. I got everything finished up at work. Larry just needs to compile everything together, finish the patent paper work, make a news release so the press doesn't fill in the blanks and then format it for transmission. Well and also transmit it of course. Larry has maybe three or four hours of work left in total, which he can finish tomorrow. However, the rest of us are done."

"Congratulations! That's quite an accomplishment."

"Thanks," said Mia, with a wide smile.

Marty smiled back, feeling very proud as Mia continued relaying the events of the day.

"This morning some guys shuttled up to the ship with the warp drive prototype, that's what we call the thing that makes the warp field now. They should be retro fitting it now. That's the last piece we are waiting on. The gamma ray laser and black hole generator won't be built for a while yet. That's mainly because it will take a while to manufacture those. They'll need the resources of Earth too."

"That is very good news. So I guess with the black hole generator it's going to take time because of the complexity and the gamma ray laser is due to how many are needed and how large they are."

"Yes, that's right, Marty. The gamma ray laser is too powerful to really do anything with it other than create the black hole to put in the generator. Gamma rays are rather dangerous too. So until you can make the generator and create several lasers, they aren't much use."

"It will be nice to have that considering you can travel twelve light years in an hour with that. But, even running just off the antimatter generator will give us a top speed of one light year per hour. That's not too shabby. That's about 150 light years in the time it took to get to Mars. Even taking your new engine design up to max would be about fifty hours to go to mars. So that's quite a difference."

"I'm glad you're excited about it, Marty," said Mia, as she smiled broadly. The guys installing stuff are going to do the initial testing, but after that, a science team will be taking it to visit a few distant locations. I'm not sure which yet, but I'm going to be on that team and so I'm, of course, taking you with me."

"Fucking A, Mia! That is going to be so fucking cool! We're going to see some crazy shit, aren't we?"

"Yeah, we'll get to at least check out a couple places. Then we have to go back to Earth. Later we might get to do some more exploring, but we aren't sure. It will be late in the year if it happens though."

"That would be cool if we get to. Late in the year is better for me anyway. I was wanting to enter the 2083 state powerlifting championship. As second runner up for 2082, I'm prequalified for it. All I have to do is sign up."

"I'll be cheering you on."

$$* * * * * * *$$

Dez sat on her couch waiting for Tucker to come up. He apparently had something important to tell her. While she waited, she rubbed her hands over one of her men, who she had positioned in front of her. She massaged his buttocks with one hand and his balls with the other. When she saw him harden, she moved her hand up and wrapped it around the shaft. She kept squeezing his buns with the other hand.

Tucker walked in at that point. He walked up to her and stood right next to the man in front of her. He acted like he didn't even notice there was anyone standing there.

"Dez, would it help if I made a funny face?"

"Huh?"

"Look, Dez, after all this time, I would think nothing of it if I walked up here and saw you playing the ol' rusty trombone, if you know what I mean."

Dez fell back on the couch laughing almost hysterically. The man she had been playing with laughed pretty hard as well. She thought she saw Tucker laughing a little at his own joke too.

When she regained composure, she said, "Go wait over on the bed for me, I'll be in a little later. Gather up a few friends while you're waiting too, honey."

After a brief pause she said, "All right, funny man, what's up?"

"Amalgam is going to start moving their guys over to the IMB in the morning. They will attack as soon as they get everyone in position. They are sending two hundred guys down there, almost everyone they have, as far as fighters. That leaves just a handful in the base and another handful patrolling."

"That will make things easy for us, but the IMB will be in trouble."

"Our attack will force them to send forty or fifty back to their base. Also, Chimera will be sending a team down there. The IMB has Forty at most, if they pull every single guard they have to deal with this. Chimera is sending seventy, which is most of what they have. They will be leaving only a few guards at their base. They are still outnumbered almost two to one. Our attack will improve the odds. It might not be enough though."

"Well, we will do what we can. How is fighting going to work out there anyway? The suits are flexible, but bullets can't pierce them. Getting shot would be painful and maybe knock you down, but it's just going to leave a flesh wound."

"I was thinking about that too. Nothing like this has ever happened. We all had guards for defense, but we never thought we would be involved in open combat. We would probably be better off carrying bits of netting and metal tubing."

"I see what you mean. Tangle them in the netting, or club them with the tubing. You might be able to break bones like that."

"If you get them in the net, you can tie them up and fasten them to something, or take them prisoner. If you want to kill, you just take off their helmets. As long as you have them bound so they can't get to their oxygen hose in the suit, they'll die in about two minutes."

"Stealth and surprise should be their other weapons. Otherwise they might have trouble getting to the Amalgam guards if they keep getting shot."

"Oh yeah, I'm planning on an ambush. If they were going to see us coming, I would probably make shields out of the clear stuff we use for helmets and parts of the base."

"Sounds good, Tucker. Thanks."

Tucker nodded and then turned to go. Dez got up to go attend the party that was waiting on her bed.

$$* * * * * * *$$

Jorge had gone back to Maria's quarters with her after their date and they sat at the end of the bed talking.

"Jorge, I'm curious about something. I figured you would have asked me about my childhood by now. Why haven't you?"

"Well, it just seems like it's not really any of my business and you'll talk about it if you want to."

"That is very sweet," said Maria smiling. "Far too many guys start with the embarrassing and personal questions right from the beginning. I want to tell you if you want to hear."

"Yes, I'd like to hear. You can tell me anything you want. I'm a good listener. There is one thing I want to know first though. When you were worried about talking to me, why were you even going to tell me you were a transgender woman? I never would have known."

"That's a good question. If I was just going to have sex with a man a few times and then move on, then I wouldn't say anything. He would never know. That's not how I like to do things though. When I am with someone, I at least want a chance of a serious relationship. A relationship must be based on honesty and trust. You can't build a relationship from lies. It's not like I can just tell you my parents lost all the pictures of me before the age of six and I had a twin brother who died about that time. That won't work, silly boy. Besides, I never want to hide from anyone. If you hide something, it means you have shame. I am proud of who I am. People can be cruel though and that is what I worry about."

It was like a light turning on in his head, suddenly it all made sense.

"Oh I see. I never thought of it like that. That makes a lot of sense."

"Now for the story. When I was born, my parents named me 'Mario'. It makes sense. You assume you have a son when your child is born with a penis. I always knew that wasn't quite right though. Something was wrong. Later I realized that I was a girl. When I told my parents, they explained about boys having a penis and girls having a vagina. They thought I was confused about the difference. When I insisted I was a girl, they started to realize what was going on, or so they told me later.

"They took me to see a doctor in a nearby city. He talked to me and confirmed that I was a girl. This was right before I turned six by the way. What I remember best, is my mother telling me that when she was pregnant, she picked out a boy's name and a girl's name and if she had a daughter, she was going to call her 'Maria'. She asked if I wanted to be called Maria. I said, 'Yes, Mommy. I am Maria.' When I heard that name, it just sounded like that's what I should be called. That is who I am. I was confused because my parents were smiling and crying at the same time. I didn't understand that sort of thing then.

"The same day they asked if I wanted girl's cloths and stuff like that. I said I did. We moved at the same time. My parents said some people in the village wouldn't understand and people can get mean when they don't understand. They said it would break their hearts to see me go through that. So, we got an apartment on the other side of the city where my parents worked. Then a couple months later, we moved to Naples because my parents found jobs there.

"They said people there will only have seen me dressed as a girl and even if they did know, most of them would understand. People understand more in the cities. It was true. I lived there for several years and nobody ever picked on me. After I was all grown up, some men would suddenly lose interest when I tell them, but they would never admit why. But I knew."

Jorge wiped his eyes saying, "I don't usually cry on dates, but that was a very touching story."

"Don't worry, I tell no one," said Maria, as she smiled and winked at him. "So anyway, when I was about nine, I got a whole other set of nanobots injected into me. All they did was regulate my hormones. They just waited until puberty was imminent and then they suppressed some hormones and introduced others. That way I went through female puberty. It happens a little faster with the nanobots, so by thirteen or fourteen, people think you're sixteen or seventeen.

"I was very happy when I got breasts. Not that they got very big, but they were the same size as my mom's, so that made me feel good. I had the surgery when I was fourteen. That was the final step. This is going to sound silly and don't you dare tell anyone, but I smile and feel happy every time I look down at my vagina."

"That's understandable. I'd feel the same way if I had been born in the wrong body and then it was finally corrected. I feel like I should tell you about how things went for me, since you shared your story. It's not very interesting though. I got a lot of acne, I had erections at random, inconvenient times and I had a few wet dreams. I soon figured out how to prevent that last one."

Maria laughed pretty hard at that. "Jorge that is one of the things I like about you, you are very funny. You know how to make me feel comfortable too."

Jorge smiled. He could listen to compliments from Maria all night. However, something better was in store for him. Maria put her arms around him and then their lips met. Soon he was kissing her and they had fallen back on the bed. This was going to be another amazing night.

$$* * * * * * *$$

Oscar watched as the men exited the base a few at a time and gathered out in front. At that moment, Bill walked over from the area where the lifts were.

"Bill, I have them all gathering outside now. They should be ready to go shortly."

"Excellent, but could you explain the odd collection of stuff they have."

"The main issue is that bullets aren't going to be very useful with the suits everyone wears. So, we took a bunch of two meter metal rods from the storage area. Most guys we arm with those. Then we have some suits with air compressors rigged up inside them. We took apart some compressed air tools and made these little cylinders you can use to launch projectiles. We are going to use them to shoot the blasting charges, which we took from the mining supplies. We rigged the detonators with pressure sensors. Firing it closes one circuit and then when it detects the impact, the signal closes the other circuit, activating the detonator."

"I see. So they detonate on impact."

"Yes, that's right. It won't be lethal to someone in a spacesuit, but after being hit with the shockwave, it will be at least a few minutes before they can get up. We need all the help we can get too. We are going to be much outnumbered."

Oscar watched as the men, who had all piled into gliders of various sizes, sped away into the distance.

Chapter Twenty-Eight

Marty walked into Dome Six and discovered quite a commotion. Over near the doorway leading to Dome Five, there seemed to be some sort of a manufacturing station set up. They were making large tower shields out of transparent carbon nanotubes, which are for all transparent applications from the domes themselves, to helmets for spacesuits.

As she got closer, she could see a bunch of sledgehammers, which were normally only used for mining. The hard under-suits, which were recently instituted for safety purposes in mines and some manufacturing sites, were also sitting out, lined up across the floor. Marty spotted Yev and called out to him.

"What the fuck is going on down here?"

"We have to get ready, Marty. We got a call from the guys at Chimera. Apparently, Amalgam is sending two hundred armed men down here to attack us. They want to wipe us out. Hence the mining equipment and the shields we are making. Chimera is sending all they can to help us, but we will still be out numbered almost two to one. Amalgam is only attacking with regular guns. So, we put those Kevlar under-suits on, well, under our spacesuits. Then, we carry these shields, which are also bulletproof. We use the sledgehammers for our weapons."

"Sounds good, I'll join you."

"You don't have to do that, Marty. You aren't on my team."

"You need all the help you can get, so I'm volunteering."

"Thanks, Marty. We could definitely use you out there. We at least need to hold them off until Larry finishes everything up and sends out the transmission to Earth."

Marty joined Yev, helping him prepare for the upcoming Amalgam Global attack.

✳ ✳ ✳ ✳ ✳ ✳ ✳

Charles Mantis practically jumped out of his chair when he heard the alarm sound. The dome was compromised and they were losing pressure fast. Someone must be attacking. He quickly recalled fifty men to help defend the base.

When he got to where the alert indicated the problem was, the alarm stopped and he saw that a maintenance bubble had been put in place to cover the hole, until it could be fixed. Outside he saw two men from the patrol standing guard. He only had those two and a few guys inside. The rest of the guys out on patrol were not responding.

It must have been Dez, that crazy bitch. She's the only one that would order a strike like that. She picked quite an inconvenient time for this. We must have done something that pissed her off. He couldn't think of anything lately though. Perhaps the deal was that if she couldn't get her hands on the alien tech, she didn't want anyone to have it.

In the end, it didn't matter. He would still outnumber the forces at the IMB more than three to one, even with the fifty coming back to base. Plus, they won't even get a chance to put up a fight anyway. His guys would be down there before they even know what hit them.

✳ ✳ ✳ ✳ ✳ ✳ ✳

Oscar Perry got a call from his men in the field. Apparently fifty men turned back to defend the Amalgam base. The communication they intercepted said that their patrol was attacked and someone put a hole in the base.

It could only be Dez. That made sense. Parasol Group would be just as big of a loser as Chimera if Amalgam Global were to get their hands on the alien ship. He sent a message over to the IMB to let them know the Amalgam force would be smaller. So, they now stood a good chance of holding them off.

✳ ✳ ✳ ✳ ✳ ✳ ✳

Marty, Yev and Darren were the last three out of the base. As they walked over to where the other thirty-seven people were, Marty felt like a knight, or a character in one of the fantasy role-playing games she played. She walked rather stiffly from the hard Kevlar she wore under her spacesuit. She carried, in one hand, a shield almost equal to her body in height and width. She carried a large sledgehammer in her other hand. She swung it with ease in the Martian gravity.

Marty was relieved that it was going to be fewer people attacking. One hundred and fifty is still a lot though. It was then that she saw gliders coming into view. They stopped more than one hundred meters away. They were now marching on foot toward them.

Once the Amalgam guys had closed most of the distance between them, they suddenly turned around. Just then, Marty saw the Chimera forces running at them from the other side. Yev pointed his hammer in that direction and took off running. Marty and everyone else ran with him.

When Marty got to the Amalgam forces, she could see that they had split into two groups. One group stood to face her as she advanced and the other was back behind the first, trying to deal with Chimera. As she charged, Marty could hear bullets bouncing off her shield and one even ricocheted off the top of her helmet. The Amalgam forces backpedaled, as they fired their weapons, trying to stay back from the countercharge.

On the other side, Marty could see shockwaves going off. Chimera was apparently hurling explosives at them. Or, maybe shooting them. They came out of some strange object Marty couldn't identify from a distance.

Finally, Marty got within striking distance of one of the guys. She swung the sledgehammer hard, hitting the guy in the middle of the chest. He flew back a few feet and landed on his back. He just lay there clutching his chest, making no attempt to get up. Having some bones in your chest broken by a hard blow from a sledgehammer tends to have that effect.

Eventually, after several guys went down on each front, the Amalgam force began to retreat to the side. They met up with the

Chimera force as they walked through the fallen Amalgam guys. Marty synced up her communicator with one of the guys from Chimera.

"Don't think this is over," he said. "They will be back later tonight with much better weapons. The only way to prevent it is to transmit."

"We should be ready to do that soon," said Marty.

"We'll follow the Amalgam retreat from a distance and let you know if anything is going on."

"Sounds good. We'll head back and see how Larry is getting along."

"He needs to make sure Amalgam intercepts the confirmation from Earth. That's the only way Charles will cancel the attack plans. Once he knows it's over, he'll send a crew down here to collect the injured and bring them back."

"I was wondering what to do about them. There are rather a lot."

"He'll come get them, but only when he knows he has lost."

✱✱✱✱✱✱✱

"So how's it going, Larry?" asked Marty.

"You look funny with that bulky mining gear on," said Larry with a chuckle. "I'm almost done. I'm getting everything about the project in there, the patent paperwork, an information packet so the press doesn't start saying something crazy, plus reports about some of the things that have gone on around here. I also made a little message, which will get sent back this way and be intercepted by Amalgam. That should prompt Charles to give up. There. That should do it. It will just take a couple minutes for the computer to package that. Then I can transmit."

That was a very long couple of minutes for Marty, but finally it was ready and Larry started the transmission. After a minute, Larry spoke again.

"All right, that's it. Now we just wait for confirmation. It should just take a minute."

Larry paused a minute and then pulled up the confirmation.

"There we go. That's it."

Marty was mostly relieved. However, she would feel better when they had a sign that Amalgam would leave them alone.

✳ ✳ ✳ ✳ ✳ ✳ ✳

Marty sat at a table in Dome Six, with Mia next to her. Larry, Smita, Brian and Yev were also there.

Larry said, "Now that the crew is back from retrofitting the ship, we are all set. We'll shuttle up to ship the day after tomorrow. You'll need to bring everything with you, because we'll be going back to Earth. This is just for people on my team though, which includes plus ones, by the way. Everyone else will go back on a regular ship at the normal time."

"I just got a message from my guys," said Yev. "Here, check this out."

Yev brought up a video on his holo-display. It was a bunch of personnel from Amalgam global. They were unarmed and going around collecting the injured.

"Fuck yeah!" said Marty. "I think we've finally seen the last of those fucking corporate cocksuckers."

"I agree," said Larry.

"I think that's reason enough for a celebration," said Brian. "I know I could use a drink anyway."

Everyone else emphatically nodded their agreement. It had been a rough day. A drink sounded like exactly what she needed.

✱ ✱ ✱ ✱ ✱ ✱ ✱

Jorge had gone to visit with Maria and he had a question he needed to ask. After she greeted him with a kiss and showed him in, he went ahead and asked.

"Maria, there is somewhere I have to go. It has to do with the project I have been working on. I wanted to see if you would be willing to come with me."

"I heard a little something about the ship with the retrofitted prototypes," said Maria with a smile. "Yes, of course I'll go with you. I was hoping you would ask me."

"It's going to be pretty cool. We're going to explore a little. We're going to the outer edge of the Kuiper belt first. Then after that, we'll go to the Alpha Centauri system. We'll stop at Proxima first and then we'll be going Between A and B, which will give us a clear view of both. Not much in the way of planets there, but it is a binary system, with a third star orbiting around the pair as if they were a single object. It's also close, of course. We can get there in just a few hours. We'll be going back to Earth after that. However, toward the end of the year, we might go out on another exploration mission. That one would be longer."

"That sounds like fun. I'm cool with going back to Earth. I can come back to Mars anytime. I just want to go wherever you go. I've become rather attached to you."

"I feel the same. The most important thing to me is having you there by my side."

With that, they embraced and shared a very steamy kiss. This whole thing had gone even better than he had imagined.

✳ ✳ ✳ ✳ ✳ ✳ ✳

Marty and Mia had all their stuff together, lugging it through Dome Six to meet with everyone and say their goodbyes. They were joined by Larry, Smita, Brian, Yev, Zahra, Jorge and Maria, who were also lugging their stuff with them. Their other friends all gathered to see them off.

"Yev, thank you again for having the confidence in me to give me this promotion," said Darren.

"You are easily the best person to succeed me as head of security. I gave you your first assignment because you appeared to be the best of the best, based on my initial assessment. You proved that was right every day."

Rachel and Hilda said their goodbyes to Marty and Mia, thanking them for helping them through the difficult situation they had been in a few months prior.

Al and JP had already left the day before. They took the last ship back to Earth. There wouldn't be any more for a few months, as the two planets would be too far apart. Magnus and Samuel came by though, shook hands with everyone and wished them well on this final phase of their mission. Even Alma and Andrew Cohen stopped by to see them off.

Nik came to see them as well and his parents, Junior and Aria were with him.

Aria said, "Nik wanted to come say goodbye and Junior and I wanted to thank you for everything. We really appreciate it."

Junior said, "Thank you very much. You have both been generous with your time and excellent mentors and role models for Nik."

"You're welcome. I enjoyed teaching him stuff and training him," said Marty. "We had a lot of fun up there in the fitness center."

"Nik is a joy to be around," said Mia.

Aria and Junior said their goodbyes and left, telling Nik to take as much time as he wanted, but not to hold Marty and Mia up.

Nik hugged Mia and wished her well on the last part of her mission. Then tears began to well up in his eyes a bit, as he put his arms around Marty.

"Marty, I'm going to miss you very much."

"I'm going to miss you too, Nik," said Marty, as she hugged him tight, feeling tears come to her own eyes.

"I hope I get to see you again someday," said Nik.

"You will. That's a promise. Until then, you have my contact info. Send me messages and let me know how you are doing. Oh and keep practicing all the things I taught you."

"I will. Goodbye, Marty."

"Goodbye, Nik."

After they had a little time with everyone who came to see them off, the group headed over to Dome Five. The shuttle should be about ready for them to board.

✳ ✳ ✳ ✳ ✳ ✳ ✳

Taking off in the shuttle was much easier than when they took off from Earth. It required much less force to reach escape velocity. It wasn't long before they felt themselves become weightless.

After the shuttle docked, everyone pushed all their stuff through into the ship. The ship was only half the size of the one in which they traveled to Mars. However, it could comfortably accommodate more than double the number of people in their group. Therefore, everyone just randomly picked a room and pushed all their stuff in. Zahra got a room to herself and there were even empty rooms.

Marty and Mia stayed in their room just long enough to tie all their stuff down. Then they floated back out, just as they heard the locks disengage, allowing the shuttle to go back down to Mars.

Everyone else had floated out of their rooms by this point too. The group floated through the ship together, exploring every part of it, becoming familiar with its layout. It was a lot like the layout of the ship that took them there, but only half the size. It had two decks of double height and then a single height deck at the top, which contained the crew's quarters and the flight deck.

There was a skeleton crew on board to assist them with piloting the ship. One of them partially floated down from the top deck.

"Just let us know when you want to get underway. We'll be up here waiting for you."

"Thanks," said Larry. "We'll be up after we get familiarized with the ship."

"That's understandable. Take your time. I do the same thing when I board a ship, especially one I haven't been on before."

With that, he pulled himself back up and the group continued looking around the ship. The bottom deck had little room for anything but the engines. There were small engineering rooms and a couple supply closets containing stuff related to maintaining the ship. No cargo area though. The middle deck was divided in half. A kitchen area and a couple common rooms took up all the space in the front half. The cargo area sat atop the single-height cabins and bathrooms, in the back section of the deck. Bits of fencing made it easy to tie cargo down with straps. There were stairs leading to the cargo areas, which were needed during acceleration and deceleration.

They went up to the top deck, which had a common room near the middle that the crew could use as a lounge. The crew's quarters were toward the back and the flight deck was in the front.

Three members of the crew were on the flight deck, the other three were probably in the back somewhere. The flight deck was a lot like the one they had been on before, it just took up a much larger portion of the top deck on this smaller ship.

There were view screens, which acted like electronic windows, showing the view outside from different parts of the ship. This was in addition to the actual windows distributed around the flight deck. There were also lots of holo-displays and controls around everywhere, which was pretty standard.

In the middle was something unusual and out of place. There were additional controls and holo-displays there. They looked like they had been added-on later. Of course, that is where they control the new stuff, which was installed on the ship.

"I love it!" said Mia. "These controls are great. This is exactly what I asked for."

"I guess we can get underway now," said Larry. "Let's Just pull out of orbit and move away from the gravitational influence of Mars."

The crew did exactly that and Marty could see them turning partially away from Mars, as the view rotated. There was now less of Mars and more of space taking up the view outside. They were starting to move away slowly with maneuvering thrusters, allowing their orbit to become larger and larger. They were now on their way to go places where no human had yet visited.

Chapter Twenty-Nine

Once the ship had spiraled out of orbit and then drifted away from Mars at about the same speed it had been orbiting, Larry indicated that he was ready to begin testing. They were going to begin by using the warp drive to warp the space at the bottom of the ship in such a way that it caused a gravitational pull from the floor of the bottom deck on up. At the same time, the top of the ship would be warped the other way in order to keep the top of the ship from attracting objects to it.

As they drifted slowly out toward the asteroid belt, Marty floated next to Mia, watching as she began operating the controls. Since everyone in the ship was now there on the flight deck, Mia called out to prepare for gravity. Everyone put feet toward the floor and held onto something. Mia increased gravity very slowly, so they gently sank until their feet were on the floor. She increased it to about a quarter of Earth's gravity over five minutes. Then, since the crew had been weightless for a couple days and had little to no gravity for a year, she set it to increase by

.01% of Earth's gravity every second and a half. This would give them time to adjust, as it would be more than three hours before it finished incrementing up to a full g. Marty was glad of that, since she had just spent the past few months on Mars.

Larry said, "Mia, when you are ready, take us to the outer edge of the Kuiper belt."

"All right," said Mia, as she worked the controls. "I'm setting it go at a tenth of a light year per hour. I'm linking to the navigation system and setting the course. It will take about thirty-five seconds to get there. It will start when I activate and collapse the field when we arrive. Activating...now!"

When Mia activated the warp drive, there was no sensation of movement at all. However, everything at the front of the ship went completely black. Everything being displayed from the back disappeared as well. On the sides, anything near the back or the front also disappeared. However, on the sides, there was a diffuse, lightly glowing rainbow. It went from black, which faded into a violet color, went through all the colors of the visible spectrum until it became red toward the back and then faded to black.

"I thought it might do that," said Larry. "Here I'll set everything around the front to ultraviolet and everything around the back to infrared. Well, the display screens anyway, obviously we can't set the front windows to ultraviolet."

Larry laughed, as did everyone else. The stars came into view again after Larry adjusted the displays.

"As you can see," said Brian, "The stars in front and behind remain clear, then as you reach the sides, they form blurry lines and then turn to this sort of diffuse glow. That's because of how quickly our position is changing relative to the stars."

As Brian finished speaking, the rainbow pattern turned back to normal stars. Larry put the displays back to the standard setting.

"Look at how small the sun appears," said Zahra, pointing to a rear display.

It looked more like one of the other stars at this distance. The biggest and brightest for sure, but it just looked like some other star. It was amazing to see the sun at such a distance.

Larry zoomed in on different areas of the space around them and they got close-up views of asteroids and comets. There were very few though and they were all very far away. One small asteroid was the only object relatively close, at about a hundred-thousand miles away. Other objects were a million miles away or more.

After they looked around for a while, Larry said, "I want to test the machine that creates matter from energy. We should get that done before we get too caught up in exploration."

"Normally this would be in an engineering room," said Mia. "However, this ship is a little too small. So, it's here on the flight deck. It's connected to the power system below."

The machine looked like some sort of an oven with a holo-display on it. Larry set it for iron, compact shape, a hundred grams. After activating it, there was a quiet humming noise and some light coming from inside the machine. After a few seconds, it indicated that it was complete. Larry opened it up and took out a small piece of iron.

"Well, I think that is successful," said Larry.

"Can we make other stuff?" asked Smita.

"Yes," said Mia. "But the more you make, the longer it takes and the more energy you need. It is also limited to raw materials. It is more for supplying our current manufacturing machines and three-dimensional printers rather than replacing them. It's not really going to be fitted on ships most of the time. It's more for industrial operations on Earth or Mars."

With the testing complete, they returned their focus to the warp drive.

Larry said, "Mia, let's go out near the outer edge of the Oort cloud."

"All right, Larry. I'll kick it up to maximum this time, which should take about forty-five minutes."

"Actually, could you angle us in the direction of Proxima Centauri?"

"Yeah, I was just thinking that might be a better idea, since we are going there later. I have the course laid in. It should take about an hour."

Marty saw Mia confirm the course and then change the light year per hour speed being displayed, from 0.10 to 1.00. Mia paused for just a brief moment and then activated the warp drive. The instant she did so, they got the same rainbow effect.

Larry said, "Well, we may as well go down to one of the common rooms below and relax for a while."

Everyone nodded and murmured their agreement. It sounded like a good idea. Marty noticed the gravity was currently at about half that of Earth. The gradual increase was helping. It felt no worse than when you first get out of a swimming pool. As the group of nine headed toward the stairs, they saw that one member of the crew stayed on the flight deck, two sat down in the lounge and the other three kept walking toward the back.

After they went down to the middle deck, they all walked into the common room nearer to the middle of the ship. There was plenty of room for all of them to sit down and even spread out a little. Mia leaned into Marty a little when they sat down and Marty put her arm around her. The mood was somewhat relaxed, but there was a little excitement in the air as everyone chatted about what they had just done and what was yet to come.

✳ ✳ ✳ ✳ ✳ ✳ ✳

They all went back to the flight deck when the warp field collapsed. Looking at displays from behind them, they just saw stars, the same as the view in front that looked out toward interstellar space.

Larry said, "Here we are, at the edge of our solar system. The sun looks like any other star behind us. In front of us, is interstellar space. Well, technically we are out about four hundred times further from the sun than where interstellar space starts, but the Oort cloud is part of the solar system. So, the way I look at it—"

"Larry," interrupted Brian. "Get on with it."

"Oh, right. Sorry," said Larry sheepishly. "I also wanted to get readings from the outer edge of Oort cloud. This will be more interesting. By the way, we are about a hundred and eighty times as far away as Voyager could be if it is still moving, which is hard to say after almost one hundred and six years."

"Larry!"

"Sorry, Brian. I'm just excited."

"Me too, which is why I'm losing my patience. I want to see what our sensors are registering."

"Me too. Let's go look," said Larry smiling.

Larry and Brian walked quickly over to a holo-display, like a couple of kids on a playground. Everyone else followed close behind. Larry and Brian gathered readings and discussed what they found. They were there for about an hour in total before they were ready to move on. By this time, the gravity was getting close to Earth normal. Marty felt kind of heavy and sluggish, like getting out of a pool after you had been swimming all afternoon. It wasn't too bad though.

Mia set the course for Proxima Centauri, leaving the speed at maximum. Then, she activated the warp drive.

"This is going to take a little over three hours," said Mia.

"We may as well go down to the galley and fix something to eat," said Yev.

Marty was definitely feeling hungry and everyone else seemed to like that idea too. So, they all headed back down to the middle deck.

✳ ✳ ✳ ✳ ✳ ✳ ✳

Marty walked with the group back up to the flight deck. They arrived just as the warp field collapsed. There on the view screen in front of them was Proxima Centauri. It had a sort of reddish orange color. It looked just a little smaller and a littler dimmer than the sun did from Mars.

Larry said, "We are fairly close to this star, because it is small and rather dim. It really only looks a little smaller and dimmer than the sun did on Mars. However, the distance from the sun to Mercury is ten times greater than the distance we are from Proxima Centauri. This is about where habitable planets would have to be if there were any."

They stayed for an hour or so studying the star and the surrounding areas. They took readings, as well as pictures and video, which they could send back to Earth. Word was probably getting around about this. So, it would likely end up being a big story.

When they were finished at Proxima Centauri, Mia set the course to put them directly in between the Alpha Centauri Binary pair, which Proxima Centauri orbited at a great distance. It would take about fifteen minutes to get there. So, everyone just hung around waiting for them to arrive.

When they arrived, they had to use filters on the display to view Alpha Centauri A and B. The combined light of both stars poured in through the windows, providing a level of luminance similar to a Martian day.

They got a visual on the planet assumed to be orbiting the smaller B star. It was a rocky planet, a little larger than Earth. It orbited very close to the star. Their readings showed a surface temperature well in excess of a thousand degrees centigrade.

They spotted two smaller planets going around the A star, which were unknown until now. The first was further out than the planet orbiting the B star, but due to the A star being larger and more luminous, it had a similar surface temperature. The second planet was much further out, but still kind of close. Its surface temperature was much cooler, but with a reading of more than three hundred degrees centigrade, this was only in a relative sense.

Marty knew it was unlikely that there would be any habitable planets here, but it was still rather disappointing to confirm this. She was just kind of along for the ride at this point, but she found it all quite fascinating. Time seemed to pass very quickly. Before she knew it, people were wrapping things up and preparing to go downstairs to unwind a little and then get some sleep.

✳ ✳ ✳ ✳ ✳ ✳ ✳

The next day, they spent the entire morning gathering data and making observations. Between that and what they had done yesterday, they accomplished quite a bit. Everyone pitched in too. Marty, Smita, Yev and Maria may not officially be part of the science team, but they were at least able to act as assistants. Mia had set the course for Earth and activated just before they went down to get some lunch. They now sat in one of the common rooms, full from their lunch and satisfied with their mission.

Larry said, "Well, I think it's safe to say: 'mission accomplished'. Good job, everyone. Now we can relax."

"We should also celebrate," said Brian.

"That sounds like a good idea," said Larry. "It's going to be hours before we arrive near Earth and probably dinner time before the crew gets us into orbit. So, we may as well have fun. We'll have a wait ahead of us, because I am sure they will not send a shuttle up until morning. I have some good scotch left that I was saving for this very occasion. I plan to get it out after dinner."

"That sounds good," said Brian. "Speaking of dinner, Yev and I will whip up something special. It will be part of our celebration. I kept a few bottles of fine wine stashed in anticipation of this and that will go nicely with what we are planning."

Marty liked the sound of that. They had much to celebrate. For Marty, the biggest reason was sitting right next to her.

Chapter Thirty

After dinner, they all sat in one of the common rooms, in the ship, which was now orbiting Earth. They were all sipping on the scotch that Larry passed out. Some people only had a small amount though, but everyone tried it. Mia just took a sip from Marty's cup, since she didn't really like that sort of thing. Marty found it to be quite tasty though. It was amazingly smooth.

Larry was flipping through news stories on his mobile device. He made a face like he found something very interesting and expanded it across his entire holo-display. Then he moved the hologram out toward the middle of the room and increased its size. He also set the audio to transmit to some speakers situated in the middle of the room.

Larry said, "Check this out. There is a whole big news story with us. There is a video too."

Marty was very curious to see it and everyone else expressed their interest. Larry started the video.

In the hologram, in the middle of the room, they saw video footage of the Mars base, with a voice-over talking about what had been found there and that it had been kept a secret for almost a year. The coverage was very fair, although some people were interviewed who did not like the way it was handled.

The video had updates tacked onto the end and it continued on into the first update. This one was an interview with Alma Cohen from last night.

In the video, Alma said, "I know some people don't like it when things are kept secret. We had to do that for our own safety though. There were people who wanted to steal this tech and patent it for themselves. I think the public would have been much more unhappy paying monopoly prices in order to benefit from our find.

"In addition, this was found by university personal, making that ship property of the university. As with anything the university does, all discoveries will be made public as soon as it is safe to do so."

Alma then elaborated on the dangers they faced and the attacks that came from Amalgam Global and The Parasol Group. She went over all of them in detail. She also discussed the charges being pressed against those two corporations and the evidence she provided.

The video continued on to the next update. This one was added overnight and featured an official statement from Chimera, given by Bill Jeffries.

"Chimera can confirm what Alma Cohen says is true. It was people working for me who supplied her with the footage of Amalgam Global's illegal plasma weapon manufacturing racket. We also sent all the security personnel we had to help defend the IMB from an all-out attack by Amalgam Global.

"The senior board members and I feel that what the IMB does is very important for our community. We have always supported that and when needed, we used all the resources at our disposal to come to their aid.

"Now that the IMB has succeeded in their mission, it is time to bring the benefits of this to all the people of the world. Chimera is here to be your partner in this. We have relationships with all world governments and seek to keep strengthening those relationships.

"Chimera has what is needed to complete any contract job ahead of time and under budget. That is my personal guarantee to all world governments. You want to research this and turn it into the products that will benefit your people as quickly as you can. Chimera is here to do that for you. We look forward to assisting everyone, just like we helped the people at the IMB."

Marty couldn't believe what she heard. Bill twisted everything around to his advantage. It is true they helped, but only when it was unlikely they could get ahold of the tech. Maybe that was in part because they were only moderately ruthless, but their entire motivation was always greed and self-interest. Marty's attention then snapped back to the video as the next update played.

This one was an official statement from The Parasol Group. They had denied the charges last night and then there was a video statement from Dez, made this morning.

"The Parasol Group is shocked at these baseless charges. I am here to respond to them. I am saddened that the people at the IMB would falsely accuse me of things and by proxy, The Parasol Group. I will admit we did grab the professor. It was a case of mistaken identity though. He was not harmed in any way. Then the woman, who was here, broke in. That's the real crime that was committed. It was understandable given the mistake we had made though. They did have to wait a little while before I could straighten everything out. But, while they waited, we took care of their every need. Here is a video of them eating the finest food to be found anywhere on Mars."

The image of Dez was replaced by a video of her and Larry eating. There was no sound and it was out of context, but it was unaltered footage. It did make it look like they were more guests than prisoners.

"As you see from that video, they were treated very well. After their meal, I was finally free to attend to them. I sat down with them, explained the mistake and apologized over glasses of my finest wine. I told the woman that no charges would be filed for the break-in and that they were free to go whenever they were ready. Here is some video from our meeting."

A video played showing the three of them drinking wine together. It did look like they were old friends. There was no audio of course. Marty had to admit that the evidence Dez presented looked quite conclusive.

"As you can see, it is just as I described. Shortly after that video, I took them down in the lift and directed them to the main airlock. Then they left. That's all that happened. I think this proves conclusively that the charges against me are all lies."

After the statement from Dez, it displayed an update message, which was added more recently. It was from just a couple hours ago. It said that the evidence presented and lack of any solid counterevidence, created too much doubt. The charges against Dez and The Parasol Group, have been dropped.

The next update was more entertaining. It was some of the images they sent back from all the places they went yesterday and earlier today. It had links to additional images, video clips and some of their data too.

The final update was a statement from Amalgam Global, made just a few hours ago, responding to the charges against them. Charles Mantis spoke for the company.

"I want to respond to these charges. On behalf of Amalgam Global, I am very sorry to say, that someone working for our company did commit all the heinous crimes, which have been reported. We have since discovered that he committed many other crimes in addition to these. He was very good at hiding it. He hid it from me, the leadership of this company and law enforcement."

A picture of Anton Griswold was shown in the corner, as Charles continued.

"This man here, Anton Griswold, was in charge of operations on Mars. Recently I discovered he had a hidden manufacturing area on the base, where he and men loyal to him were creating plasma weapons for sale on the black market. Apparently, he also wanted to get his hands on the alien ship. I didn't realize he even knew about that. I heard rumors about things people overheard at the IMB, but Mr. Griswold wasn't one to fraternize with the staff. He knew though. I suspect he was engaged in espionage there as well.

"When I discovered the plasma weapons, I made a plan to capture the men involved, destroy the weapons and then turn Anton Griswold in. The few men who were there tried to kill the security forces sent to stop them. They were killed in the firefight. I destroyed the weapons by exposing them to high voltage, which fried their circuitry. I will turn these over to law enforcement as soon as they can travel to Mars.

"After seeing to the weapons, I discovered Mr. Griswold sent men loyal to him down to the IMB to wipe them out and take what he wanted. He and a few men barricaded themselves in a room when I moved to put an end to all this. They all died in an exchange of fire with security personnel, including Anton Griswold.

"With Anton Griswold dead, I was able to gain control of the force attacking the IMB and I ordered them to stop and return to base. They were very willing to do so, once they saw Anton Griswold was dead. I think all, or at least the vast majority, were acting under duress to one degree or another. I have uncovered evidence of direct and indirect threats, made by Anton Griswold, to employees working under him. If you follow the link I will include in this video, it will show you the evidence I have sent to law enforcement. I warn you, it is very graphic.

"All the evidence you will see there, I discovered after his death. It is truly horrible. He tortured and murdered several people. He has dismembered people and thrown them out of airlocks to die. He has thrown them alive into the grinder in the greenhouse. People have reported that they were told they would get the same treatment if they refused his orders.

"I wish I could have stopped him sooner. I just arrived on Mars a few months ago. So, I had no idea what was going on. I promise you though, that as soon as I discovered what he was doing, I put a stop to it. Again, I would like to apologize on behalf of Amalgam Global, for what was done by one of our employees.

"The contact information included is to our corporate legal department. If you have any evidence at all that you were harmed directly or indirectly by the crimes of Anton Griswold, we would be happy to settle with you. In addition, your attorney can bill his or her time to our company, so it will cost you nothing out of pocket."

When the video ended, an update message was displayed. It was from about an hour ago. It said that due to Mr. Griswold being deceased, the criminal case had been closed.

Marty was pissed. She couldn't believe that little weasel was going to get away with it. Do what they want and then pay people off if they get busted. That was infuriating. She couldn't hold it in anymore.

"That fucking lying piece of shit! That was a massive load of fucking bullshit. What the fuck? Why does anyone believe that? Each one of those fucking assholes was worse than the one before. I didn't think anything would piss me off more than what that fucking cunt, Dez, said, but fuck me if I wasn't wrong as shit. That Charles Mantis can fuck off and go eat a dick! The only good part about it, was knowing that I gave him that big ass bruise on his stupid fucking face."

Everyone just nodded in agreement. They looked like they agreed with her, but weren't sure what to say.

Marty said, "Sorry, I didn't mean to totally lose it like that. It's just that first Bill got on my nerves, then Dez was even worse than that and then Charles blew them both out of the water. I was ready to explode by the end of that."

Larry said, "It's understandable. I was feeling angrier by the minute too. I'm just glad that you waited until the video was over."

"See, I'm making progress."

328 \ D. B. DREW

Everyone chuckled a little at that exchange and the mood started to lighten again. People discussed their anger a little and then the conversation turned to the parts of the video about them. After a while, that brought them all back to celebration mode again.

✳ ✳ ✳ ✳ ✳ ✳ ✳

Marty and Mia stood next to a large window, looking out into space. They had a very nice view of Earth, as the ship circled around in its orbit. Marty put a hand on Mia's back, rubbing it affectionately.

"Marty, this is such a nice view. You never realize how beautiful the Earth is until you are looking at it like this, from orbit."

"I find it quite captivating as well. You know, there is something I have been thinking about, that has been on my mind a lot lately. It's something I wanted to ask you."

"Oh? What's that?"

"Well, I just wanted to ask," said Marty, pausing for just a brief moment, taking Mia's hands in hers and looking into her eyes. "Mia, will you marry me?"

Marty hadn't even completely finished her sentence, when Mia gasped and put her hands up to her face. After Marty got the whole question out, tears came to Mia's eyes and she started trembling a little.

"Oh, Marty—"

She paused for just a moment and then continued.

"Yes! Yes, of course I'll marry you!"

Marty felt tears coming to her eyes too. She took Mia in her arms. They embraced and had a quick kiss.

"I love you very much, Mia."

"I love you too, Marty. You have made me so happy today."

They both took a moment to wipe their eyes and then held each other tight again. They kissed passionately for a few minutes. It was a single long kiss, expressing the love they had for each other. Then they just stood there, with their arms loosely around one another, each looking into the other's eyes.

"Should we tell everyone?" asked Mia.

"Yeah, I think we should."

Marty took Mia's hand in hers and together they walked into the other room, where the rest of the group was hanging out.

"I have some news," said Marty, pausing to see that everyone looked up at her. "I asked Mia to marry me."

"And I said, 'yes'."

Everyone got up and congratulated them all at once. They each told them how happy they were for them and wished them well in their life together.

Larry said, "A few months ago, I never would have thought a day like this would come. Then, after I saw your relationship with Mia begin to unfold, I knew this day was only a matter of time. It makes me feel good to see you so happy, my friend."

Everyone else also took a moment to say something, without the others talking over them. Mostly it was congratulations and well wishes. Marty and Mia thanked everyone for their kind words. After that, they sat down together and the outside world seemed to fade away, as they held hands and looked into each other's eyes.

****

Marty lay in bed, with Mia next to her. They were all snuggled into the covers together. It had been a very long day and it sounded like Mia had just fallen asleep. Her breathing was deep with an even rhythm, a clear sign of sleep.

Marty was tired too, but her mind was still thinking about things, so it would probably take a little longer to fall asleep.

That morning, a shuttle took them back down to Earth. Then they had backtracked along the same path they took to get there a few months ago. They used the same methods of transportation as well. It ended with them being taken to the same hotel they originally left from. The university had booked rooms for them, at Larry's request. There they would stay, until they made other arrangements.

That is exactly where she was, up in her room, lying in bed, with Mia by her side. She thought about what sort of place she might get. She wanted to rent something fairly large. She would have her stuff coming out of long-term storage and she would be moving in Mia's stuff as well.

This whole trip had been amazing, all the things she had seen and done. It really was the trip of a lifetime. Of everything that happened though, meeting Mia and falling in love with her, was the best thing by far. Her adventure of a lifetime included finding the woman of her dreams. Sometime later in the year, they would be married too. What a different and better place her life was in now, compared to when all this had begun, a few short months ago.

There were differences on the inside. She realized that she had really grown as a person. She owed it all to Mia and in return, she helped Mia grow as well. Now she felt at peace and her life felt complete. As she thought about it, she realized that all these things, this entire chain of events, had been set in motion early last year, millions of miles away. Or, another way to look at it, was a billion years ago, from the center of the galaxy. Either way, it all happened because of what was found, buried in one of the caverns of Mars.

About the Author:

D. B. Drew lives with a spouse and cats. The Midwestern native enjoys writing and has a lifelong love of science fiction. D. B. Drew hadn't written a novel before, but was compelled by the characters, and how they seemed to come to mind so frequently.

Facebook:

https://www.facebook.com/Author.DBDrew

https://www.facebook.com/The-Caverns-of-Mars-486116911568479

Twitter:

https://twitter.com/dbdrewauthor @dbdrewauthor

Web:

http://dbdrew.com

http://cavernsofmars.com